Weddings

Can Be

Murder

Connie Shelton

Books by Connie Shelton

THE CHARLIE PARKER SERIES
Deadly Gamble
Vacations Can Be Murder
Partnerships Can Be Murder
Small Towns Can Be Murder
Memories Can Be Murder
Honeymoons Can Be Murder
Reunions Can Be Murder
Competition Can Be Murder
Balloons Can Be Murder
Obsessions Can Be Murder
Gossip Can Be Murder
Stardom Can Be Murder
Phantoms Can Be Murder
Buried Secrets Can Be Murder
Legends Can Be Murder
Weddings Can Be Murder
Holidays Can Be Murder - a Christmas novella

THE SAMANTHA SWEET SERIES
Sweet Masterpiece
Sweet's Sweets
Sweet Holidays
Sweet Hearts
Bitter Sweet
Sweets Galore
Sweets, Begorra
Sweet Payback
Sweet Somethings
Sweets Forgotten
The Woodcarver's Secret

Weddings
Can Be
Murder

Charlie Parker Mystery #16

Connie Shelton

Secret Staircase Books

Weddings Can Be Murder
Published by Secret Staircase Books, an imprint of
Columbine Publishing Group
PO Box 416, Angel Fire, NM 87710

Printed and bound in the United States of America
ISBN 1523680903
ISBN-13 978-1523680900

This book is a work of fiction. Names, characters, places and
incidents are either the product of the author's imagination or are
used fictitiously. Any resemblance to actual events or locales or
persons, living or dead, is entirely coincidental. Although the author
and publisher have made every effort to ensure the accuracy and
completeness of information contained in this book we assume
no responsibility for errors, inaccuracies, omissions, or any
inconsistency herein. Any slights of people, places or organizations
are unintentional.

Book layout and design by Secret Staircase Books
Cover image © Sebastian Czapnik
Cover silhouette © Ayutaka

First trade paperback edition: February, 2016
First e-book edition: February, 2016

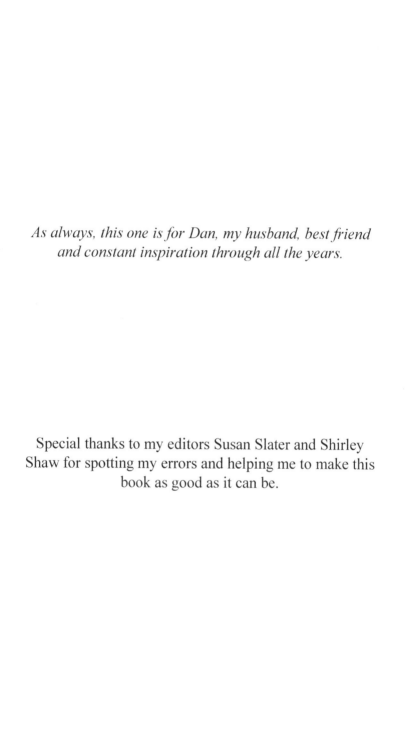

As always, this one is for Dan, my husband, best friend and constant inspiration through all the years.

Special thanks to my editors Susan Slater and Shirley Shaw for spotting my errors and helping me to make this book as good as it can be.

Chapter 1

The first Saturday in December was going to be the happiest day of my brother's life. Ron and my husband, Drake, were all tuxedoed up and presumably picking up the flowers on their way to the chapel. My matron-of-honor dress hung on a hook on the closet door, all snug and clean in its garment bag. Victoria had helped me choose it but had not jammed her own opinions down my throat. I've seen so many disastrous, puff-sleeved, low-waisted bridesmaid dresses in every color from baby pink to violent purple that I truly appreciated it when she let me pick one that might serve double duty for the upcoming holiday season—in case we actually got invited to a dressy soirée. My deep burgundy, knee length dress was demure enough for a wedding and low-cut enough for a party. I picked up the accessory bag containing my shoes, jewelry and makeup, mentally running through my to-do list as I called Freckles in from the backyard, hustled her into her doggy crate and headed for the front door.

Pick up Victoria at her house, arrange both of our dresses in as unwrinkled condition as possible in the back seat of my Jeep Cherokee and get us to the chapel with time to spare for putting them on and applying finishing touches to hair and makeup. In my case, that last part would consist of an extra swipe of lipstick and hair-spraying any errant strands from the complicated up-do that my local hairdresser had been kind enough to create at eight o'clock this morning. Believe me, I felt decidedly overdressed walking out of there.

The noon ceremony with approximately fifty guests would be followed by a very classy luncheon at the country club, an afternoon of champagne and dancing, and a quick exit by the bride and groom in time to catch their plane to the east coast. Ron had confided that he'd told Victoria only to pack for warm weather. Their destination was a surprise for her, but I knew he'd booked them a room at a very chichi hotel in Miami with a side excursion to Disney World because he truly did believe the ads that promised it's way more fun without the kids. Besides, his three boys are already beyond the kiddie-ride phase and well into the blasé, you-can't-impress-me stage.

I stashed my things in the back of the Jeep and gave a final stare at the house. Had I locked the back door? Yes. The front door? Fairly sure I did. No sense worrying about the iron—I don't do ironing. The toaster had long since been put away and the coffee maker emptied when I got back from my hair appointment. Ron had been a nervous wreck for two days but Drake—bless him—was a model of organization. It's what makes him an extraordinary pilot and the logical choice as Ron's best man. Our brother Paul, his wife Lorraine and their two kids had stayed the night next door at Elsa Higgins's house, and they would give our elderly neighbor a ride to the ceremony. With a houseful of disorganized house guests, I had a feeling my surrogate grandmother would be the happiest of all of us to see this weekend to its completion.

The Jeep cranked to life with a little reluctance and I wondered if she was going to make it through another winter. The night temperatures were already dipping below freezing and the old girl was getting a little testy about that. I pulled my wool dress coat more tightly around me as I waited for the heater to thaw my toes.

Victoria's house sits less than two miles away, a cute little three-bedroom bungalow on the fringes of downtown. Convenient to Ron's work, it's one of the reasons they've decided to move into her place rather than his—that, and the fact that he's been in a dumpy, depressing bachelor apartment in the northeast heights ever since his divorce from Bernadette, I don't know how many years ago. My brother is hardworking, loyal, and kind; he is not a homemaker. The dreary apartment doesn't look a whole lot different from the day he moved in.

Victoria, on the other hand, has put all her professional interior decorator skills to work on her place, so even though it's an older home she has added all the modern conveniences without sacrificing the original ambiance. Last I heard, Ron had moved quite a bit of his stuff over there and was ready to vacate his apartment by the end of the month. Pretty much everyone thought he couldn't leave the old dump a moment too soon.

I drove up Lomas, noting that the Saturday morning drivers all seemed to be moving sluggishly along the frosty streets. This was our first real cold snap of the season and

I supposed none of us were really ready to say goodbye to the gorgeous autumnal blue skies and Indian summer temperatures we'd experienced all the way through Thanksgiving. I turned off Lomas and took a couple more turns into Vic's 1950s neighborhood where, thanks to a recent revival of interest in Albuquerque's downtown area, the homes had undergone a wave of renovation and renewal. Tired facades had been updated, withered landscaping replaced and updated for greater curb appeal. All in all, it was a charming little area where anyone would want to live.

Stopping in front of her mushroom-brown house with its dark chocolate trim, I started to tap my horn before realizing how rude that would be. Besides having a lot to carry, she most certainly had a zillion things on her mind and would appreciate a hand with some of the tasks. I braced myself against the chilly breeze and climbed out of the Jeep.

Boxwood hedges lined the flagstone path that meandered with a charming curve to the front door. The drapes appeared closed, but beyond the transom window the entryway light was on. Victoria had probably been up since before dawn putting the final touches on whatever it was that perfectionist brides put touches on. I'm not a fusser and my own wedding had been thrown together very last-minute, so I have no clue about a lot of this stuff. I pressed the doorbell.

Not a sound came from inside. She must be back in her bedroom. With a shiver against the breeze, I buttoned my coat up to the throat and hit the bell again. This time I distinctly heard it echo off the hardwood floors and through the spacious living room. I let a full two minutes go by. Maybe she was in the shower. After awhile, though, I began to wonder. She knew I was coming. She'd been very specific about the schedule, allowing time to get to the chapel and dress for the ceremony. I was not a minute late, but I wasn't early either. I began to feel slightly irritated as I reached for the doorknob.

The solid wood door swung inward without a sound.

"Vic? It's Charlie. You ready?"

From the basement I could hear the furnace running but a chill breeze skimmed my ankles. I closed the door and took a few steps into the entry hall, reminding myself that I'd left my Jeep running out on the street.

"Vic? Hurry up, time to get going," I called out. My voice ricocheted back at me.

With one ear tuned to the idling Jeep and the other to the sounds within the house, I walked into the living room. A puddle of white silk caught my attention first. Victoria's wedding dress, lying in a heap on the floor. Something was very wrong.

Chapter 2

I took a shaky breath and called her name again, this time with a definite waver in my voice. No response.

Okay, Charlie, stop and think. There could be a lot of reasons for this. She's on the phone, she ran to a neighbor's place for something, she realized Ron would forget the flowers and went to pick them up herself. But she would never leave her beautiful wedding gown lying there on the floor. I'd gone with her to the designer's shop to choose that dress. With Victoria's usual flair for the chic, she'd chosen this one because it so perfectly fit both her figure and her style. She looked like a sophisticated princess in it. She loved this dress.

I wandered over to the pile of white and picked it up, looking for the hanger. That's when the disarray in the rest of the room caught my attention. The overstuffed sofa, normally at a precise angle to the fireplace, sat off-kilter. Brightly colored pillows, always neatly plumped at the corners of the couch, had fallen to the floor and an arrangement of seashells from the coffee table lay strewn across the blue and cream area rug. A sharp odor, somewhat familiar, hung in the air.

My heart went into overdrive. I dropped the white gown onto the sofa.

"Vic!" I yelled, racing down the hall toward the bedrooms.

No sign of her in the boys' room or the front one she used as her home office. The master bedroom showed a neatly made bed, a makeup case on the dresser with her white satin shoes sitting nearby, and a packed airline suitcase with the lid up just waiting for whatever last-minute things she intended to pack. Both bathroom doors stood open; neither held a wisp of recent steam or a hint of soap or shampoo scent.

Down the hall again, I went into the kitchen where there was no sign of breakfast, not that Victoria wouldn't have immediately cleaned up after herself. I did find the source of the chill I'd felt earlier. The back door stood partway open.

My pulse pounded in my head as I reached for my cell phone. But I'd left my purse in the Jeep which, given the city's notoriety for missing vehicles, was an incredibly stupid move on my part. I ran out front and yanked open the driver's door, sliding into my seat and grabbing for the purse on the floor of the passenger side. My hands shook as I tried to tap numbers to reach Drake. Two misdials before I finally got it right. I took a deep breath as his phone rang.

"Have you and Ron heard anything from Victoria this morning?" I asked, amazed that my voice sounded as calm as it did.

"Why? She's supposed to be with you."

I breathed. "I know that. I'm at her house. She's not here." At that point, my fake calm left me. "Something's really wrong, hon. I don't know what, but things don't look right."

A moment of silence. "We'll come. Wait where you are. Fifteen minutes, max."

I nodded, as if he could hear it over the phone, but the connection was already dead.

The Jeep was warm inside, and it was tempting to take Drake's instruction literally and stay there, but unanswered questions bug me to death. When they involve a loved one, there's no way I can sit quietly by. I pulled my keys, grabbed purse and phone, and even remembered to lock the car as I headed back to the empty house.

This time I paid close attention to every detail. Nothing at the front seemed out of place. Small, potted evergreen shrubs flanked the red painted door. The fact that the door was unlocked when I arrived was troublesome, but there really had been no sign that Victoria had not left it that way. Inside, the entry hall with its console table, trio of Nambé candlesticks, antique mirror and arrangement of fall foliage appeared exactly as I'd seen them on previous visits. Still, the condition of the living room worried me. The wedding gown on the floor would have never happened with Victoria in control. Someone else had been here.

I sniffed the air. Again, that noticeable acrid odor. I stepped into the grouping of sofa and side chairs, the area I'd only observed from the doorway earlier. From this angle

I saw it—a long smear of red on the wheat-colored sofa. Closer, I could tell it was blood. Below the smear, on the blue and cream area rug, a puddle had formed. Drops led away from it, dripping their way toward the dining area and kitchen.

I swallowed hard, my toast and coffee threatening to rise. My index finger reached toward the spot, wanting to test whether it was wet. *Stupid move, Charlie.* I yanked my hand back.

Other things began to catch my attention. Slivers of wood on the hearth, shreds of stuffing from a pillow that had fallen to the floor. A small statuette of a Franciscan saint lay on its side on the mantel, nudged there by some force not quite strong enough to knock it to the floor. I knelt and held a hand to the glass fire screen. It was cold.

A sound at the front door startled me and two seconds later Ron and Drake walked in, catching me on my knees at the hearth staring up at them.

"What's going on?" Ron demanded.

"I wish I knew." I pointed out the red stains.

"Where's Vic?" Ron demanded.

"I was hoping you could tell me. I got here to pick her up and found this. The front door was unlocked. The back one is standing open …"

"Shit," he murmured, rubbing his hands through the somewhat sparse hair on his head.

"We have to call the police," Drake said. "Something could have happened to her."

"Maybe she got scared and went to one of the neighbors," I suggested.

"And didn't call me?" Ron paced the room, his eyes flitting every direction.

I looked toward the dining table, surrounded by six antique chairs. The purse Victoria normally carried hung by its strap over one of them.

"Maybe she couldn't call. Here's her purse," I said, checking and verifying that her phone was inside.

"Charlie, she could have gone to a neighbor, used their phone."

Good point—stupid me.

"She's missing and there's blood. We have to get the police involved," Drake repeated. He was already pulling his phone from the pocket of his tux. "Meanwhile, it's probably good if none of us touch anything."

My hubby is quickly learning the finer points of crime scenes after only four years on the periphery of Ron's and my private investigation business. I left Victoria's purse where it hung and tried to think of everything else in the house I might have touched, while he dialed 9-1-1 and gave the dispatcher the basics.

Ron continued to pace and there was something about his expression that bothered me.

"You going to tell me what's going on?" I finally asked.

"Nothing! Nothing's going—well, obviously, something went on here."

"Ron? You've been tetchy all morning. I hardly noticed it at our house, with all our rushing around to get ready. Is this wedding day jitters or something else?"

He glanced toward Drake then back at me.

In the distance I heard a siren.

"Is this something you want to tell the police, or would you rather get it over with while it's just us three?"

The siren grew louder, making the turn onto this street.

"It's just—I don't know—Vic and I had an argument last night." He glanced toward the front door as the cop car came to a stop at the curb.

"You guys never fight. Was it a bad one?"

"I don't know, Charlie. I've never seen her like that. We were talking about today and about our honeymoon trip. She'd found the tickets and I was a little put out that she wasn't happy with my surprise. That's all, I swear."

Footsteps approached the front door.

"Did the fight get loud?" I kept my voice low. "Could the neighbors have heard it?"

"No! I don't think so." He shuffled his weight to the other foot. "By the time I left everything was okay. I swear, she fully intended to go through with the wedding."

The doorbell rang.

"I'll get that," Drake said. "Maybe you'd better shush about this until we see what the police say."

Both Ron and I took that as excellent advice.

Chapter 3

Two uniformed officers stood at the door when Drake opened it, a tall, dark-haired man standing slightly behind the other, a woman with her blond hair twisted into a bun at the back of her cap. They seemed a bit surprised at the appearance of Ron and Drake in formal wear at eleven o'clock in the morning. I suppose I looked a little off-whack too, with my hair elaborately done up, wearing jeans and a flannel shirt under my woolen dress coat.

The female officer spoke first, verifying that the call had come from this residence, and Drake basically repeated what he'd said to the dispatcher. Victoria Morgan owned the house and was supposed to be getting married this morning but was missing and we'd found things out of order inside the house. I led them into the living room and went through the list of things I'd noticed out of place. Other than the blood and wedding dress, most of the other items could easily be explained away, I supposed, by someone rushing through the room in a hurry. I did my best to impress upon them that Victoria wasn't the type who rushed about knocking things over, nor would she have left the room in disarray. Not to mention that she was expecting me to pick her up this morning.

In a standard divide-and-conquer move, the male officer took Ron to the kitchen and the woman, whose badge merely identified her as P. Lacey, shuffled Drake and me back toward the front door where we went through a raft of questions of the sort they were probably required to ask although they were stupid. In my opinion.

"Could Ms. Morgan have simply left to do a quick errand before the wedding?"

"No, her purse is here and her car is out in the driveway."

"Maybe she meant to meet you at the church?"

"Leaving her dress, shoes and everything else behind? Really! Not to mention that she would have phoned with any change of plans."

Officer Lacey must not have liked my tone of voice. She turned to Drake.

"When was the last time any of you saw her?"

"The rehearsal dinner last night," he said with a smile that was intended to say, Don't mind my wife's attitude. She's always a little short-tempered in situations like this. "Other family members are in from Arizona and we met at Pedro's for dinner. Ron drove Victoria home afterward."

Ms. Lacey wrote all this into her little notebook along with our phone numbers and address. "I'll need a complete list of those at the dinner. Did either of you speak with Ms. Morgan this morning?"

We both shook our heads. I felt as if I'd done something seriously wrong by not staying in closer touch, but really—we're only talking a matter of twelve hours or so.

Through the archway to the living room, I could see the other officer—I think he'd introduced himself as John Blumenthal—with a guiding hand at Ron's elbow, steering him toward us. The man's eyes, however, were aimed toward the blood-stained rug.

"I'm calling in a 10-28," he told P. Lacey. To the rest of us, he said, "You all will need to leave the house now. We have your contact information."

"What? We can't leave until we know where Vic is," Ron sputtered.

"We're investigating the fact that she's missing. Meanwhile, I meant what I said," Blumenthal replied. "You can go home now."

The two of them herded the three of us out the door and down the front steps. Then the door closed between us, just after I noticed Blumenthal speaking into his shoulder mike.

"So. What now?" I asked.

"Well, I'm not going home," Ron said. A flicker passed over his face as he looked up at the bungalow. "This is my home. Aside from a few things back at the apartment, I'm almost completely moved in here."

"We could go to our house," Drake said.

"No!" A rush of rebellion ran through me. "There's no way I could sit around, wondering what's going on. I'm staying here."

Ron ran his hands down the sides of his face, then glanced at his watch. "The wedding's supposed to start in thirty minutes." He looked completely lost.

"Okay, here's what we'll do," I said. "I'll call Paul and tell him to keep everyone entertained, tell them there's a little delay. That will buy us some time."

Neither of the men had a better plan, so they merely nodded.

"Then, on the off chance that she really did pop over to a neighbor's house, forgot the time, didn't notice the arrival of two cop cars …" It sounded lame. "We should ask around. You guys take the houses on either side, I'll go across the street. Ask if anyone has seen her, if they heard or saw anything unusual at the house last night or this morning. Ron, what time did you leave her here last night?"

"Eleven-thirty? Midnight? Something like that."

Unfortunately, I couldn't corroborate what time he'd gotten to our house. I'd been dead asleep by ten.

"Okay, so use that as our timeline, the last time we know for a fact that she was okay. Ask people if they noticed anything after midnight."

"Charlie … the police will want to ask the questions," Drake said.

I ignored him and pulled my cell phone from my purse. Ron started moving. Drake shrugged and I watched the two guys head in opposite directions, practically hopping through the frosty winter-brown grass in their woefully inadequate dress shoes and clothing. In five minutes, I'd informed our other brother, Paul, that there would be a delay and asked that he take over and keep folks busy for another hour or so. He dithered—he's a great ditherer—wondering aloud what he should do until I got impatient and told him to figure it out. Sheesh!

The sun began to peek out through the clouds as I walked across the street, and I hoped the day would warm up a bit. I rang two doorbells where no one was home; Saturday errands apparently took precedence over the excitement in the neighborhood. At the third house, really the only other one with a clear view toward Victoria's, an elderly lady answered. My hopes dimmed when, upon asking my question, I had to stop so she could turn up her hearing aids.

"I never sleep a wink anymore, honey," she said. "Some nights I just lay there in bed. Sometimes I get up and bake. Would you like to come in for a cookie? You look cold, dear."

I glanced back to see if I could catch sight of Ron or Drake, but neither was near enough to rescue me. The sun wasn't hitting the covered porch where I stood and a gust of wind nearly took my breath away.

"A cookie would be lovely," I said.

The moment I stepped inside I had to peel off my coat. The place felt like a hundred degrees. I hoped the old woman's Social Security covered such a heating bill.

"I'm Gladys Peabody."

"Charlie Parker. My brother, Ron, is marrying Victoria, across the street."

"Charlie? That's a funny name for a girl. You ain't one of them who's changed herself from a man, are you?"

I chuckled at the suspicious going-over she was giving me.

"No, nothing like that. My name is Charlotte—Charlie's a nickname I've had since I was a kid."

She led me through a living room that would have been the dream of any Depression-era collector. Carnival glass candy bowls, sets of pink and green sherbet dishes and a metal tureen with intricately etched designs filled bookshelves and glass-fronted curio cabinets. In spots, I had to turn sideways to squeeze through the dining room as we headed toward a kitchen that sported a slope-shouldered refrigerator (amazing the thing still ran) and a dinette set of chrome edges and yellow leatherette seats.

I already knew there was no way she could have seen Victoria's house if she'd been baking. The kitchen's only window faced a backyard full of elm leaves and crispy rosebush canes. But she'd forgotten my original purpose and was intent on pouring hot water from a kettle on the gas burner into a teacup. I tried to make little hurry-up noises, picturing Ron and Drake standing out in the cold waiting for me. But Gladys was not to be rushed. She found an old fruitcake tin and opened it to reveal the most scrumptious-looking pile of butter cookies I've ever seen. Oh well, Ron and Drake could sit in the truck and start the heater.

Between bites of melt-in-the-mouth cookie, I tried to ascertain what times Gladys was up and whether she had actually looked out her front windows at all during the night.

"Well, I always do," she said. "You know, just keep an eye on things and make sure the neighborhood looks all right."

The tea scalded my tongue and I didn't even mind. I took a second cookie.

"My brother brought Victoria home after their rehearsal dinner and stayed until around midnight. Did you see him leave?"

"I think I must have been asleep then. See, the thing about getting older is that you fall asleep at the oddest times. I drift off in front of the TV then go to bed and can't catch a wink."

I wanted to hurry her up. I could only eat so many of

these cookies before I'd have to unbutton my jeans.

"But last night I actually went to bed around ten-thirty, right after the news. It was about two o'clock when I woke up and couldn't go back to sleep. I got up and started my baking about three in the morning. I noticed a light on over there, across the street."

"Was that unusual?"

"Yes. Come to think of it, it was peculiar. I don't know the young lady all that well, but I do have to say that I've never seen her lights on late like that. She'd told me she was getting married. I suppose I thought she was doing something to get ready for the wedding. Or maybe she was just sleepless, like me."

We could speculate along those lines all day long and I really did need to get going. I thanked her for the treats and edged my way back through the cluttered dining and living rooms. The icy blast at the front door actually felt good and I raised my face to the breeze before realizing I'd better put my coat back on.

Across the street, I saw Ron and Drake sitting in Drake's truck in Victoria's driveway. I started toward them, pausing at the curb when a sterile-looking white car came slowly down the street. I recognized it as belonging to Kent Taylor, an APD detective.

Homicide. The realization sent a chill right through me.

The car pulled to the curb in front of Victoria's, parking behind my Jeep. Ron's startled face showed that he, too, had recognized Taylor's car. He got out of the truck and the two of us approached Taylor as he started toward Victoria's front door.

"Ah, the Parker duo," the detective said. He seemed older than when I'd last seen him, the lines in his face more pronounced and his fringe of hair grayer. He wore a flat cap, like a golfer's, and a long wool overcoat against the chill air. "I thought that was your Jeep."

Ron spoke up. "Kent, why are you here?"

Realizing how abrupt that sounded, I inserted that there had not been a homicide, that Victoria was missing. That was all.

"I can't speak to the facts until I've been inside," Taylor said. "I came because the responding officers reported finding a significant amount of blood and some bullet holes. The Crime Scene Team should be along any minute and we'll see what the evidence shows."

As if they'd heard his voice calling out to them, a large black van turned the corner and pulled in behind Taylor's plain sedan. This was becoming all too real, all too quickly.

Bullet holes? "Kent, are you sure?" My breathing felt ragged.

He turned to me. "We aren't sure of anything, Charlie. That's our job, to gather evidence and put it all together and then to catch whoever is responsible."

He started walking toward the van and I automatically trailed along, until he spun around and pointedly asked me to wait at my vehicle. I didn't realize Ron had also followed; when I turned I ran solidly into his chest.

Detective Taylor began issuing orders to the crime scene folks using a low voice that, frustratingly, I could not hear. Ron and I stood frozen in place, huddling there, our eyes fixed on the police team. Thoughts ricocheted through my head—bullets, blood, crime technicians—along with the picture of Victoria's white gown I'd found on the floor inside.

All the officials disappeared into the house. I wanted

so badly to go along, to explain and show what I'd found earlier, but even I realized they would never go along with that. Although the sun had come out, the air had not warmed much at all. Without consulting each other, we three climbed into my Jeep and I started the engine for some heat.

A very long half-hour passed before Kent Taylor came back outside. He held a small notebook in one hand and a cell phone to his ear with the other. He stared toward us as he talked for about a minute, then stuffed the phone in his pocket and strode over to the Jeep.

Ron started to get out but Taylor asked if we minded talking in the car. Without waiting for an answer he walked to the remaining empty passenger seat and let himself in. I turned in my seat to watch.

"Ron, your registered weapon is a Beretta 9 millimeter, isn't it?"

My brother nodded.

"Is it in your possession?"

"Well, considering I was at the wedding chapel, no, I'm not wearing it right now."

"Don't get snide with me." Taylor sounded resigned, rather than angry. "I'll need to test it. Where is it and when was the last time you fired it?"

"It's in my car back at the chapel. I went to the gun range about two weeks ago and that's the last time I fired it. I cleaned it the next day."

"Okay." Taylor was jotting this down in his little notebook. "Why the car? Don't you normally keep it at home when you're out on social and family occasions?"

"I'm a little unsettled right now. I've moved most of my stuff here to Victoria's house, but there are still a few things at my old apartment. It just felt safer to keep it near me, that's all."

"Why does this matter?" I piped up.

"I'm afraid the bullet holes in the house are nine millimeter."

"There are at least a thousand nine millimeter guns in this town. Probably more," I said.

"Charlie …" Ron's voice held a warning but I'm not very good at staying quiet.

"You can't seriously think Ron would go shooting up his own home!"

A little smile formed on Taylor's face. "You'd be amazed at how often that very thing happens."

"Wait a second," Drake said. "Are you saying Ron is a suspect in a crime?"

"I'm saying we have more questions than answers at this point. We'll do tests. We'll do interviews. We'll find out what happened." He flipped back to the beginning of his notes. "So, for starters, tell me how you all happened to be here this morning."

I ran through the quick version of the wedding day plans, how I'd arrived first, finding the door unlocked and the bride missing.

"After the other officers kicked us out of the house, we went to the immediate neighbors to see if maybe Victoria had gone to someone's house. I figured I'd look pretty silly if it turned out she'd just run next door for a cup of something and came home to find the cops all over her house."

He sent me a look. "Charlie, there's a lot of blood in there. There are bullet holes. No matter where Ms. Morgan

is, there's plenty of reason for the police to be involved."
Taylor shuffled in his seat, reaching for the door handle.
"Hang out here until I get back but don't go around
questioning any more neighbors. I mean it."

The three of us sat in a thick silence as Taylor got out
and went back to the house. Before the door closed, one of
the uniformed cops came out and posted himself on the
porch to watch us.

"What the hell is this about?" Ron fumed.

My mind was racing ninety miles a second. The rest of
the family and friends were still at the chapel, thinking the
wedding would happen any minute now. I'd purposely not
told Paul anything he could misconstrue, so his logical story
to the gathering was probably that there'd been a delay with
the bride's dress or the flowers or something. The ceremony
should have started a half hour ago and I could picture the
crowd getting restless.

"Let's think about what might have happened," Drake
said, the one cool head in the bunch. "Victoria has her own
pistol, doesn't she? She went to the range with us a time or
two. Maybe she was doing something with it, cleaning it or
something and it went off and injured her. But she was able
to get to medical care somehow."

The idea of Victoria, the night before her wedding,
deciding to clean her gun sounded way far-fetched to
me, but it provided a ray of hope. I suggested we call the
hospitals, since we had nothing else to do but worry. With
three of us on cell phones, we went through the list pretty
quickly, then the urgent care centers in this part of town,
receiving negative answers all around.

"What else might have happened?" I asked when the

hospital scenario didn't pan out.

"Maybe she heard an intruder, got out her gun, wounded the guy ..."

"And she wouldn't call me right after this happened?" Ron grumbled.

He was right. Victoria might have been cool-headed enough to confront and get rid of an intruder on her own, but there was no way she wouldn't have reported this to Ron and the police and—if I knew her at all—she would have immediately set out to clean up the mess in her house. She was gone, and although none of us wanted to voice the thought, it was beginning to look as if someone had taken her. Dead or alive.

Chapter 4

It felt like forever before Kent Taylor came back out, a stretch of time in which I could only repeat to myself: she's alive, she's alive somewhere.

"Okay, Ron," Taylor said. "I'll need you to come with me and make a statement. We'll stop by and pick up the gun from your vehicle, then we'll be downtown." Something told me he'd found out about the argument between Ron and Victoria last night. There was a certain firmness in the detective's expression.

"We'll come along," I said to Ron.

"You can't ride with us," Taylor said. "I've already got my hands full here. But I suppose I can't stop you from driving down to the station yourself."

He had that right. While Ron got into Taylor's car, Drake and I quickly made a plan. We would swing by our house and leave his truck there, then take my Jeep to the police station. The extra stop was only a few minutes out of the way.

While we were at it, I'd better accept the fact that the wedding wasn't happening today. That meant calling Paul again and also contacting the country club and letting them know the reception and luncheon were off, too. With a heavy heart, I dialed Paul's number. Officially calling off the wedding made it too real.

"Let the guests know it's time to go home," I told him. "Take Ron's boys back to their mother's house. This isn't the time for them to become an added distraction for Ron. He's, um, going to be busy for awhile. I'll fill you in when I see you back at Elsa's place."

I could picture the gorgeous cake Sally had driven all the way to Taos to pick up at Sweet's Sweets, my favorite pastry shop on the planet. We were *not* going to let that fabulous confection go to waste.

"I'm going to stop by the club on the way home and save their cake," I told Drake.

Forty-five minutes later, the two of us were carrying the splendid three-tier cake into our house and setting it on our dining table. If everything went well, we would have Victoria back in our midst by tonight and could figure out some way to pull off this event tomorrow, with the cake none the worse for the delay.

I repeated it to myself as I hung my matron-of-honor dress in the closet, as I set my makeup case on the dresser, as I stared in the bathroom mirror at the newly formed dark circles under my eyes. Face it, things were not looking good. Our beloved Victoria was missing and my brother was being questioned by the police. My haggard face reflected the otherworldly feeling in my head.

"Hon, where are you?" Drake called out.

I dabbed at my eyes and applied fresh lipstick to draw attention away from my reddened nose.

"I'm in the bathroom," I said. "Almost ready."

Drake had traded his tux for jeans and a sweatshirt and he handed me my warm parka as we headed for the front door. Our casual clothing felt wrong, a symbol of the entire day gone off track.

We were halfway to the Jeep when Elsa's 1968 Mercury, quite the sporty thing in its day, pulled into the driveway next door. My brother Paul was at the wheel, Elsa beside him, with Lorraine and their two kids crammed into the narrow backseat. Paul brought the car to a jolting stop when he saw we were about to leave.

"What happened? Where's Ron? What's with Victoria?" He didn't stop questioning the whole time it took him to cross the lawn.

My condensed version of the story was becoming more concise with every telling. For this group, only the very basics: Victoria had not been home when I got there this morning, it appeared there'd been some kind of mishap, Ron was talking to the police about it and we were on our way to pick him up.

Elsa Higgins, my ninety-year-old neighbor who has been more like a grandmother over the years, had followed Paul and now stood shivering in the wan winter light because of her lightweight flowered chiffon dress and beautiful-but-flimsy matching autumn-gold coat. She obviously hadn't figured out that October has been gone for awhile now.

"Oh, dear," she fussed. "Poor Ronnie. Will Victoria be all right?"

I didn't want to even begin to address that question so I changed the subject.

"I'm so sorry about the cancelled luncheon," I told them. "Maybe when we get back we can get take-out food or something."

"Don't you fret about it at all," Elsa said. "I thought about it on the way home. I've got a pot of chile that I'd made for tomorrow. It'll warm up in a jiffy and feed us all. And it won't take but twenty minutes to bake a fresh pan of cornbread to go with it."

"You all go ahead and eat. I know it's late for lunch and you must be starving. Drake and Ron and I will check in with you when we get home." I held to the faint hope we'd be back within an hour or so.

As we drove toward police headquarters downtown, I couldn't stop picturing the scene in Victoria's house. The blood, the disarray, the gown. Add to all this the fact that they were now questioning Ron. I was glad we had passed up the invite for lunch. My stomach was in such a twist, there was no way I could imagine putting food in there.

I navigated the one-way streets downtown until I reached the station. Luckily, Saturdays are fairly quiet around here and we were able to snag a decent parking spot. As we approached the main entrance, it looked like some kind of speech was taking place. Media people from all the local stations aimed microphones at a suited man with a two-hundred dollar haircut. Politician or lawyer. I didn't recognize him, but he had the look. We swerved around the cluster of excitement and climbed the steps.

I've been to Kent Taylor's office before. Several of Ron's cases have overlapped with APD's and most of the time we've managed to work effectively together, if not always cordially. In general, the police would love it if private investigators and ordinary citizens stayed out of the way and allowed the officials to do their jobs. Most of the time I'm perfectly cool with that. Most of the time I don't have a relative who's being questioned.

Drake and I made our way through security but were stopped short of getting down the hall where the detectives' quarters are. I had to put my name on a list and wait for a sergeant to come out and listen to our story. He stepped away and apparently made a call. When he came back we were told that Ron Parker was a 'person of interest' and we would have to wait until questioning was completed.

"Does he need a lawyer?" I hated the fact that I had to ask the question.

"Mr. Parker has not requested one," the sergeant informed me, "although he certainly has the right to."

Something about his tone gave me an uneasy feeling. I waited until he left and I turned to Drake.

"I think I'd better call someone for Ron."

"Charlie …"

"Even if he doesn't want an attorney now, I think he needs good advice. The fact that they brought him here, rather than covering the questions back at Victoria's place … I don't like it."

He didn't argue with me.

I thumbed through the contacts on my phone coming across the name of Ben Ortiz, one of the attorneys our firm had dealt with on multiple occasions when RJP Investigations performed background checks and other investigatory errands connected with various clients of Ortiz's. Mainly, I liked the fact that Ben was a bulldog in court and had pulled off some amazing feats of defense. I tapped his number.

Court. Just having the thought go through my head rattled me. Surely this thing would never go that far.

"Ortiz." His voice was crisp and matched what I remembered of the man who wore tailored suits and expensive shoes.

"Ben, it's Charlie Parker—RJP Investigations." I went into the condensed version of where I was and what I was doing here.

"I can be there in a half hour," he said.

I repeated that Ron had not yet officially requested counsel but I would certainly pay for Ben's time, whether or not it turned out he took the case—if there was a case. We agreed to meet in the building's lobby where I could bring him up to speed with the little I knew.

Meanwhile, Drake had disappeared somewhere and came back with two cello-wrapped sandwiches from a vending machine.

"You haven't had anything other than toast and coffee all day." He pushed one of the sandwiches and a canned soda into my hands, ignoring my protests that I wasn't the least bit hungry.

I choked down the dry bread and unadorned turkey, knowing he was right about needing nourishment, hating that we weren't all at the wedding reception having champagne and cake right now. We walked the halls as we ate, each wishing we could think of something to say to comfort the other. The best I could come up with was to repeat what a great attorney Ben Ortiz was and that he would help us think of what to do next. The part I left unsaid was the worry over Victoria, where she might be, what condition she might be in. Those thoughts hung over me like a dark, ominous cloud.

* * *

"Tell me again, exactly what was said during this argument between you and your fiancée?" Kent Taylor asked Ron.

They were seated in an interrogation room Ron had never seen up close before. Previous visits to APD headquarters had always taken place either in Taylor's glassed-in office or the main squad room where the bustle of officers and the torrent of questions had always been about someone else. The closest thing he'd experienced to a personal tragedy was when Charlie had been taken by desperate robbers from the lobby of a bank eighteen months ago. It had been nerve-wracking and terrifying, but he'd been on the right side of the law. This felt completely different. The stainless steel table and chairs, the large two-way mirror on the wall, the recording equipment … it all felt antagonistic. His hands were like ice.

He sighed and went through the story again. "Victoria had found the tickets I bought for our honeymoon trip. I wanted the destination to be a surprise—Florida. Neither of us has been there and it seemed like such a great destination this time of year. I was going to pull them out when we got to the airport this evening."

Airport. That was another thing to cancel and probably lose his money on, the airline tickets.

"But she disagreed?"

"I don't know. She didn't really say so. She seemed, all at once … she just got all agitated, argumentative, and started pacing the room."

"She didn't want to go?"

"I got that feeling. Something was really bothering her about it." Ron ran his hand through his hair for the fortieth time in the last hour.

"But you don't know what, and you swear she'd never said anything against Florida in the past?"

"We've both been edgy for a few days. The wedding, my moving into her space. Little things that we each snapped about." Ron nearly bit his tongue. He had to remember that Kent Taylor was not his friend this time. He'd not been charged with anything and he'd not been given the official warning, but Ron knew his words would be used against him later if he kept blabbering away.

Taylor took a different tack, asking about the Beretta, getting Ron to repeat what he'd said earlier about the last time he used it and when he'd cleaned it. They had stopped at Ron's car and picked it up, Taylor taking it into evidence to be tested against the bullet holes at Victoria's house. Ron still didn't know what evidence they'd gathered at the house, what unknowns were possibly lurking to condemn him.

A knock at the door distracted Taylor and he went to speak with the uniformed officer standing there. The two chatted for a moment in low tones. Some new bit of information was being delivered but Ron couldn't hear what it was.

* * *

I spotted Ben Ortiz through the heavy glass doors facing the street. The earlier political hubbub had dissipated, the sleek-suited man gone and the remaining media people either milling about or packing their cameras and gear into vans at the curb. A couple of the journalists perked up when they recognized Ortiz but he ignored them and walked directly into the building.

Drake and I hung well back from the entry, waiting for Ortiz to pass through security before stepping from behind a large metal sculpture to greet him.

"Don't talk to that bunch out there, whatever you do," he warned us after shaking hands. "Let me handle them."

He probably remembered that I tend to say what's on my mind, not always at the most opportune times.

"Charlie, I'm serious. They're like vultures waiting for fresh meat. You and Ron do not want to provide it."

I nodded, reluctantly agreeing.

"Shall we go see what's happening upstairs?" Ben asked.

Drake and I gave each other a look. Neither of us is good about waiting for the wheels of procedure to turn. We like results—getting out there in our helicopter or raking through stacks of paper to uncover evidence. I need to be *doing* something. I caught sight of the large clock hanging from the ceiling in the lobby. Mid-afternoon already and I couldn't see that one thing had been accomplished toward finding Victoria and getting her home again. I itched to go back to her house and start a systematic search, to figure out a way to retrace her steps and learn where she might be now. But with the cops treating her home as a crime scene, there was no way they'd let me do what I needed to. Drake and I followed along as Ben Ortiz pressed the button for the elevator.

Kent Taylor emerged from the interrogation room and the lawyer strode purposefully toward him. I noticed Kent's eyes harden when he saw who we were with.

"I've been retained by the family to represent Ron Parker," Ortiz said. "I understand he hasn't been charged, so don't go into all that."

Kent Taylor was a cop who detested what he saw as those guys in the system who routinely mucked up perfectly good police investigations. I knew this—I'd heard his comments about Ben Ortiz and his type on more than one occasion.

"We're merely asking questions at this point," Taylor said, putting a diplomatic tone in his voice.

Ortiz had a way of facing the larger man as if he were actually the taller one. "Mr. Parker and his family have been through sheer hell this morning and it's time to give them a little peace. You know where to reach us if you have more questions later on. I want him released now."

"He's not being held. We're just crossing a few Ts, that sort of thing."

Ortiz sent a little nod my direction, a tilt of the head indicating he wanted to talk to the detective alone. Drake and I shuffled off to a row of chairs down the hall and watched as the conversation became more animated. After a good ten minutes of gesticulating and comments delivered through clenched teeth, Taylor walked away and the lawyer came toward us.

"Should just be a few more minutes," he said.

It was more like a half hour, but Ron emerged looking like a pup who'd been tossed into a roomful of angry cats, intimidated and relieved to have escaped. The sight of him in his wedding tuxedo felt especially wrong. I ran over and gave him a hug, a gesture that probably hadn't happened more than a dozen times in his life—we're typically not a huggy family. He kept an arm around my shoulders and sent Drake a bedraggled smile. When he started to tell us what had happened, Ben Ortiz cautioned him to wait.

We rode the elevator in silence and came out in the lobby.

"I want you to get a good night's sleep," Ben told Ron.

As if that would be possible.

"Tomorrow, come by my office at ten and we'll go over the whole story." He shook hands with his new client and left us.

My steps faltered. How would any of us get a wink of sleep with Victoria missing and this ridiculous cloud of suspicion from the police? I wanted to storm back upstairs and demand that Kent Taylor tell me what was being done to find her, what actual evidence he had to implicate my brother. Drake's words interrupted that train of thought as we walked toward the exit.

"Look, everyone, he's right. We all need some rest if we're going to act rationally. Let's go back to our house, eat something, think things through. Ron, the wedding will happen yet. We'll find out who got into her house and where they took her."

Ron stepped ahead and held the door for me and I belatedly noticed a man with fakey-perfect hair and thick makeup approach.

"Excuse me. Blake Moore, Channel 12 News." When he flashed the smile I recognized him immediately. "I just heard about your fiancée—you are Ron Parker, right? It's tragic, her going missing like that. Is there some way we can help?"

Ron's mouth opened, just as I jabbed him in the ribs. My first thoughts were: What the hell? How did this guy hear about it? How did he know who we were? Not necessarily in that order.

"What are the police saying?" Blake Moore continued. "Do they have a suspect in her death?"

"She's not dead!" My rib-jab and vise-like grip on Ron's arm didn't stop him from protesting loudly.

At that moment I saw Ben Ortiz approaching at a fast clip. He hadn't got as far away as I'd imagined and must have overheard. Unfortunately, it looked as if all the remaining media folks had also taken notice. In less time than it takes to think about it, we were surrounded.

Chapter 5

It was awful," I told Elsa.

We'd escaped police headquarters—with another dire warning from Ben Ortiz about keeping quiet—and made our way home, where Paul, Lorraine and Elsa waited.

"The attorney says we'll issue a public statement in the morning. Meanwhile, we aren't to answer the phone or the door to anyone who isn't a close friend or relative." I stared into the refrigerator, heedless of the cold air and waste of electricity, feeling that I should be coming up with food for the group.

Ron had gone into the guest room to shower and change clothes. Drake was outside, having said something about making sure our vehicles were locked.

"The attorney's advice is surely for the best, dear," Elsa said.

At this moment I had no idea what was for the best. Dusk had fallen quickly and Lorraine had dropped the hint that her kids were hungry. I didn't have a scrap of appetite and knew Drake and Ron felt the same way because we'd discussed it on the way home.

Lorraine bustled into the kitchen, on her way to the back door, a twenty dollar bill in hand. "Annie texted. They've given up on us and ordered themselves a pizza."

I hadn't even thought to ask where Annie and Joe were. Obviously, they were doing a better job of focusing on dinner than I was.

"We all had chile three hours ago," Elsa reminded. "I couldn't hold another bite."

"Okay, then. Anyone who's hungry can join the kids." I said in a half-hearted effort to simply get the problem solved. I closed the fridge door and turned toward the living room.

Paul had slumped into my favorite corner of the sofa, taking possession of Drake's TV remote as if he actually lived here. Ron emerged from the guest room wearing the jeans and rugby shirt he'd had on last night, and in one of those horrible bad-coincidence moments the six o'clock news blared forth with the lead story: "An Albuquerque woman is missing, on what would have been her wedding night. No one is saying the fiancé, Ron Parker, is a suspect *yet*, but defense attorney Ben Ortiz was at the man's side this afternoon at police headquarters."

I froze. Ron froze.

Drake stepped inside with, "Did you know there's a—" He stopped midsentence and took in the scene. "—news van outside?"

Ron headed for the front window.

"Don't do it," Drake said. He pulled the drapes shut. "They're already setting up cameras."

"I'm gonna tell them—"

But Drake grabbed his arm, reminding him what Ben Ortiz had said earlier.

"Shh," I hissed. "Let's listen."

Channel 12 finished with a short clip of Blake Moore standing in front of the building where we'd been this afternoon, footage obviously taken shortly after we'd bolted. As is too often the case no real news was given, just a lot of speculation about what authorities *may* be investigating. As far as I could tell, their only hard facts were that police were called to Victoria's home this morning when the bride-to-be was reported missing and the fiancé had been questioned. Of course, those tidbits were bad enough. Our phone immediately rang.

"Don't answer it," Drake advised. "It's probably reporters from other stations."

A sinking feeling hit the pit of my stomach. How could our lives have changed so much in the last twelve hours?

I heard a sound at the back door and immediately felt myself go on the attack. But when I raced in there, ready to bean some reporter with my handy brass candlestick, it turned out to be Lorraine, looking clueless as ever.

"Who wants pizza?" she offered. "We ordered two but you better get there before it's been devoured."

"You'll have to ask the others," I said. With an iron grip on her arm, I gave her the twenty-second version of how we needed to lock ourselves in and not answer doorbells or calls.

"Seriously? Even at Elsa's place?"

"Especially at Elsa's place. They'll try their best to get

the neighbors to talk to them. Do *not* do it!"

"Thank goodness the pizza guy got through before all this happened."

Whatever. I followed her into the living room, where Paul was the only person interested in eating. Repeating my warnings, I saw the two of them out the back door and locked it behind them. We agreed that anyone wanting to go between the two houses should call ahead and we'd each do our best to sneak through the hedge in the dark of night.

The TV was off when I went back to the living room with Ron, Drake and Elsa sitting in gloomy lumps on the couch.

I joined them. "I feel like we have to do something. We can't just let this whole thing happen without taking any action."

"You three weren't here for the chile earlier. You need food," Elsa announced. "No wonder you have no energy."

She got up, went to the kitchen and I heard cupboard doors opening and closing.

"She's right." I followed, discovering she'd already located fruit, cheese and crackers.

"It's not the wedding buffet but at least it might give you the energy to think straight." Once again I knew why I adored this lady.

We called the men and all sat around the kitchen table. Ron looked like an already-condemned man; Drake kept sending glances my way, silently asking how to handle this. I hadn't a clue. Luckily, Elsa began to recover first.

"I say we spend the evening making posters with her picture. We'll go around all over town tomorrow putting them up."

It felt a little embarrassing that a private investigator, a search-and-rescue pilot and little old me had not thought of this much earlier.

"All we need is a good picture of her," I said. "I can lay out a flyer on the computer and I'd bet Drake would let us have some of his office paper."

"Take all you want." At least we had a few bright eyes around the table as enthusiasm picked up.

"While I'm doing the computer stuff, Ron, you and Drake start calling her friends."

The plateful of cheese and crackers quickly disappeared as we now had tasks ahead of us. The phone had not stopped ringing since the news story hit the airwaves and, much as I hated to, I volunteered to listen to the messages. One of them could be from a friend who knew something or, ideally, maybe we would hear from Victoria herself.

Even as I had that thought, I knew better. Vic would have called Ron's cell phone if she was able to. Second choice would probably be mine. Both of those had stayed dreadfully quiet. As I listened, Drake's earlier statement proved to be true. Seventeen messages were from media people, from the four local stations, two national networks, and a handful of newspapers. I dutifully jotted down all the names and numbers—we couldn't know yet whether any of them might actually be of help.

Elsa cleared the plates away while I booted up Drake's office computer. Ron had dozens of pictures on his phone and we quickly chose a couple that looked most like Victoria in natural light with a pose that wasn't overdone. I soon had the facts and phone numbers typed below it and started the printer to crank out a few dozen. If this thing went on longer than a day or so (heaven forbid) we could have hundreds more done up at a print shop.

"Okay, thanks," Ron was saying to his cell phone. By the look on his face, I knew it was another disappointing call.

"Here's a list of the people I've called," he said, handing it over to me. "Everyone wants to help but no one's seen her."

"Most of these would have been at the wedding," I said.

My throat tightened at the thought—Ron and Victoria's big day ruined, the friends and family disappointed, the unopened gifts, the uncut cake still sitting on my dining table, her gown. I wondered if the police had taken it away or just left it there in its sad heap of fairy-princess white. I suppressed a sniffle and pretended I had an urgent need for the bathroom.

"I can try a couple of her clients," Ron was saying as I ducked out.

When I returned after a stern lecture to myself about holding it together, Elsa had found thumb tacks and tape, and had set them beside a nice stack of flyers on the table. We would be ready to hit the streets first thing in the morning.

"Okay, thanks," Ron said to the phone. "If you think of anything she might have said in recent days, any ideas where she might have gone, please give me a call." He gave the number for our office as well as his cell phone.

Drake handed me his written list of calls, mostly names Ron had provided, people I didn't know personally. I felt myself spiraling downward again, wondering what else we could do. The thought that *nothing* could be done hung at the periphery but I refused to let it take hold.

By nine o'clock we'd cross-checked our call lists and compared notes, all with no results. I wanted to snatch up the phone book and start with the A's to dial every household in the city, but realized that would not only be futile but rather rude. I peeked around the edge of the drapes to find that there were now three news vans out front.

"I'd better walk Elsa home," I said. Having my elderly neighbor caught in the glare of those awful lights was unthinkable. Plus, I needed to reiterate some things to the rest of the gang. Who knew what two pubescent kids who thrived on reality TV might do when someone turned a camera and microphone on them?

"Of course we know better than to talk to the press," Paul said, a little indignantly, when I brought it up to the little family I'd assembled in Elsa's living room.

"I'm just saying. No talking to anyone about any aspect of this. Our attorney will be giving a statement in the morning and that's that." I aimed my words toward thirteen-year-old Annie who, alarmingly, seemed more titillated than horrified by what we were going through.

The kid had never shown me a lot of respect, but Paul and Lorraine both promised to rule with an iron hand. Since they'd never done this in the past, it was with a lot of trepidation I left and tippy-toed through the break in the hedge to my own back door.

The men were on the sofa, their cell phones sitting dark and silent on the coffee table in front of them, glasses of Scotch resting on coasters. Maybe it was a sign that Ron was beginning to unwind a little.

"Elsa said something to me while she was stacking those fliers earlier," Drake said after offering me a drink. (I opted for the wine.) "She asked if Victoria had always lived in Albuquerque."

"She has." Ron didn't even look up from his lap.

"I suppose we could try going way back in her past," I

said. "See if she's been in touch with old school chums or previous co-workers?"

This time Ron did look up. "I wouldn't know where to start. Ever since she opened her own business, it's all been about clients and suppliers. It's been years since she worked for an employer and she rarely talks about her childhood. All I know is that her mother raised her alone and died fairly young."

"Maybe Kent Taylor will let us get to her business files so we can search out some more names." Drake offered the idea but I had my doubts.

If Taylor had any reason to believe Victoria's disappearance was tied to her business, he'd have already confiscated those files.

Chapter 6

October, 1978 – Miami, Florida

Juliette Mason gave her curly brown hair a shake and plumped the long spirals into place. Dark eye makeup, pale pink on the lips—getting this aspect of her appearance right was the easy part. She glanced toward her bed where she'd laid out several clothing choices. The short skirt with lime-green diagonal stripes was cute, her favorite outfit, but was it right for a job interview? *This* interview?

She'd received the inside tip from a neighbor whose brother's son's best friend worked for Pro-Builder Construction. The city's largest contractor was looking for a secretary, and rumor had it the boss liked them young and pretty. Juliette knew that attitude was sexist—half her friends considered themselves feminists and were in on the bra-burning craze—but at this point she needed a job, one that paid better than the minimum wage position at the auto parts store. Hell, the guys at the store hit on her all the time, anyway. Why not let some old geezer flirt for a lot more pay?

The blue pantsuit was the most businesslike, the one her mother would have chosen if she were still alive. The belted jumpsuit was classy, a tangerine polyester that looked almost like silk, but it really was more appropriate for evening with a few gold chains added around her neck. She reached for the short skirt and matching pullover top.

Forty minutes later she stepped off the bus, hiked her faux-leather bag strap over her shoulder and walked the half block to the address she'd been given. The squatty concrete building didn't say much about the success of the contractor, but the Pro-Builder sign was right there. She supposed a construction firm could build fabulous steel and glass high-rises for others even if they operated their own business out of a couple thousand square feet on a few acres of fenced dirt lot.

The concrete structure was free of ornamentation but there were wide windows on all sides and she saw desks inside. With luck, she might get one of those. Anything that showed blue sky and palm trees would be better than her current cubbyhole on the mezzanine above the auto parts store, where the nauseous reek of new tires never went away. She pulled the tinted glass door open and went inside.

She barely had time for a quick impression of the interior—nicer than she'd imagined, with some kind of stone flooring, earth-toned upholstery on the chairs, good quality wood furniture. A hallway led toward the back of the building and two closed doors concealed other rooms.

"Can I help you?" The husky voice came from a receptionist who was in her forties with blond hair in a classic upsweep from a decade ago. Her makeup was perfect, her clothes stylish and her nails painted to match her lips. While Juliette searched for the name of the man she was to see, the woman took a long draw on her cigarette.

"Um, yes. I'm here for an interview with Mr. Proletti." Juliette prayed she was pronouncing his name correctly.

"Al's out on a job. He told me to talk to you. Go ahead, have a seat." Ash fell from the cigarette when the woman—whose nameplate said her name was Sheila Page—pointed to the chair in front of her desk.

Juliette sat, tucking the hem of her skirt under her legs and setting her purse on the floor.

"The job is basic secretarial," said Sheila, "typing, filing, dictation. Sometimes the bookkeeper needs extra help with ledger entries. You ever done that before?"

Juliette cleared her throat quietly. "I had excellent grades in school in both typing and shorthand." Well, fifty words a minute on the old manual typewriters in class. "I've never done ledger entries but I'm very good at filing. I'm sure I can learn whatever's required of me."

Sheila stubbed out the cigarette and let her eyes travel over Juliette's chestnut curls, hazel eyes and the V of flesh at the top of the lime-green blouse. A flicker of something resembling acceptance crossed her face.

"You'll start at a thousand a month," she said. "If you want the job."

A thousand dollars a month! It was double what she was making now and the office was so much nicer.

She opened her mouth. *Don't seem too eager.* "Could I see where my desk would be?"

"Sure." Sheila stood, towering over Juliette on five-inch heels. She led the way toward the hall Juliette had noticed earlier. "That office there is Al—uh, Mr. Proletti's," she said with a wave toward the closed door to the right of the hall. "The one on the left is his father's, but the old man isn't here all that much. He pretty much retired a few years back."

Juliette followed Sheila down the hall. The first door on the right stood open, revealing a small office with one desk, a row of brown metal file cabinets and a closed door that must connect to Mr. Proletti's office. But the big attraction was the window. It faced the edge of the property and, once you got past the driveway that ran beside the building and the chain link fence surrounding the whole place, the view showed a lush park filled with flowering oleander and tall trees.

"How many people work here?"

"The whole crew? A lot. It varies by how many jobs we got going at the time. If you mean just the office staff, besides the owners there's me, the bookkeeper, a couple guys who handle shipments of materials. And Mr. Proletti's secretary—that's you, if you want the job."

Juliette couldn't believe her luck. "Yes, absolutely."

"Get yourself some decent clothes and plan to start Monday morning at eight o'clock." Sheila turned back toward her desk.

The comment about her clothes stung a bit but Juliette wasn't foolish enough to question. She studied her co-worker's outfit, a tailored pantsuit of obviously good material and shoes that probably cost what Juliette currently earned in a week. She would have to work up to those, but she could come up with something to get started. She practically flew back to the bus stop.

She stayed with the bus, past her own neighborhood, until it stopped outside the Surfside Mall. Near the mall's food court she found a pay phone and made two calls. Her boss wasn't happy that she'd phoned in sick this morning and was now informing him that she quit. He let out a string of curses and she hung up, wondering belatedly if she'd just lost out on her final paycheck.

Her second call went to Carol Ann Dunbar, her best, and only, friend who'd moved to the big city with her after graduation from Dalhart High. Juliette posed her question. Thirty minutes later she spotted Carol Ann weaving through the crowd and waved her over.

"I told Bob I had a dental appointment during my lunch hour, so I can always tell him it ran late or the gas made me woozy or something. I doubt he'll get too mad if I'm not gone more than an extra hour. What's up?"

Juliette explained about the new job and the need for wardrobe changes.

"So, my silly little courses in fashion design are coming in handy now, huh?" Carol Ann teased.

"Hey, don't knock secretarial work either." Her friend's eyes bulged when Juliette revealed her new salary. "But what I need now are the right clothes."

"It's a construction company?" Carol Ann seemed puzzled.

"But the boss is really successful and you should see the way the receptionist dresses. If I'm his personal secretary I have to look at least as good as she does."

"True." Carol Ann nibbled at her lower lip, studying the shop fronts nearby.

"But I can't spend much, at least right now. How classy can you dress me on a budget?"

Carol Ann led the way to one of the department stores. "Once you start earning some money you can head for the fourth floor. For now, we're over here." She headed deeper into the store.

Ninety minutes later each of them carried two huge shopping bags. With two suits—a brown and a black—a variety of blouses and a couple of skirts she could switch out with the pants, plus two dynamic pairs of heels, Juliette knew she could handle the new workplace. She got out of Carol Ann's car in front of her apartment and walked through the shabby courtyard to her place. Removing her new clothes from the bags, she got a dizzying bout of sticker shock. She'd run her new credit card up to the limit. What would she do if the job didn't work out?

She decided to only take the tags off each item as she wore it. She smoothed the store receipt and stuck it under the lamp on her dresser. If the new boss took a dislike to her she could at least return the unused clothes and go beg for her old job back. The smell of the tires came back to her, unbidden. No. The new job had to be great—she wouldn't let it be otherwise.

She ate a grilled cheese sandwich for dinner and tried to follow *The Rockford Files* on TV but her mind was on a hundred other details. Saturday morning, she scrounged ten dollars from various pants pockets and walked to the nearest low-price salon where she had three inches trimmed from her unruly hair. It would be an extra five bucks to have the beauty student style it in an up-do, which wouldn't last a whole day, so she skipped that.

Sunday, she did her own manicure and practiced trying to get her hair into a sleek upswept style like Sheila's, but it was impossible. She settled for pinning it up and letting the wavy tendrils go where they wanted. Maybe after a paycheck or two she could afford to have it straightened. For now she was counting bus fare and checking the peanut butter supply to get her through the first week. Sheila hadn't mentioned whether the pay was weekly—what if she was only paid every two weeks? She should have foregone one pair of shoes and made a grocery trip instead. She couldn't sleep that night.

By six forty-five Monday morning she'd showered and wrestled the springy hair into a semblance of a French roll. Her lipstick from the dollar bin at Walgreen's wasn't a name brand but it was a good shade to go with the vivid turquoise blouse she'd chosen to wear with her black pantsuit today. Stepping into the high heels, she stole a glance in the mirror and felt more grownup and confident. She paced her tiny apartment for forty minutes, until her feet began to ache in the new shoes, and finally it was time to leave for the bus stop.

What is it about the first day at a new job, she wondered as she dragged herself to the bus that evening. The boss hadn't showed up—some business had come up near Ft. Lauderdale, they said. She'd met the bookkeeper, Marion Flightly, a churchy lady in her forties whose eagle-eyed glare made Juliette think the woman didn't believe such a young kid could handle the work. Sheila had greeted her with a stack of folders and said it was filing to be done. Juliette spent an hour poking through the drawers in her new office, figuring out how the filing system worked. Mainly, the folders seemed to contain bids for jobs, information on new clients and invoices for materials. When she asked if the invoices should go to Marion, the older woman dismissively said, "You'll have to figure it out." What a witch. Juliette blew off the insult and concentrated on straightforward filing. In total, it took less than an hour.

About the time she was looking for something to do the phone began to ring.

"I'm transferring all of Al's calls to your desk. Just take messages. You won't know any of the names but that'll come with time," Sheila said.

Three lines immediately lit up at once. Juliette put on her best voice and pressed the button for Line 1.

"Mr. Proletti's office," she said.

"Where is he?" The gruff voice had a strong New York accent and she almost had to ask the man to repeat.

"I'm sorry, Mr. Proletti is out of the office today. May I take a message?"

"Who're you?"

"My name is Juliette. I'm Mr. Proletti's new secretary. How may I help you?"

More gruff words. Finally a name and phone number. On to Line 2, then Line 3, then back to Line 1. By lunch time she felt as if her head would explode. She asked Sheila if lunch was a full hour, then took her sandwich and walked to the park. Tomorrow, put a pair of comfortable shoes in a bag and bring them along, she told herself. She could learn the job. Surely, she could.

Tuesday, the office was abuzz already when Juliette

walked in at 7:49. The door to Albert Proletti's office stood ajar and she caught a glimpse of a good-looking, dark-haired man, younger than she would have expected. For some reason when Sheila had referred to the boss's father as 'the old man' Juliette assumed he must be in his eighties, putting the sons in their fifties or sixties. Mr. Proletti glanced up, spotted her, flashed a smile.

She greeted Sheila and headed toward her own office. This morning the connecting door to the boss's office stood partway open. A cassette tape sat on her desk. She picked it up, leaned out into the hall and waved it toward Sheila, shrugging her shoulders. The receptionist came and showed Juliette the transcription machine, whipping the cover off an IBM Selectric. Juliette figured out the headphones and playback mechanism which operated with a foot pedal. By the time Mr. Proletti got off the phone she was halfway through the first letter he'd dictated on the tape.

"You'll find that I often work at night," he said, leaning on the door frame to his own office as he nodded toward the dictation machine. He wore a sleek-looking suit with wide lapels and a bold-printed tie that was surely real silk.

She gave a nervous smile, unsure if he meant what the inflection in his voice seemed to hint.

"So, Sheila tells me you have a lot of secretarial experience," he said.

She did? Juliette merely smiled.

"I'm glad. The work here can get crazy at times. We have deadlines that cost tens of thousands a day if we miss them. Sometimes I yell. Sometimes I curse. I hope that won't bother you." He winked one of those brilliant blue eyes as he said it.

Juliette shook her head. She'd noticed that Marion Flightly kept her own office door closed. Was this part of the reason?

"You'll do great, sweetie. Don't worry about it."

Carol Ann would have piped up and objected to a boss calling his secretary sweetie. Definitely a sexist remark. It absolutely would have been if her old boss had uttered it. But here Juliette didn't mind. His tone was warm, yet professional. She had a feeling this was a boss who really cared about his employees.

"Mr. Proletti—"

"Al. We're all on first names here."

"Thank you. I, um, I hope all the messages I took yesterday were all right?"

"Perfect, Juliette. Just perfect." He turned back toward his desk but that time she was fairly certain his tone was not quite appropriate.

Chapter 7

I woke before dawn with that feeling that I'd never been fully asleep. The past twenty-four hours still had a surreal feel. Yesterday morning I'd awakened with anticipation. The wedding and reception were just ahead of us and my main concern had been about feeding the guys and getting us all out the door on time. For one moment I relived that, *almost* capturing the feeling that I would walk into the kitchen and begin an ordinary Sunday. A sound from the living room cancelled that.

Ron was huddled into the corner of the sofa, wearing the same jeans and rugby shirt he'd put on last night.

"Did you even go to bed?" I asked, slipping my arm around his shoulders as I passed.

He shrugged. "Tried. No point to it."

In the far corner Freckles stirred in her crate, giving an

impatient whimper. I let her out and followed her to the back door, where she bolted to her favorite corner of the yard. I pressed the button on the coffee maker and when I came back through saw Ron in the same spot. His face was haggard, eyes bloodshot with huge bags underneath.

"I take it there's been no call from the police?"

He shook his head desultorily.

"Let's get some coffee in us and then we'll go put those flyers out." I splayed my arms to show that I was already dressed for the chill outdoors.

He stared out into empty space and I finally plopped myself beside him on the couch. "There are lots of things we can be doing, Ron. Sitting here doesn't accomplish anything."

My normally action-oriented brother sitting like a lump was really beginning to worry me. A sound came from behind me as our bedroom door opened and Drake emerged.

Talk to him, I mouthed, tilting my head toward Ron as I headed for the kitchen. Freckles had long since finished her business and was scratching at the door, and I saw the sky had lightened considerably. I tended to her desire for some kibble in a bowl, reached for three coffee mugs, and checked the bread box where a package of Danish pastries still looked relatively fresh. Within a couple minutes I had a tray loaded and carried the meager breakfast to the guys.

Drake had switched on the TV and a way-too-cheery ad was touting all the Christmas goodies to be had at one of the department stores.

"Come on, you two. We are not settling in at home today. We've got flyers to distribute and don't forget Ben Ortiz was going to schedule a news conference so we can get the word out. Once everyone in Albuquerque is looking for Vic, we'll find her." My best upbeat voice barely made it through to them but the smell of coffee and pastry had at least grabbed Drake's attention.

"According to police, thirty-six year old Victoria Morgan disappeared from her northeast heights home and hasn't been seen in a day and a half," came the voice from the television set.

All three of our heads whipped around to look.

"We're here in front of the house where her fiancé, Ron Parker, is said to be staying …"

The rest of it was lost on me as I realized in horror that the house behind the reporter in the picture was, indeed, my own. I pulled back the edge of the drapes—yep, there were four news vans and bright lights aimed at the various reporters.

"… most likely suspect in her disappearance."

Ron's face had gone pasty gray, so I could pretty well guess the gist of the sentence I'd half missed.

The kitchen phone began ringing but I couldn't tear myself from the screen and the news story with its unwelcome intrusion into our personal lives. Five minutes later it became apparent the news folks had used up their set of facts; they began rehashing the same information, trying to freshen it up by rearranging the order and person delivering it. But there was really nothing new to be learned. Drake didn't respond to my request that we switch off the set, so I headed for the kitchen and picked up the phone to see who had called.

The mechanical voice told me I had two messages. Two? I swore it had only rung once, and we'd cleared everything last night. I pressed all the right buttons. "First message," the voice said. A faint clatter, a rustle, the hiss of static. Not even the courtesy of informing me the caller had gotten the wrong number. "Second message." This one came from Ben Ortiz, informing us that he'd scheduled a ten o'clock joint press conference with the police to give information about the case. It would be good for Ron to be there. We were to meet him at nine forty-five at his office for a short briefing. The address was a five-minute walk from the steps of police headquarters. I grabbed a pen and jotted down the details.

A tap at the back door caught my attention and I jammed the message slip into the pocket of my jeans. With the debacle out front, I didn't take any chances. Peering through the sheer curtain at the kitchen door I saw it was Elsa.

"Come in," I whispered, practically pulling her by the arm.

"You've seen them too?" she asked.

I merely clenched my teeth.

"Have you all had some breakfast? I made pancakes for Paul's family. It's easy enough to whip up another batch," she said.

"That's okay. We had a little something. No one's very hungry anyway."

"Mainly, Paul wanted to know if they should change their flight."

I'd entirely forgotten about their plans. Had the wedding gone off without a hitch, we would have had breakfast together and then sent the Arizona group home.

"What time is their flight?" Normally I'm good with this stuff but at the moment my mind felt like mush.

"Ten o'clock."

I did a little backward math and figured we ought to be

heading for the airport in an hour or so. It wouldn't leave much time for sticking up our flyers all around the area.

"I could—" Elsa started.

"No, I don't want you doing it." A woman whose recent driving experience only includes the grocery store and church? No way would I put her in the midst of the free-for-all the airport can be.

"Let me think. Drake can take Paul's group to the airport. Ron and I are heading out now to do the flyers and then we have to meet the lawyer." I didn't elaborate on that part of it. "Don't let anyone go out front until Drake has the car in your driveway. We cannot, *cannot* talk to these reporters."

She started to open her mouth, thought about it— picturing Paul's two kids, no doubt—and nodded. "I'll keep them all inside, if I have to throw myself in front of the door."

The mental picture of tiny Elsa spread-eagled to block the door made me smile, I realized, for the first time in awhile.

I worked out the logistics. Drake would need my Jeep for the four passengers and luggage, so Ron and I would drive the pickup. Ron's very recognizable car would surely be noticed and followed by the reporters. Of course, that could happen to any of us. What a boondoggle this was turning out to be.

In the end, we sent Drake as the decoy wearing Ron's normal Stetson and jacket. He dashed out to Ron's red Mustang, hopped in and drove away. A couple of the reporters bit, jumping into cars and following. They would surely be disappointed when they ended up right back here in fifteen minutes, but the little window of time would let

Ron and me make our break.

Stockier Ron sucked in his gut and put on one of Drake's bomber jackets and ball cap with our helicopter company logo on it. We didn't give Drake's pickup much chance to warm up, and I only had to say "no comment" once before we were on our way. I don't know how these news crews normally spend their days, but this had to be among the most boring and chilly ways to do it.

We headed first for Victoria's neighborhood, scanning carefully to be sure her house wasn't also a media target. Although the yellow tape remained over the front door, luckily there was not a van in sight. They must have gotten all the footage they wanted of the crime scene. I sighed and forced myself not to think of it that way.

Ron parked the truck a block off the nearest major street and we began taping flyers to light posts, bus stops, and any other unmovable object where people might pause a few extra moments. I covered six blocks east and four south, with Ron doing the same in the opposite direction. It felt like a meager effort. We really needed these all over the city. The television coverage might accomplish that—getting her picture and the story widely broadcast—and my heart became a little less hardened toward their intrusiveness. We couldn't have it both ways, I supposed.

My phone bleeped at me from down in my jacket pocket. Ron. He'd finished his distributions about the same time so we agreed to head for our vehicle. We only had about twenty minutes to make the appointment at the lawyer's office, which made me glad I'd convinced my brother to change into something a bit more reputable than his slept-in clothes. He'd even shaved for the occasion. I got to the truck first so I drove.

Ben Ortiz's office sat on a side street about a block from the cluster of municipal buildings downtown, in an area that was once residential about a hundred years ago. Now, the small former houses that escaped demolition have become oh-so-cute restaurants and offices. The one we were looking for was a two-story upright box with brown siding, dark green trim, and a waist-high wrought iron fence around its postage stamp of a lawn. A narrow driveway led to the back where, presumably, the old backyard had given over to employee parking—our own office a half mile away has a similar arrangement.

For customers, there was the street and not much of it. Each narrow property did well to accommodate two vehicles. We had to go three blocks west and around a corner to find a spot. By now we were running late and Ben was waiting at the door when we approached. Sending us a look, he suggested that we talk as we walked toward the police station. The narrow sidewalk necessitated that Ron and the lawyer walk side by side, so I dropped back and barely caught the gist of their conversation.

Basically, Ortiz had prepared a written statement for Ron to deliver. "Don't deviate from this message and don't extemporize," was one of the phrases I did catch. I gathered that I was to hang back, look supportive, and keep my big yap shut.

Ron attempted to read while walking, with a couple of stumbles due to old sidewalks buckled by ancient tree roots.

"I'm sure Detective Taylor will have something to say first," Ortiz said as we approached the steps of the police department where a podium and scads of microphones waited. "Then I'll give a brief statement to paint Ron as the devastated fiancé. Then Ron's going to make his plea for help from the community."

The first part went according to plan, anyway.

Kent Taylor, to his credit, remained very neutral in his words. He told the gathered crowd basically what we already knew. Victoria Morgan, on her wedding day, had disappeared from her home in the northeast quadrant of the city. There had been signs of a struggle. It was feared that she had been injured because she'd made no attempt to contact her family. Her whereabouts and condition were unknown at this time. He didn't use the word 'abducted' but his message sort of left that impression. He gave the number of a special hotline which had been established and asked that anyone with information please call.

I stood where I could watch Ron during Taylor's briefing. He was bravely trying to hold it together, his mouth clamped in a firm line to avoid trembling, his eyes straight ahead. I wished I'd taken the time to review his outfit a bit more closely. The jeans were rumpled and the plaid shirt was one he'd plucked from his overnight bag. My iron and I are practically total strangers but I could have run them through the dryer to take out some of the wrinkles. I sent him a tiny smile of encouragement.

Cameras clicked away as Ben Ortiz took the podium. I could only pray that the attorney's vigorous reputation would work in Ron's favor. I still wasn't convinced that showing up this early in the game with an attorney was the best move. Wouldn't my brother appear more innocent, less defensive if he simply got up there and spoke from the heart?

By the time he finished speaking, however, I had to admit

Ben Ortiz's words had gone a long way to explain Ron's disheveled appearance and sleep-deprived face. Ron took a deep breath, clutched his prepared speech in his hands and stepped to the front. I scanned the crowd and didn't see a lot of sympathy out there in the gang of reporters.

"Thank you for coming this morning," Ron began. "As you may imagine, the disappearance of my fiancée has come as a shock to our family. We have heard nothing from Victoria since Friday night and we fear for her safety. We very much appreciate this opportunity to connect with the community and to ask your help in locating our loved one. Vic did not leave the house of her own free will, of that I am convinced. It's not a case of a runaway bride. We were looking forward to our life together."

Beside me, Ben Ortiz tensed. Ron must have gone off-script, but I had no clue what he'd said that the attorney didn't like.

"Please keep Vic's picture visible. Please let every citizen of Albuquerque—of New Mexico—know that we are searching for her, that we want her back. Even a phone call, anything to assure us that she's all right."

"Mr. Parker," one reporter called out, "how is it that no one knew Ms. Morgan was missing until just an hour before the wedding? Did you know she was gone but withheld that information from the police?"

Ron's mouth flapped open mirroring, I'm sure, my own astonishment. Ben Ortiz stepped up quickly.

"Since this is an ongoing police investigation, we cannot comment on details." He took Ron firmly by the elbow and led him off the podium.

My mind spun. Wouldn't it have been better to set the

reporter straight? I'd arrived at Vic's house exactly as planned a couple hours before the wedding and had immediately informed the police. Well, almost immediately.

I turned and followed closely behind Ben Ortiz, who led us inside the municipal building. Outside, Kent Taylor stood facing the crowd, hands up, apparently telling them the meeting was over.

"What just happened?" I demanded as soon as Ron, Ben and I had stepped into a small alcove.

Ben faced Ron, his face tense. "Didn't I tell you to read the statement verbatim?"

"I said everything it said. Reading aloud always sounds wooden and fake."

"There are reasons. You referred to her in the past tense. You *were* looking forward to a life together. Somebody's going to construe it to mean things changed between you."

Seriously? One word?

"And the runaway bride comment? Ron, that thought was never out there—now you've planted it. They'll start looking for proof the two of you were unhappy."

Ron's expression closed. He'd heard enough. I took a deep breath and ran my hand down his arm.

"Let's go." I was trying to fix a map of the surrounding streets in my head, wondering the best way back to the truck without being waylaid by the media throng, when Kent Taylor walked into the lobby.

"Let's talk a minute," he said.

I braced myself for another lecture on what to say and not to say.

"You all can visit the hotline room anytime you want," he told us. "We have people to man the phones, so don't worry about that. Just saying—if you want to know what's going on. I want all of you to have your phones with you at all times. Leads can come from friends and family as well as the 800 number."

Ron and I both patted our pockets. "I've had this with me the whole time," Ron said. "Vic will call me. I know she will."

I wished he'd displayed the same emotion and sincerity outside a few minutes ago. It was nerves—I knew that. I just hoped everyone else could see it.

Taylor started toward the elevators and I caught up and tapped his shoulder.

"We wanted to see if we could get into Victoria's business files, Kent. Ron felt we should notify her clients … let them know there might be delays in their projects."

"Charlie, we picked up her calendars and current files as evidence. I have no idea where this will go. Once we've checked out the leads we need, we'll release everything, but I have to warn you it may be awhile."

"How about getting into her house? I just feel like … I don't know … there might be something a family member would recognize as being of value. If nothing else, I should clean up the mess before she gets home."

His expression was momentarily unguarded. Clearly, he believed there was a good chance Victoria would never come home. I swallowed hard. He turned and punched the elevator button. On the far side of the lobby I saw Ron and Ben Ortiz standing near a side entrance. I caught up with them and we walked to the lawyer's office in silence.

The news conference was the hour's top story on the radio as I started the truck.

"I can't think straight," Ron said.

"You need some rest."

"I need to get busy. Let's go to the office."

"Ron—"

He shushed me and I drove. Luckily, it didn't appear the media people had discovered our offices yet. The gray and white Victorian sat dark and quiet in weekend mode so I pulled down the side driveway and parked behind. I started coffee brewing, wishing we'd at least pulled through some drive-up and brought food with us.

Upstairs, I could hear Ron clumping around in his office, then the sound of canned laughter. As I approached, a commercial for laundry detergent blared, then the familiar voice of the noon newsman who promised an update on the sensational story of the missing bride. Great, Ron. Can't we stay away from the damned television? I started to voice my opinion but the introductory music was already on and there was my brother's face on the screen in his office.

"Our lead story this weekend, the frightening events surrounding a bride who never made it to her wedding, and the groom who wants the whole thing to go away."

"What!" I stormed into the room and reached for the remote.

"Charlie, we have to know what's being said."

My gut churned as we watched. The edited film showed Ron stammering—his one hesitation—during the interview. His past-tense reference to Victoria was quoted intact. His expression seemed uncertain, his face haggard and unflattering in contrast to Ben Ortiz's. The lawyer's use of makeup made him look smooth and camera-ready. When the talking heads came on to opine on the subject, of course it was Ortiz's past defenses of guilty-looking defendants which was brought up first. I thought I would throw up.

Chapter 8

November, 1978

Juliette took the cassette from the dictation machine and put in a fresh one, ready and waiting for Al's next batch of letters. A month into her new job and she was beginning to feel more confident. She'd bought a plant for her desk, taken all the tags off the new clothes, and had even gone out to lunch with Sheila a couple of times. She knew how Al took his coffee and which files he preferred to keep in his own office, although she still hadn't a clue why some were different than others.

"Juliette, I need five copies of this bid." Al Proletti walked through the connecting door from his office, wearing a long-sleeved dress shirt for the first time with today's cooler weather.

"Certainly, Al. Right away." She reached for the sheaf of pages, which he shifted slightly so their fingers touched as she took them.

She blushed and pretended she hadn't noticed.

"Put those on my desk when you're done," he said. "I'll be at the Bingham site for an hour or so, then I want you to go with me out to the Rossmoor job."

He turned away, plucking his jacket from the back of his desk chair before walking out the other door into the lobby. She could hear him giving instructions to Sheila, then the outer door opened and closed. Juliette headed for the copy machine which sat in an alcove off the hallway, placed the bid sheets on the paper feed and set the controls.

While paper hummed through the machine she went back to the boss's office where she picked up his sticky coffee cup and stuck three stray paperclips into the little magnetic holder where they belonged. Sheila spotted her through the open doorway.

"You know where the Rossmoor job is, don't you?" the older woman said with a sideways grin.

Juliette shrugged.

"Out near Al's house." Sheila glanced toward the closed door of Marion Flightly's office and lowered her voice. "All the new girls eventually get a tour of Al's house."

"What are you saying?" Juliette carried the dirty coffee cup and detoured to stand in front of Sheila's desk. "That he's coming on to me?"

"Al comes on to all women. Surely you've already noticed. He means nothin' by it. It's just his way."

"Have you been to his house?"

"Sure." Sheila took a long drag on her current cigarette then tapped the ash into the ashtray that already held four butts. "Once on a private tour, four times for the company Christmas parties. It's quite a place."

Juliette carried the cup to the little kitchenette, last door at the end of the hall, where she rinsed it and placed it on the drying rack before going back to check on her copies. As she collated and stapled the bid pages she wondered what Sheila had meant by 'tour.' She'd watched, in the early days of the new job, assessing the office relationships, speculating on whether Sheila and Al might have had something going. She'd pretty much come to the conclusion they didn't—Sheila was a few years older than the boss, and she was married—until the remark about getting the tour. Then again, she'd said Al didn't mean anything by it. Juliette shrugged it off and returned to the pile of files on her own desk.

It was after eleven when Al breezed in, picked up the bids Juliette had stacked on his desk, and peeked into her office. She shut off the dictation machine and removed her earphones.

"Ready for the Rossmoor job?" he asked. "Bring a note pad."

Well, that sounded safe enough, she decided as she neatened her desk and picked up her steno pad and sweater. Outside, the day had warmed a bit and she ended up draping the sweater over her shoulders. Al led the way to the back lot where he bypassed the company pickup trucks and ushered her to the passenger side of his Porsche. Her heart did a little flutter.

Back in Texas muscle cars were the dream of every boy in high school but none of them dared set their sights on a car this magnificent. Bobby Ray Jackman's Competition Yellow Boss 302 Mustang was the coolest car she'd ever set foot in, going to the Cree-Mee Drive In for a burger. She touched the door of the sleek black Porsche and settled into her seat. It smelled like expensive leather and the tinted windows sealed her into a private little world.

Al slid into his seat, turned the key and put the car in gear, almost in a single movement. A second later they were making the right turn onto Greenlee Boulevard. He whipped through the lane changes with a swiftness that nearly took Juliette's breath away. When he pulled into the fast lane of the Interstate, Juliette let herself slip into a little fantasy where the Porsche flew past the yellow Mustang, with Billy Ray gaping at her in astonishment. She smiled through the side window as if he were really there.

"Nice, huh?" Al Proletti said, catching her in mid-smile.

She flushed. A glance at the speedometer told her they were at least thirty miles per hour over the speed limit. Proletti shot a glance toward his side mirror and zipped across three lanes of traffic to take the next exit. Ten minutes later they pulled to the curb in front of a chain link-fenced job site. A sign showing an architect's rendering of a huge Spanish-style building announced that Pro-Builder Construction was general contractor on the new Rossmoor Golf and Country Club.

Juliette knew bits and scraps of information about the job, the pieces she gleaned from letters she typed and documents she copied. The fifteen million dollar bid was only the beginning, enough to cover earth-moving to form the curving fairways and greens of the golf course. The clubhouse/restaurant pictured on the sign would be added separately. For a girl who'd been living on a little over five hundred dollars a month until recently, those kinds of numbers were surreal.

Al got out of the car and came around to her side. She picked up her notepad and swung her legs around. She struggled a moment to get out of the low car. He didn't say anything but she hadn't imagined where his attention went as her skirt slid upward. She smoothed it down and squared her shoulders, standing beside the car and staring out at the massive earth-movers and trucks in the distance.

While the machines crawled over the pale dirt hills, Al had already headed toward the cluster of metal trailers at the front of the property and Juliette followed, tottering on her high heels over the uneven graveled drive. He climbed four steps at the front of the first trailer, opened the door and held it for her. She clutched her steno pad and entered a room with linoleum flooring and walls covered with tacked-up notices and permits. A desk, its surface strewn with papers, sat at one end of the room, but the largest feature was a long worktable where rolled blueprints were unfurled and held in place with two staplers, a metal tape measure and several rocks. A stocky man sat behind the desk, phone to his ear, leaning so far back in his swivel chair that Juliette was surprised it didn't take off beneath him. He gave her the once-over as she stepped into the room, before he noticed Al behind her.

"I, uh, I'll call you back, Mr. Sciatone," he said, snapping upright in his seat, dropping the phone to its cradle. "Mr. Proletti. Didn't know you was stopping by today."

"I know," said Al. His eyes traveled the width of the desk before he turned toward the worktable. He stared at the blueprints, smoothing the top sheet with his hand. "Why aren't we in phase three yet?"

The man edged his way past the cluttered desk, giving a nod toward Juliette as he passed.

"Sorry. Where are my manners?" Al said. "Juliette, this is Ernie Batista, job foreman."

Ernie gave her a tentative smile. She never recalled making a man nervous before, but this one was walking on eggshells.

"So?" Al's question was more pointed this time. "Phase three, Ernie. Talk to me."

"Well, Mr. Proletti, there was that delay with the concrete delivery …"

"Old news. We got that straightened out three days ago. Why am I not seeing a foundation out there yet?"

"The trench is there, sir, it's just we had all that rain. An alligator came onto the site and got itself stuck in the trench and none of those bas— uh, guys on the crew would go anywhere close. Finally, Tommy the Shark shot the thing … but they didn't make such good progress this week."

Al gave the man a silent stare with his intense blue eyes. "Next guy shirks his duty around here, the gator's gonna get him." A long, silent beat went by before Al laughed. "Can you see it now? Some guy shows up to put forms in that trench and there's this big old gator?"

Ernie's laugh started as a shaky chuckle but soon he was roaring. Juliette put on a polite smile, not quite sure whether she was meant to be in on this conversation. All at once, Al's laugh went dead silent.

"Wait outside," he said to Juliette.

The humor had drained out of the room as if there were a whirlpool in the floor. She dipped her head in a slight nod and did as he ordered. Three seconds later she heard a crash from inside the trailer. She hustled toward the car as quickly as her high heels allowed.

Al's face was serious when he came out of the trailer

but at the car he turned to all smiles. She took her seat and tucked the unused steno pad beside the console.

"Okay," he announced. "Business done. We're gonna have some lunch. I got a little something to show you."

It was as if there had never been a tense moment in the man's life. She decided whatever had passed between Al and Ernie back there was something purely between them, something that was none of her business. Maybe the men had been friends forever, maybe they joked around like this all the time. She put the whole thing out of her mind as the Porsche roared onto the freeway once again. With her head back against the headrest and the cool breeze from the sunroof, she felt there wasn't a care in the world she couldn't handle.

They drove to a part of the city she'd never seen, crossed a bridge and entered a drive where a guard saluted Al and a gate swung silently open revealing large lots with mansions set well back from the streets. He took the turns confidently. Juliette watched for a restaurant, wondering if her simple black skirt and purple blouse would be elegant enough for any place around here.

"Don't worry about it," he said, his fingertips light on her forearm. "You look beautiful."

She gave a hesitant smile but felt the tingle of the touch long after he'd returned his hand to the wheel. Now he could read her mind?

The sleek car turned right at a narrow drive where straight rows of royal palms formed a colonnade with a tall fountain sparkling in the distance. Al took the lane slowly and swung around the circular drive at the end. A fawn colored building with red tile roof spread out in two wings with a central portico held by tall pillars. Juliette looked for a placard with the name of the place but saw none.

"Home, sweet home," he said, pocketing the car key and coming around to her side.

This is a house?

She allowed him to take her hand, assisting her out of the car. He let go, shut the car door, and they walked together up a set of stone steps. The massive wooden door led to a foyer larger than her entire apartment. Overhead, a rib-vaulted ceiling showcased painted scenes, like something from the medieval cathedrals she'd read about in novels. Double staircases rose on each side of the entry, with carved pillars and white stonework forming arches that framed a view through two-story-high windows at the back. She could see a shady veranda and gardens that stretched out of sight and had to remind herself not to gape.

"What do you think?" he asked. His blue eyes crinkled at the corners as he smiled.

"I think the construction business must be very good."

He laughed aloud at that. "Just one of my many endeavors, sweetheart."

Voices from another room snagged their attention. A crease marred Al's smooth forehead for a moment.

"Hold on a minute." He left her standing there and crossed the marble floor, his heels clicking solidly. He pushed open a carved door she'd barely had time to notice, and the voices grew louder.

A low exchange of words, deep male voices. Al returned, leaving the door open, and took her elbow.

"Business that can wait," he murmured, steering her toward the back of the house and the tall glass doors with the veranda beyond.

She caught sight of two men in dark suits emerging

from the room where Al had spoken to them. They seemed large and not especially friendly, but they didn't say a word as they exited by the front door.

"Hungry? Let's eat first, then I'll give you a little tour." He held the wide glass door open, calling to someone unseen as they walked outside.

A table had been laid with china, linen and silver, an enormous arrangement of tropical fruit in the center. He led her to the chair positioned for maximum enjoyment of the view, while he took the one facing the door.

"Ernestina," he said to the Hispanic woman who appeared at Juliette's side. "We'll have our lunch now."

* * *

"You wouldn't believe his place," Juliette said later, nearly upsetting her wine glass as she described the afternoon to Carol Ann. Her friend had insisted they meet somewhere for happy hour the minute they got off work, and this little wine bar was closest to the bus route.

"Lunch was lobster salad. But, I mean, there was shrimp and crabmeat in there too, and some kind of herbs or spices ...or something. I can't even describe it. And the fresh fruit! And a bread that just practically melted ..."

"In other words, you never had anything like it back in Texas, huh?"

"Oh my god—no. It was amazing."

"Sounds like something completely fitting for the way you described the house."

"It was like some castle in Europe, Carol Ann. Seriously, seriously fit for a king."

Carol Ann's eyes showed a hint of skepticism as she

picked up her wine glass.

"And this guy, your *boss*, is interested in *you*?"

"Don't say it like that. He's just nice. There was nothing inappropriate or forward about the whole day." Except maybe the nagging doubt Sheila had put into her mind, the remark about how Al came on to all women.

"Come on … he showed me this huge living room where he said they move the furniture out of the way for dancing at parties, and there was a dining room with the longest table you ever saw. And a library—talk about classy books! They all had leather covers and gold print on the backs." She left out the part about the two men who'd come out of that room. "He didn't even take me upstairs. If he was making a move on me, don't you think he would have wanted me to see the bedrooms. I bet they are totally swanky."

"I'm just saying, it would be dumb to get involved with him. Guys like that just use girls like us. There's no future in it."

"I'm not looking for a future with any man. Not yet, anyway."

"We've been out of school almost five years, sweetie. The girls who went to college are already staking out their men, getting married. The girls who didn't are married already and have a kid or two. I'm just thinking it's time to start looking around for the guy who'll be the one, the man you stick with."

Juliette drained her glass. What if Al Proletti did turn out to be the one for her? She could certainly do worse. But she didn't say so to Carol Ann.

Chapter 9

I stomped into my office the minute the newscast ended and dialed Ben Ortiz's number. His secretary said he was busy but once I gave my name in a none-too-friendly tone, she managed to put me through.

"What was the purpose of that stupid press conference if we get this kind of coverage from it?" I demanded the moment I heard his voice.

"Charlie, settle down. I don't have to talk strategy with you. Ron is my client."

I shouted across the hall for Ron to pick up the phone.

"Charlie, just settle down," Ortiz said, his voice impossibly calm. "These things always happen. Media people are notorious for sensationalizing everything. They need a story and they need it to be as tantalizing and salacious as possible. We can't stop that. They would do it whether we appeared at a news conference or not. The important thing is that we've got Victoria's face up there on every TV screen in the state. With luck, the national networks will pick it up."

Luck? My stomach did a flip at the thought of this pack of lies being spread across the whole country.

"We're getting Victoria recognized everywhere. That's the main thing. Her abductors won't be able to keep her hidden. Someone, somewhere will see her. If she's hurt or doesn't remember what happened, at least somebody out there can get her back to us."

"Charlie, he's right," came Ron's voice on the line. "Once Vic is back and we're together, the wedding will go forward and this whole story will do a one-eighty. We'll be America's luckiest couple because we found each other again."

Since that was far more optimism than I'd heard from my brother in a lot of hours, I let the statement stand right there. Maybe he was right. We let the attorney go—no doubt that phone call had just cost another few hundred dollars.

Ron appeared in my doorway. "We'd better eat something. I'm exhausted and I can hear the frazzle in your voice."

"I don't want to go out. That broadcast is still too fresh, and I'm afraid I'll say something Mr. Lawyer won't approve of."

No argument from Ron. I dialed Drake's cell; he would have finished the airport run a long time ago and I was a little surprised I hadn't already heard from him.

"Hey, hon." He sounded a little breathless. "Sorry I didn't call earlier."

"Everything okay?" I pictured a last-minute airline screw-up that sent Paul's whole family back to our house for a longer visit.

"It's great, actually. I just got a call from Fish and Game and they got approval for an elk count up north. They want to start at daybreak tomorrow, so I'm packing. I need to pull pitch by three o'clock."

"Do you need me to come along?" *Please not, please not.* Ron needs me plus there is already snow in the high country and I'd been in on enough game counts already, thank you. Staring at the ground while the helicopter circles the herd, trying to count animals that look like black dots on the ground … well, the tummy tends to go all queasy.

"Nope, I'm good. I'm just throwing my winter gear into a bag. I'll head out to the airport in a few, preflight the ship … I'll call you right before I take off. Where are you guys anyway?"

I gave him the short version of the morning's events and the fact that we were basically hiding out at the office.

"Probably wise," he said. "The news vans were gone awhile but now they're back in front of the house."

"Great. We'll probably hang out here until dark. Maybe they'll give up on us. Look, can you bring Freckles by the office on your way out?"

Bless him, my hubby is the best. He agreed without even taking an extra breath.

"I got the gist of it," Ron said from the doorway. "I've already called Sal's and ordered a pizza. They said forty minutes."

I glanced at my watch, noted the pizza ETA, and turned on my computer. I might as well get something useful done since I was stuck. My attempts at accounting entries held my attention for less time than it took for the pizza guy to drive up. I answered the door and took the box, which gave off waves of pepperoni and mushroom.

Ron met me in the kitchen. Drake drove into our back parking area just as I was rummaging in a cupboard for extra napkins, and Freckles bounded out of the Jeep.

"Glad you suggested this," he said, snagging a slice from the box. "I needed to trade vehicles with you anyway. Forgot some of my tools are still in my truck."

Freckles kept her huge brown eyes on each move of his pizza slice—up and down as he raised it to his mouth. It dawned on me how movie directors can get a dog to nod yes to a question. Her focus was total.

Ten minutes later, I sent Drake on his way with a kiss and a promise to track his flight once he let me know that he'd taken off. When I walked back from the truck Ron's expression was glum.

"Sorry. I wish I knew what to do." It had to be excruciating for him to watch Drake and me, happy and safe together.

He shrugged and balled up his third paper napkin.

"Want to talk about it? Maybe we can make a plan."

"If this was happening to anyone else, a missing loved one, I'd tell them to do everything we've already done. Get flyers out, get media coverage if possible … I just never knew how it would feel from the inside."

"What else can we do?" I finally got my second bite of pizza.

"If I had access to her files, I'd start looking for names, calling people she'd recently contacted. See if anyone could tell us something we don't already know."

"She told me she'd scheduled most of her decorating jobs around the wedding and the trip. I don't recall her saying there was anyone she needed to tend to until after the holidays."

His eyebrows knotted in a way I know so well, his thinking mode. "She has a couple of shipments coming in, some tile for a bathroom remodel and drapes or something for somebody else. But she had talked to Sally about accepting the packages here at the office, stashing everything in one corner of the conference room until we got back from our trip. The customers were not expecting to hear from her. Both had agreed to holding their completion dates until after the first."

I pushed the food aside and closed the box. "None of that sounds even remotely connected."

"I agree."

"So, it seems that we're left with two possibilities. She was taken forcibly …"

"We would have received a ransom demand by now," he argued.

"Or, she had to leave, to escape someone who came after her." I didn't dare mention the idea that not everyone who is kidnapped is taken for ransom. The thought of Victoria abducted, probably raped or killed, was too horrible for me to get my mind around.

Ron massaged the sides of his head, raising spikes of hair at his temples. "I can't help but think it's something to do with our argument. That she had second thoughts about the wedding and just had to get away and sort it out."

"Really? At the press conference you said this was no runaway bride scenario."

He sent me a look.

"Okay, I get it. I wouldn't say to them what was really on my mind either." Especially since the police were already thinking badly of Ron. "So, let's go over the days before the wedding and see if we can figure it out."

"It's just what I *have* been doing." His voice was miserable. "She talked about the plans—cake, flowers, invitations. I guess that's the stuff all brides talk about. I don't know."

"Sounds like it to me."

"What about when you gals were alone? Did she say anything at all, anything beyond that day's events?"

I wanted to rub my temples too. I honestly hadn't heard Victoria give any clue that she wasn't a hundred percent in love with Ron and ready to get married. I told him so, if for no other reason than to get a trace of a smile to show on his face.

It didn't really work.

I went back to my computer but my heart wasn't in it and my mind wasn't on the work. Rather than make a bunch of mistakes I would have to find and correct later, I decided to take the dog for a walk. The fresh, chilly air stimulated me and a plan began to hatch, not one I could tell Ron.

Back at the office, he was on the phone. I held my breath, hoping for good news. Well, really, any news. When he hung up I could tell it hadn't been anything of importance.

"So, what do you want to do?" I asked. "Tonight, you need to make some decisions. Most of your stuff is at Vic's but you can't go back there yet and your old place is out of the question. You should sleep at our place for awhile yet."

I could see him picturing his crummy apartment, worse now because it was mostly empty. He nodded at my suggestion.

Drake called to let me know he was heading north and would be staying the night in the little town of Eagle Nest. In the background, rotor noise almost obliterated his voice.

I told him Ron would be with me and he wished us luck.

"We both need some rest," I said to Ron. "All this has been too much."

He nodded again, too wrung-out to make conversation anymore.

"Let's go home, settle in, ignore the news people. One of us should call Kent Taylor and find out the status, if they have any new leads from the hotline."

"What about Ben Ortiz?"

"I'm not asking permission. I think this needs to come from family. Make the call."

Of course there was no real news. Taylor would have let us know. He did say calls were starting to come in, but so far none of the leads were specific enough to be of value. He thanked Ron and told him to take care, which I thought was nice.

I drove the Jeep home and hustled Ron and Freckles into the house without a glance toward the vans at the curb. The temperature had dropped at least ten degrees—good news for us because it kept the reporters in their vehicles. Inside, I closed all the drapes. It would be dark soon anyway, and I wanted lamps on without feeling that the whole world was watching me.

The clock ticked. Our phones stayed silent.

Ron finally crashed, face down, on the bed in the guest room. From the living room I heard his snore so I went in and did the sisterly thing--I removed his boots and pulled the comforter over him. I set his cell phone beside his hand, knowing it was probably the only thing in the world that would wake him up at this moment. I made myself a cup of tea and stretched out on the couch to enjoy it. When I woke up the tea was cold, Freckles had curled up at the base of the sofa, and I had a horrible crick in my neck from sleeping at the odd angle. The light-up face on my phone showed it was almost five a.m.

I got up and checked on Ron. He hadn't moved a muscle in more than ten hours and didn't appear likely to. I gently closed the door to his room and thought again about the plan I'd hatched the previous afternoon. I didn't dare tell Ron. It was better he not know what I had in mind. He could claim ignorance and his innocence would be assured.

I fed Freckles a super-early breakfast which she gobbled without question as I bustled about, gathering supplies. She went willingly into her crate and I peered out the front window before opening the door. The news vans had given up and gone away, but I had no illusions that they wouldn't be back by daybreak. I closed the front door behind me and crunched across the frosty lawn to my Jeep.

I was on my way to Victoria's house, police and lawyers be damned.

What none of them knew was that I already had a key to the place; I'd volunteered for plant-watering duty while the newlyweds were to have been honeymooning. All I had to do now was get to the front door and past the yellow crime tape without being spotted. It was the reason I'd changed into black jeans and hoodie. My flashlight had a semi-covered lens and I'd even remembered to tuck latex gloves into my pockets.

I parked around the corner at the nearest cross street. A hooded figure in black wouldn't exactly be a welcome figure in this neighborhood in the pre-dawn hour so I adopted the few little things I could do to look more like a jogger or some other kind of health nut—pushed my hood back and let my ponytail swing as I walked merrily along as if I had every right to be there. It didn't much matter—no one was out and about at this ungodly hour anyway.

As I approached Victoria's place I spotted a light on across the street. Good old Gladys Peabody must be baking again (I have to admit my mouth watered slightly at the memory of those butter cookies). The lit window was on the side, facing a neighbor's house. I kept my jaunty pace until it was out of sight. Her street-facing living room window was dark. I scoped out the street lamps at either end of the block. Neither cast enough light to illuminate my target so I edged toward the door, disguising myself as part of the large arbor vitae by the porch until I could get the key in hand.

It took a little gymnastic maneuver to ease myself between the crisscrosses of police tape without ripping any of them, but in under thirty seconds I was inside. I locked the door; a quick getaway would be easier through the backyard anyway. I didn't want to be flashing a light around but risked a quick look to orient myself to any changes that might have happened since my last visit.

The furniture was exactly as before, coffee table skewed, the sofa a little out of place, pillows strewn. The blood-stained rug had been removed and her wedding dress was gone. For some reason, that made me sadder than anything else. I took a deep breath. This was not the moment for thoughts of what might have been. It was Monday morning and the neighbors were likely to begin stirring within the hour.

I decided to skip the living room and kitchen entirely.

No doubt the police had been through them and had taken anything of interest. At a glance, for instance, I could see that Vic's purse was gone, which meant the invaluable contact list on her cell phone would be out of reach too. I paused at the hall. Where to start?

Her home office would have the records Ron and I had discussed so I headed that direction. Not surprisingly, Victoria's desk was uncluttered and immaculately clean. On top, only a phone, a notepad, an in-tray and a cup holding pens and pencils. She'd told me her laptop would be locked away in her home safe in the basement while she was gone. I would check that, except I didn't know the combination. Would it be worth waking Ron to ask? I needed to give that a little more thought. If she'd had an appointment book or desk calendar they were gone now.

I picked up the phone receiver and listened as the quick dial tone indicated unheard voicemail messages. "You have two new messages," it told me. I pressed the series of buttons it asked for. "First message." A perky female voice spoke: "Congratulations, you've been selected to win—" I hung up before learning what the fantastic prize would have been. "Second message." Another woman's voice: "Hey, Victoria. Just calling to check on my drapery fabric but I realized you are away on your honeymoon. Congrats to you two! I'll talk to you when you get back." The woman didn't leave a name so I could only assume Victoria would recognize the voice. I hung up without deleting either message.

I sat in her chair and opened the drawer on my left. It contained files tabbed with client names. Ron had mentioned her working with several current clients but he didn't know most of their names. One of those little details that probably wasn't important enough for her to tell him—until now. The drawer on the right contained business files of the sort everyone has—paid bills, tax information, supplier data. I grabbed a couple, laying them on the desk.

Along one wall were shelves filled with decorating books, the kind with wallpaper samples and color swatches. A display of tile samples dominated a corner of the room, and a huge paperboard-covered book held fabrics. There were paint chips, more fabrics and scads of catalogs—nothing I could imagine relating to our present problem. I flipped through the books on the shelf quickly, in case a secret diary or a note written in code should fall my way. Nothing did.

Victoria's bedroom was much the same as I'd seen—except her packed bag had been rummaged by police, with lacy underthings now water-falling down the sides almost to the floor. There, too, if there'd been a trove of information in her travel stuff, it had been taken away. Same with the nightstand drawers. Even the bed pillows had been disturbed and the mattress was cockeyed showing someone had lifted it.

Odds were, the safe was the only untouched place in the house, unless the police had obtained the combination or a safecracker. Against my better judgment, I decided to call Ron.

"Where are you?" he asked with a querulous note in his sleepy voice.

"Don't ask. I just need one bit of information and you can deny you ever gave it to me."

Either he was too sleepy to process the implications or he'd taken my attitude—the hell with waiting for the police to solve this. He gave me the numbers.

I'd only been in Victoria's basement a couple of times, and she had recently redecorated it as a little man-den for Ron's sons. On one of my visits she'd needed to put something away, so I knew the safe was a floor model in a corner. A square of the flooring could be lifted once you moved a heavy floor lamp with a big base. The recessed dial presented itself and the information from Ron worked. The lid was heavier than I expected but it came up and I spotted the laptop computer right away. As long as I was blatantly breaking the law I figured I should go for it, so I pulled everything out and stuffed it into the knapsack I'd brought from home.

With the safe lid back in place and neatly concealed once again, I went back to her office to gather the files I'd pulled. They joined the rest of the plunder. I'd no sooner crossed the living room on my way to the back door when a set of headlights hit the wall. A car had pulled into the driveway.

Chapter 10

December, 1978

Juliette stared at the oblong velveteen box on her desk.

"What's this?" she asked when she sensed Al standing behind her.

"Let's just call it an early Christmas present."

She opened the box and gasped. A thin bracelet of diamonds glittered against the black background.

"Al ..." She kept her voice low, although she knew they were alone in the office. Sheila had left for the day but what if she forgot something and came back? "You can't be buying me gifts like this."

"It's not much. Just a little tennis bracelet. You're supposed to wear it when you play tennis."

She laughed. "I don't play tennis, Al."

"Then you can learn. There's a court at my house. My coach can teach you."

"Don't be silly. I'd be no good at it. Plus, you don't take up a sport just to have a place to wear jewelry." She closed the box and started to hand it back but he stuck his hands behind his back, refusing to accept it.

"Look, it didn't cost much. I got it wholesale from my cousin's shop." He reached for the box, opened it and took the bracelet out. "Let's put it on and see how it looks."

The moment he fastened the clasp at her wrist she lost the desire to refuse the gift. It was the most beautiful thing she owned.

"Like I said, early Christmas." The other women had received potted poinsettias on their desks.

For a second she thought he meant to kiss her. "I can't— I can't become involved, Al. It's not right."

"Another boyfriend?"

"No, it's not that. Just … you're my boss." She kept her eyes down.

"I don't force myself on women. Even ones as beautiful as you." He turned toward his own office. "Enjoy the bracelet. It looks a lot better on your wrist than in the box."

Juliette covered her typewriter and picked up her coat, putting the velveteen box into her purse. She hoped she hadn't hurt his feelings.

"Thank you, Al. It's lovely, a very thoughtful and extravagant gift."

He gathered his jacket and switched off his light. "Don't forget the Christmas party tomorrow night at my place. You can bring a date if you want."

The party had been the talk of the office for weeks. Juliette didn't have a date. She'd thought of inviting Carol

Ann but her friend never had a nice thing to say about Al, so why should she get to see the fabulous mansion? Forget her.

Sheila knew Juliette hadn't bought herself a car yet and had offered a ride. It would work out fine, the two women going stag, since Sheila's husband couldn't get away from his restaurant-management job. Juliette saw herself doing her co-worker a favor, as much as the other way around.

Al locked the door and walked toward his Porsche, noticing Juliette heading toward the street.

"I can give you a ride home," he called out.

She shook her head. "That's okay. I have a stop to make."

He looked as if he would gladly take her on her errand but she merely smiled, waved and kept walking to the bus stop. She didn't really have any other plans. The gift of the bracelet and Al's increasing attention were too much distraction already. She was half afraid of her own actions if she were to get in the car with him.

Friday night. She plopped into her seat on the bus, mildly annoyed, bored, uneasy … she couldn't define the feeling exactly. No doubt her edgy mood was partly due to Al's gift just now. She stretched her arm slightly so the bracelet showed below her cuff. But her discontent was not entirely his fault.

Every Friday night for years she and Carol Ann had plans—movies, shopping, dinner at one apartment or the other. If nothing else, they would simply hang out and enjoy glasses of wine and talk about the latest books they'd read. But the last few weeks, things had cooled. Part of it was Carol Ann's attitude about Al—true—but then another guy had come along.

Juliette had met her friend's new boyfriend twice. First

impression was he was exactly that, a boy. Tommy was their age but seeing Carol Ann with him took Juliette right back to Texas and the drama of boy-girl stuff there. He'd been away at college, come home to Florida at Thanksgiving, and was now talking about not going back to school after the winter break. Stupid. He had a semester left to graduate but couldn't do without Carol Ann another six months? How high school was that?

Compared to Al, Tommy seemed like such a kid. Juliette bit her tongue every time she talked to Carol Ann anymore. Things were changing. One side of her said it was inevitable—life changed, things happened. The other side couldn't believe it. Your very best friend since second grade just didn't do that to you. Tears blurred her vision and she nearly missed her stop.

She stumbled up the street to her apartment and let herself in. The beige walls she had once thought fresh and clean-looking were now just bland. The rental furniture depressed her. The one piece of art on the living room wall was a cheap printed thing from K-Mart. She'd been so wrapped up in her job that she'd not even brought home a houseplant. Now that she was earning more money she could afford a better place. She turned on a lamp, put a frozen dinner in the microwave and went into her bedroom. Moving, she decided, would be her New Year's resolution.

Hanging from her closet door was the one bright spot in the apartment—the dress she'd bought for tomorrow night's Christmas party. The red satin fit her curves precisely and the low neckline accentuated the best parts. Together, the dress and shoes had cost nearly half a paycheck; she couldn't afford to do that again, not if she wanted a new apartment.

From her tiny kitchen alcove the microwave dinged. She grabbed a fork and peeled back the wrapper from her meal. The idea of new surroundings excited her and she pulled out her bank book, going through it while she ate. There wasn't a sufficient amount in savings for much in the way of furniture, but she was determined not to go for another furnished place. Enough with the saggy couches, stained upholstery and take-what-you-get mattresses that always came with these places. With her salary she could qualify for a loan to get her own things.

The empty evening looked brighter now. She turned on the TV and let Donnie and Marie sing to her while she tidied the kitchen. *Dallas* would be on later. Who needed Carol Ann when she could immerse herself in whatever evil plot J.R. Ewing was up to?

She let herself sleep late Saturday morning and promised herself a nap later if she felt like it. Being fresh and sparkling for a late night out was the goal. She imagined the mansion decorated for the holidays and saw herself dazzling the crowd in her new dress. The mood dropped a notch when she reminded herself this was a company party, the same crowd she saw every day plus, most likely, some of the workers from the crews. Not exactly a glamour event.

She began to second-guess herself about the dress—maybe it was overkill for this particular party—but then remembered Sheila saying she'd bought a new dress. Juliette decided to skip her hairdresser appointment and put away the faux-jeweled collar she'd found on sale. She could do something simple with her long curls—the dress, shoes and Al's diamond bracelet would be understated but elegant. She polished her nails and read a magazine of home decorating ideas while they dried.

By the time Sheila tooted the horn outside her apartment window at seven o'clock, Juliette had reconsidered her outfit three more times. Aside from a whole new shopping trip—which she refused to do because of the expense—her original idea was still the best. She pulled a cashmere wrap around her shoulders and ran down to the car.

"Wow, you look like a million bucks," Sheila greeted.

The car contained a cloud of cigarette smoke and Juliette flinched a little, holding the door open longer than necessary to get rid of it. She thought of her freshly shampooed hair and hoped she wouldn't reek by the time they arrived.

"I hope I can remember exactly how to get there," Sheila said as she pulled out of the parking lot.

Juliette found it oddly reassuring to know Sheila wasn't a regular visitor to the mansion. Then she chided herself for feeling this way.

"Now, if only the guys don't all hang out at the bar and talk about concrete pours and earth-moving equipment. Of course, Marion hardly knows any subject but accounting. Boring if you're a regular person, but if you need advice on your taxes just get her into a corner. She'll go on and on."

Juliette had already noticed that about Marion, from being around the office.

"Will everyone be there with spouses or dates?"

"Most of the men on the crew are married, so there'll be women to chat with. The wives tend to give us office girls the eye, wondering if we're flirting with their husbands all day. All you can do is be friendlier to the female half of the room than the male side."

Aside from the day she'd met Ernie Batista out at the Rossmoor job, Juliette couldn't remember meeting any of the crew. There weren't more than one or two times any of them had come inside the office. Watching heavy equipment move in and out of the back lot was about her only exposure to that side of the business.

The rows of royal palms along the drive were now lit by twisted strands of white lights around their trunks. Driving between them felt like entering a fairyland. The front of the mansion had electric candles in every window, wreaths on every door, and a giant topiary ball suspended above the door. Al Proletti himself met each car, giving the ladies a quick kiss on the cheek and joking about the mistletoe overhead, while valets moved the cars out of sight. He wore a white dinner jacket and tie, setting off his dark hair and vivid blue eyes.

"May I take your wrap?" Al asked, his voice a low murmur in Juliette's ear. She noticed a uniformed maid had offered to take Sheila's. "I like your bracelet."

His fingertips brushed her bare shoulders as he lifted the shawl but they didn't linger. Nothing inappropriate. He handed the cashmere piece to the maid and offered an arm to each of them.

"Ladies, shall we join the others?"

A decorated tree, at least fifteen feet tall, filled a corner of the room he'd described on her last visit as the living room. True to his word, the furniture had been moved along the walls and into small groupings, the oriental carpet taken away. A fire in the marble-fronted fireplace added a cheery note.

Of those present, Sheila's prediction appeared true— the men were gathered, drinks in hand, near the door and she caught words like 'fill dirt' and 'the D-9 Cat.' The women hung close to the Christmas tree, pointing and commenting on the ornaments. A string quartet played quietly in the corner near the door, although she noticed a turntable and stack of vinyl albums nearby. The crowd was definitely more Creedence Clearwater than Bach—she noted with relief.

"Let's get you ladies a drink," Al said. He steered them toward a bar just inside the dining room, where Juliette noticed the side console loaded with covered dishes and the long dining table set with gleaming china and crystal. "Dinner will be announced in a half hour or so, although it's a completely casual buffet. People can serve themselves whenever they like."

Completely casual? Juliette almost laughed. In her world, casual was paper plates and barbeque. She'd never seen a table set this way in real life, only in magazines. She wondered what it would be like to host a party like this. In her new apartment she would have proper glassware and at least a few place settings of real china. It would be fun to have Carol Ann over and do it up right, pretend they were classy ladies and practice their table manners. Then she remembered Tommy and the whole picture faded.

The bartender poured her a glass of white wine, while Sheila opted for a martini. "Come on, I'll introduce you around," she told Juliette.

Al had drifted back to the front door, apparently expecting more guests. Sheila left it to the men to introduce themselves, about thirty of them. On the distaff side of the room, they interrupted the discussion of which department stores put their decorations on sale before Christmas for another quick round of introductions. Juliette supposed with time she might remember them, but likely not. She knew the company had three fairly major jobs currently underway and wondered at the turnover among the crews. She suspected there was no reason to become chums—they must come and go often.

With the choice of only Sheila, Marion and Al to talk to, she wished it had worked out to bring Carol Ann as her guest. The large room was beginning to feel stuffy so she wandered back to the foyer, admiring the paintings on the white walls. A small bell chimed a few times and she heard Al invite everyone to come to the buffet. She didn't feel hungry at the moment so she stepped toward the library as the crowd went into motion. The quiet room felt refreshing after the drone of voices and she made her way around the room, looking at the book titles. A tiny sound near the door caught her attention.

"Dinner's ready," Al said.

"I know. I thought I'd let everyone else go first."

He nodded. "Not one for noise and crowds, huh?"

"Oh, it's not that. Well, I am surprised how many employees you have. It's quite a crowd. I mean, I assumed … maybe some of them are clients?"

"No, these are all company people."

"I thought so. I didn't see those two men who were here the day you brought me out for lunch."

His forehead wrinkled for a moment. "Oh, them. No. They're … they're not." He picked up a letter opener from a small table, then set it down again.

Funny answer. She half expected him to elaborate, to tell her who the men were, but he didn't.

"Well, I suppose I should get something to eat," she said, passing him on her way to the door. "I'm sure it's fabulous food, if lunch was any indication, and someone went to a lot of trouble to prepare everything."

"You're very considerate, Juliette. That was a nice thing to say." His tone was almost one of wonder.

She let it pass and headed toward the dining room where voices rose in laughter and the clatter of dishes and silverware filled the air.

At the long table there was an empty chair beside Sheila's. "Get your plate, hon. I saved you a place."

Juliette almost couldn't fathom the amount of food. She helped herself to shrimp and rice and an interesting-looking salad, knowing she would be miserable if she attempted more. People who'd finished were getting up from the table and places were almost magically reset in time for the next person to come along. In the living room, the classical players had left and pop music tunes began drifting through the open doorway.

"I'm taking a little smoke break out front," Sheila said. "See you in there afterward." A nod toward the music.

Juliette was not incorrect in her guess about the amount of food she could hold. She couldn't even finish what little she'd chosen. A maid noticed that she'd set down her silverware and quietly asked if she wanted the plate removed. A nod, and she stood up. Already, she was a bit bored with the crowd. The women had covered the topics they had in common and those who were friends had split off into their own little conversation groups. Couples were beginning to fill the dance floor. One of the burly construction workers raised his eyebrows toward Juliette, an unspoken invitation to dance, but she wasn't in the mood. She motioned that she would be right back, as if she had to find the bathroom. All the while, she wondered how late Sheila planned to stay.

They should have discussed it. Juliette should get a car. She needed an escape hatch right now.

She wandered along the foyer, trying to remember which door was the bathroom—any place for a few minutes alone. Ahead of her, she noticed decorative lights and inviting furniture on the veranda beyond the tall glass doors. She tried the doorknob, wondering if it would be locked. It turned in her hand and she gave a glance over her shoulder to see if anyone noticed. She was alone.

The air was cool and still, the aqua glow from the pool calming everything in sight. She took a deep breath, let it out. Her bare shoulders felt chilly but she couldn't bring herself to go back to the noise and crowd. She rubbed them with her hands.

"Aren't you cold out here?" Al's voice. She knew it without turning around.

"It's not bad. Christmas where I come from, in the way north part of Texas, you couldn't even be outside right now without a heavy coat."

"Take mine," he said, shrugging out of his dinner jacket and draping it across her shoulders before she could object.

He was standing close enough she could smell the familiar aftershave. He wore it every day but out here, alone, the nuances of scent were so much more pronounced. The hint of musk and spice went into her lungs, her brain, her soul. Her eyes closed as she drank in the fragrance. The next thing she knew, his lips were on hers. Lightly at first, then firmer. Then … gone.

When her eyes came open, he had turned away. He gave her shoulder a squeeze and walked into the house. An urge to run after him, the hint of his scent wafting on the air.

She breathed deeply, taking in the last of it, before she went looking for her ride.

   I wish I knew what I wanted. But until I do, this is too dangerous a game to play.

Chapter 11

I arrived at my Jeep, panting like crazy, wondering where my stamina had gone. I'm definitely getting too old to be racing through backyards and jumping fences with a heavy knapsack banging against my legs. I could only hope the police hadn't spotted me. Most likely all our questions to Kent Taylor yesterday had prompted him to come back and look for more evidence in Victoria's house. If Taylor had spotted my Jeep or had seen me making my awkward exit, I'd be up against all sorts of evidence tampering charges. I jammed the key in the ignition and got the hell out of the neighborhood.

The sun sent a sharp beam of its topmost light over Sandia Crest as I pulled into the driveway at the office. With a guilty glance over my shoulder I hot-footed it to the back door and let myself in. I used the gray light from the windows to make my way upstairs, not wanting to reveal my presence with a lightbulb, and went into the bathroom where I locked myself in and finally risked hitting the light switch. Silly, I know.

I set the pack into the sink and sat on the toilet, partly nature's call and partly to catch my breath. A bit after seven a.m. and I felt as if I'd already put in a full day. I shed the hoodie, zipped up the black jeans and set to work at finding out what little treasure I'd brought back.

The files from Victoria's desk would be self-explanatory once I had time to read the contents. The laptop, if it was anything like mine, contained her whole life story in one form or another—banking, taxes, personal and business correspondence, and maybe some hobbies. If she had any sense at all, she'd password-protected it, which would be my challenge of the day later on. I set it aside. The rest of the bounty consisted of an envelope containing a couple hundred dollars in cash, a spare credit card, a small notebook with what appeared to be computer passwords (woo-hoo!) and an address book with a flowered fabric cover and yellowing pages. I wanted this last item to be our answer key but at a glance it appeared the entries were very old and faded, perhaps not even in Victoria's own hand.

I stared at the little stack of items. The cash and credit card being locked away seemed a bit puzzling; why hadn't she planned to take them on their trip? Of course, for all I knew she had extra money in her purse, now in police custody, and this little stash was either mad-money or had lain in the safe, forgotten, for awhile. At any rate, I couldn't see it as a clue to what had happened.

The notebook of passwords I set with the laptop. The

old address book would bear further examination and I didn't want to do it standing in the bathroom. I opened the door and checked out the upstairs hallway, as empty as usual but now there were oblongs of daylight coming through the doors to Ron's and my offices. Looked like the coast was clear enough for me to work at my desk so I piled everything back into the knapsack and carried it there. And as long as I was officially working I wanted coffee. A noise in the kitchen caught my attention when I reached the top of the stairs. I paused, senses immediately on alert once again.

I eased the swinging door open and spotted Sally, our part-time receptionist. She was measuring coffee into the filter basket. A scatter of grounds flew over the countertop when she caught sight of me in the doorway.

"Sheesh, Charlie! I can't believe you snuck up on me." She wiped the grounds and slipped the basket in place, hitting the button to start the brew. "I saw your Jeep out there. How's Ron today?"

"I'm not sure. He was asleep when I left the house. Yesterday was rough."

"I can imagine. Sorry Ross and I skipped out without seeing you guys. The kids were fussy enough as it was."

"No problem. Saturday went by in kind of blur for all of us."

She reached into a reusable shopping bag and pulled out a package—whole grain bran muffins—along with some bananas and oranges.

I'm more of a cholesterol and fat sort of breakfaster, but I can go for the healthy stuff when truly hungry—like now. My tummy rumbling at the sight of a bran muffin meant it had been a lot of hours since my last meal.

"I suppose you've seen the news coverage?" I asked, digging my nails into orange peel.

"It's ridiculous, of course. I'm so sorry for what they're saying about Ron."

"The news conference didn't go well. And of course they have to keep playing it over and over, highly edited toward the worst."

"Hasn't there been anything useful from the hotline?" Sally pulled two mugs from the cupboard as the coffee maker did its final round of hissing.

"Not that I've heard. Kent Taylor isn't saying much. I don't know if he's being secretive because Ron's a possible suspect or just because they really don't know much yet." I doctored my coffee sufficiently to make up for the lack of artificial ingredients in the muffin and took breakfast and mug up to my office.

My little haul of stolen goodies waited for me and I began to organize them. I hadn't thought to look for a power cord for Victoria's laptop—wasn't sure how long I might have with it—but felt sure I could come up with a spare cord somewhere around here. I opened the top and pressed the power button. It began to boot up.

Meanwhile, the two file folders containing supplier data and paid bills appeared to consist entirely of ordinary stuff. It didn't take long to figure out her favorite sources for fabrics and furniture for her clients. She dealt almost exclusively with two tile and carpet suppliers. The few odd invoices were apparently for custom-order items where the client wanted something specifically British or Irish or Indian. Nothing made me think the orders or suppliers could pose a danger to Victoria in any way. Taking these had been a long shot, I had to admit, but most any lead was worth checking.

When the computer asked for a password I paged through the little spiral notebook. She was organized, I had to admit. There was a section for online shopping sites, one for financial institutions, one for business sites such as the suppliers whose invoices I'd already found in paper form. Although I went through the whole list several times I didn't find the one thing I needed first—how to get onto the computer. Maybe Ron would know.

Speaking of my brother, I wondered how many hours a person could sleep before his family should become concerned. He'd been out cold for almost twelve hours when I left the house, and that was close to four hours ago. I told myself to lighten up—he'd been through hell and was entitled to all the sleep he could get.

I turned to the address book with the flowery cover. It didn't seem Victoria's style and because of its apparent age I wondered if it was something she'd hung onto since childhood. I opened it to the tab marked A. The entries were few—the letter A only had two names on the page— and were not done in a child's hand. The handwriting style reminded me of my mother's, a genteel woman raised in the '50s, schooled in an era when precise cursive handwriting was considered a virtue. Had the book belonged to Victoria's mother? I paged further into it.

Many of the entries had no addresses, only phone numbers, telling me the listing was someone the book's owner knew well. Of those with street addresses, many gave no city—again, probably because it was something the owner already knew—or the city was abbreviated. The zip codes might give a clue, once I had time to look them up. A lot of the phone numbers were written as seven digits, which had to mean they were located in whatever town the owner lived—they weren't local numbers for Albuquerque, I knew. It had been a lot of years since it was common not to list the area code for nearly every number in your contacts list. These days, many large cities have more than one. Of the numbers that did give an area code, I certainly didn't recognize them. Aside from the fact that Ron said Victoria grew up here, giving further credence to the likelihood that the book belonged to someone else, all I could say is that the book was interesting, although I couldn't figure out what it might prove. I set it down and reached for my coffee, which had gone cold already.

Back in the kitchen I'd just topped off my mug, staring out the window as I sipped, mulling over the items on my desk, when Ron's car pulled into his usual parking spot. He looked marginally better this morning, I noted, having showered and put on unrumpled jeans and plaid shirt under his sheepskin jacket. He'd even thought to bring Freckles along. Poor baby had been feeling pretty much left out the past few days. She's used to spending her days with me at the office or trailing along on whatever I'm doing at the time. She raced to the door and waited for Ron to catch up.

"Hey," he said when he walked in. "Thanks for the extra shut-eye this morning. I guess I needed it."

I handed him a full mug after he'd draped his jacket over the back of one of the kitchen chairs.

"I don't suppose there's been any news from Kent Taylor?" I asked.

He shook his head. "I'm avoiding the radio and television."

I didn't blame him a bit.

"Look, I've been thinking that we really need to work on this ourselves," I told him. "The police are going to gear all their efforts toward arresting the criminal."

His jaw tightened. "Which they believe is me."

"But it's not you, so we need to figure out who it really is. Toward that end, I've been doing a little footwork. But before I show you what I've got, I think we need to adopt a don't-ask-don't-tell policy here. Or as Elsa would probably say, don't look a gift horse in the mouth."

He sent me a puzzled look. I waved him upstairs to my office. Freckles bounded ahead and found her favorite stuffed toy near the bay window, where she settled onto her bed. Of course, Ron recognized the laptop right away and his expression went all judgmental on me.

I put up one hand. "Stop. Don't ask. Just take this information as something we can hopefully use. With luck, we can come up with an angle the police aren't working on, and we'll offer them our leads when the time is right."

"Charlie, you've broken—"

"Uh! Remember, don't ask."

"If you're caught with this—"

"It'll be locked away in our safe here when we aren't actually using it. If we come across something the police really need to see, I can always say that Victoria had asked me to keep these things here for safety while you guys were away." The police evidently didn't know about her basement floor safe because there was no sign they'd even tried to open it, but my knowing that was something which fell under our "don't tell" policy.

"What I need now is the password to get into the computer," I said. "It seems to be the one subject not covered in her handy book of passwords."

"I don't know it."

"Well, help me think. It's got to be something pretty straightforward."

"Do you think I'm limited on the number of tries I can give?" he asked, sitting in my chair and pulling the machine toward him.

"Mine doesn't have a limit," I said, "but it would depend on how she set it up. Some only let you try three times then you're locked out."

"Great." He stared at the little box with the cursor blinking in it, his fingers wiggling nervously above the keyboard.

"Think about it awhile. There's no need to rush and do the wrong thing. You can take it into your office."

He stood up and reached for the laptop when I remembered the address book. I showed it to him and he shook his head. "I don't recognize it."

It was at the very bottom of the safe, with other stuff piled on top—again, I better not tell him this little fact. "While you're thinking about the computer, I'm going to try calling some of the numbers in this book."

He gave me a knock-yourself-out shrug and carried Victoria's computer across the hall. A moment later his face appeared at my doorway again.

"Let me take that notebook of passwords," he said. "Maybe there'll be a pattern."

Good idea. I handed it over and turned to the address

book. Might as well start with the numbers which provided me with area codes. I got two recorded "This number is no longer in service" messages before a real human answered.

"I'm with RJP Investigations in Albuquerque, trying to locate someone at this number who knows a woman named Victoria Morgan," I began.

"Victoria Morgan?" The voice was gentle, probably an older woman, the accent faintly southern. "I don't believe I've ever heard of such a person."

"Take a minute to think about it," I suggested. "It's really important."

"I'm sorry dear, I just don't know her."

I couldn't very well bully the old lady if she didn't remember, so I gave her our office number in case she thought of something later, thanked her for her time, and let her go.

The same thing happened, with minor variations, for the next dozen calls. Either the number was an old one or the person had never heard of Victoria. The area codes, it turned out, were mainly in Texas or Florida, which told me nothing. Clearly, the address book had not been hers. Which begged the question: why would someone have an address book belonging to someone else and why would it be kept in the most secure place in the house?

I'd reached the letter N, past any Morgans who might be related, and was mulling the whole situation when two things happened at once.

Ron appeared in my doorway with a triumphant look on his face. "Found the password—we're in."

And Sally called out from downstairs. "Charlie, Ron, you better come see this."

Her tone grabbed our attention and we both clattered down the stairs. In the conference room she had the TV set on, the one we normally only use for viewing evidence videos. This time it was turned to one of the local stations, where a Special Report banner ran across the bottom of the screen in attention-getting red. White letters spelled out Victoria Morgan Missing Person Hotline and the number.

A man in a suit, with a detective badge clearly visible on his belt, was talking.

"… a number of leads phoned in. Unfortunately, none of them have led us to Ms. Morgan. Sheriff Beau Cardwell from Taos County has even come down to go through leads with us, as several of the more viable sounding calls came from his jurisdiction."

In the background stood a tall man in a brown and tan uniform with a felt Stetson. Something in the back of my brain told me he was connected with Samantha Sweet, the baker I'd met, the one who had made Ron and Victoria's wedding cake. Which, I made a mental note, really should be put into the freezer soon if we hoped to save it. While I was sidetracked on that thought, the camera switched away from the law enforcement men.

The reporter on scene was talking. "And that's all we know, officially at least. But seem to be things the police are keeping very close-mouthed about, Jill, and we plan to ask the difficult questions."

Cameras in the newsroom took over, where popular anchor Jill Maldonado was seated at the news desk in a low-cut dress that bordered on unprofessional, her hair and makeup so perfect it made me think of a Barbie doll. Behind her, a huge screen flashed pictures of Ron talking with Ben

Ortiz in what appeared to be a very hush-hush conversation, alternating to a shot of Ron in his tuxedo looking completely disheveled after the long day of interrogation.

"Yes, Scott, there are difficult questions. Questions such as, where was bridegroom Ron Parker during those hours when something horrific obviously happened at Victoria Morgan's house? Why, if he's innocent, did Parker hire noted defense attorney Ben Ortiz practically before the investigation team had left the crime scene? And why is the man some are calling the Killer Bridegroom not behind bars today?"

Jill Maldonado presented a serious facial expression to the camera right before she flicked it over to a smile and informed us that she would be right back with the station's legal consultant to give his take on the case. In a flash, a loud-mouthed car dealer came on, with flickering lights and fireworks to announce his holiday specials.

The Killer Bridegroom? I literally saw red as Ron aimed the remote and shut down the offensive pictures. How dare they! I spun around, ready to pick up the phone and get the perky Jill Maldonado on the phone. Sally turned, her face white with shock. Ron's was a mask of steel. He stood so still I momentarily wanted to make sure he was breathing.

Chapter 12

Juliette stretched under the featherweight comforter, reaching to the other side of the bed, finding it empty. No surprise. A little disappointment. She rolled to the side facing wide sliding glass doors where she could see the ocean through white sheer drapes.

I must be the luckiest woman in the world right now, she thought, massaging the thick quilted mattress cover beneath her. How life had changed in these last few weeks. Ever since New Year's Eve.

Al had come into her office right after Christmas, during Sheila's lunch hour when the place was virtually deserted. With a hip propped on the corner of her desk, he sent one of his brilliant smiles her way.

"Do you have plans for New Year's Eve?" he asked.

She shook her head. Every year she and Carol Ann had

done something together—dancing at a club, taking in a purely chick-flick movie, going somewhere with friends—but with Tommy in the picture Carol Ann had given the no-argument impression that the evening was already planned and the plans didn't include Juliette.

"Hm?" He'd apparently seen a flash of irritation on her face. "I thought maybe a nice dinner, some dancing, just you and me."

What the heck. Why not? She nodded enthusiastically. She was not sitting home alone in that drab apartment just because Carol Ann couldn't be bothered with her anymore.

Al had picked her up in the Porsche and without explanation drove straight to his mansion. She expected his kiss this time. Even though he'd been very proper at the office, ever since the Christmas party she'd felt the burn of his eyes upon her, every bit as potent as the heat of his lips against the chilly evening, out on the veranda. This time they'd hardly gotten inside the door when he pulled her into his arms.

"I've never wanted a woman the way I want you," he said, his breathing hard, his voice hushed.

"Al—we talked about this."

"We aren't at the office. We don't have to answer to anyone. I want you Juliette. I want to take care of you, to give you everything."

This time the kiss probed to her very soul and she felt herself swept away. He led her upstairs to the master bedroom, which looked like something out of a palace, complete with canopied bed and satin sheets. Hours passed. A short break for the promised dinner, back to the bed, a moonlit night on the veranda with soft music and slow dances. Back to the bed. The evening stretched into two days in which he truly did take care of her.

When he took her home Sunday night, walking into her old apartment was like being thrown against a dirty concrete wall. The rooms, the furnishings ... it all depressed her. She had gone straight to bed and closed her eyes, putting herself back into the fantasy world where she shared time with Al.

Monday morning at the office he handed her a tape of dictation and a plain white envelope.

"Look inside," he said with the grin she'd come to adore.

The envelope had contained a sheet of paper and a key.

"It's the lease to your new condo."

"What? Al, you can't—"

"I can, and I did. We'll go see it at lunch time. If you like it, I'll get a crew over to move your stuff in."

And that was it. Spacious rooms on the eighteenth floor, living room and bedroom facing the ocean, a kitchen far bigger than she needed, a bedroom larger than her entire apartment. The look on her face said *yes*, long before she found the actual words to thank him.

"It comes with the furniture," he said, "but if you don't like any of it I'll have it changed for you."

"It's—it's perfect. I'm speechless."

"Well, we don't have to *talk*." He led her to the bedroom and they officially made the new residence hers.

For the first two weeks he was there every night, usually staying until midnight or so, only staying all night on one occasion. When her monthly inconvenience came, he stayed away for a few nights, but the days were filled with passionate kisses behind closed doors at the office.

She'd received a raise, to cover additional expenses he'd said. A brand-new red Camaro convertible appeared in her assigned parking slot in the condo garage. The existence of the condo and her new lifestyle was never mentioned in front of the other employees, but Juliette had a feeling Sheila had figured it out.

"I want to invite Carol Ann and Tommy for dinner one night this week. I can cook and it'll be fun for the four of us to socialize."

"What night? I'm pretty booked this week."

"Thursday or Friday?"

"Do what you want. I'll see if I'm available." He reached for the door which connected their offices. "I've got a meeting right now."

The words stung. She was fairly certain he'd planned to be with her each night. Obviously, he didn't want to spend time with her friends. Then again, she wasn't a hundred percent sure they wanted to be around him. She'd introduced Carol Ann once when the girls had plans for lunch and Carol Ann had dropped by the office to pick her up. Al had been distracted that morning anyway so, yeah, he didn't exactly exude personality at the moment. And her friend's reaction had been especially weird—disdain, almost contempt. But surely, that was a one-time thing. They just needed to get to know one another.

Juliette had called her friend in early January to tell her everything that had happened and got a lukewarm reception, and Carol Ann had been occupied whenever Juliette suggested a girl's movie or lunch. Well, those things happened. Friends didn't always stick with you through thick and thin. Just surprising that her best high school friend had certainly been there during the lean times. Maybe it was jealousy over Juliette's good fortune. That must be it.

Behind Al's door, male voices droned. She looked at her desk calendar to see who the appointment was with, but there was no note of it. She turned to her dictation. Al was that way—didn't always tell her who he was seeing. She fed paper into the Selectric and began a letter.

The more she thought about her little dinner party idea, the worse it sounded. She decided to blow it off. Let Carol Ann be the one to call. Maybe Juliette would just *happen* to be busy and give her a taste of how it felt.

On the other side of the door, the stranger's voice rose. Al's voice responded but Juliette couldn't make out the words. The outer office door opened, followed by the door to the street—all familiar sounds to her. Then Al's outer door slammed. Hm … something had not gone well.

The letter was ready for his signature and he'd told her it was important, so she tapped at the connecting door.

"Come!" It was definitely a command.

She held the letter up, not saying a word. He scrawled his name on it, barely looking at her.

"Everything okay?" she asked.

"Just business. Don't worry about it."

Since her job was to worry about his dealings and appointments she felt a little excluded but took a deep breath and resolved not to dwell on the man's visit. Even though their personal lives were increasingly intertwined, there was no reason for her to know every single aspect of his business.

"Um, just to let you know … I decided not to do the dinner party with Carol Ann and Tommy. We're too busy and it's a hassle."

His mood brightened immediately. "Good. I like it better when it's just you and me."

She walked back to her desk and put the letter into an envelope. Yes, she had made the right decision.

Al pulled on his jacket and headed for the door. Juliette carried the stamped letter to Sheila's desk to join the other outgoing mail when the postman came by. Marion, the bookkeeper, stood there with a stack of her own envelopes.

"Who was that man earlier, the one who kind of stormed out?" Juliette asked.

The two older women exchanged a glance. Sheila gave a half-shrug and picked up a can of Coke from the coaster on her desk.

Marion, who rarely interacted with Juliette at all, was the first to speak. "His name's Elmer Reddick. He's with the county sheriff's department."

"Sounded like they had words."

"They always have words," Marion responded before dumping her mail on Sheila's desk and walking back to her little cave-like office.

"Okay … What did she mean by that?"

Sheila sent her an inscrutable look, as if there was something she didn't quite want to say. "Al and Elmer don't always see eye to eye."

"I gathered that."

"It goes way back, apparently. I get the impression they've known each other since they were kids." The phone rang and Sheila reached for it. The conversation was over.

Juliette wondered if the men's differences were personal or professional. She didn't have long to think about it. The call was for Al and Sheila had already transferred it to Juliette's desk.

That night Al came to her condo after nine o'clock, loosening his tie and heading straight to the built-in bar for his usual nightcap. While he poured expensive Scotch from one of the pricey bottles he'd brought when she moved in, she thought again of the visit by Elmer Reddick.

"Hey, baby," he said when she mentioned it. He slipped an arm around her waist. "What have I said about business and pleasure? We don't mix 'em. I'd whole lot rather see you in that little lacy thing I gave you for Valentine's Day than talk about some jerk who don't know what he's talking about."

Juliette blushed a little at the memory of his presentation of the 'little lacy thing.' He'd brought in a shopping bag from Neiman Marcus and right there in the office he'd pulled out a red lace teddy that left absolutely nothing to the imagination. He held it up and Sheila caught a good look at it as she'd walked down the hall. Her co-worker had not said a word about it, thank goodness.

"Go on now, scoot." Al tossed his jacket over a dining chair and removed his tie, undoing a couple of buttons and stretching out on the huge sectional sofa while Juliette retired to the bathroom to cut the tags off the teddy.

* * *

A month went by and Juliette had heard nothing from Carol Ann. Nights when Al stayed late, her world felt complete. But his increasing absences left her edgy and lonely. She called Carol Ann's number one evening, only to find the number had been disconnected. What on earth?

She realized Carol Ann must have moved in with Tommy. She struggled to remember his last name, finally coming up with Henderson. Found the listing and called. An overly-cute message answered: "Hi, you've reached Tommy and Carol Ann (both voices chiming in). We're busy (suggestive giggles). Leave a message and we might get back to you when we're not so … busy! (raucous laughter)" Then a beep. Juliette hung up without saying anything.

Back in Texas she'd always had a library card. She should get one here. Reading might help fill the long nights. She'd never heard Al talk about books at all. The library at his house seemed full of classics he'd never read—nothing that interested her. She waited up until eleven and went to bed alone.

Good Friday came. Al had declared it a half-day at the office but then he left without making any plans with her for the whole weekend. Marion was out the door precisely at twelve noon and Sheila had already covered her typewriter and put the telephone's holiday message on.

"Even though my kids are teenagers now," she said to Juliette, "we always do a little something special Easter weekend. We said we'd take them to Disney World this year. I better get out of here. The traffic's going to be murder."

Juliette looked up from her typewriter. "No problem. I've got one letter to finish and I'll lock up."

The front doorbell chimed as Sheila left. Juliette had barely typed two more lines before it jingled again.

"Forget something?' she called out.

Movement at her doorway caught her attention; she started when she saw a large man standing there. He wore tan pants and a plaid shirt, had a shiny bald top and a paunch that hung over his waistband.

"Where's Al?"

"I'm sorry, the office closed early today. May I set up an appointment for you next week?"

He glanced around, his attitude more proprietary than menacing.

"Nah, I'll just stop by when I'm in the neighborhood."

"May I tell him who called?"

His round face widened into a grin. "My, aren't we the formal ones. You must be the little girlfriend."

How could he possibly know that?

She stood up, preparing to usher him out. "Is this business or personal?"

Another of those glances around the office. He pulled a leather case from his hip pocket and flashed a badge. His voice dropped, barely above a whisper. "Al's going down one of these days, hon, and you don't want to be there."

"What are you talking about?"

"Nice. Keep up the innocent manner." He raised his voice to normal tones again. "Hell, I don't care if he does have the place bugged and he gets every word of this. Al Proletti, we've got your number and you're going down one of these days soon."

Juliette felt her jaw sag. What did that mean?

"Elmer Reddick, ma'am." It was all he said but he reached into the badge case, silently handing her a business card. Dade County Sheriff's Department.

Chapter 13

Making all those dead-end phone calls gave me a headache. Even though I hadn't made it through the entire alphabet I set the address book aside, looking for something more productive to do. Freckles convinced me the best thing would be to hand her a dog cookie from the tin canister on my shelf. I did so, then took her for a short walk around the block to clear my head. Ron had retreated to his office after the television newscast, looking as if he might put a fist through the wall.

When the dog and I returned from our walk, Ron was on the phone. Once I figured out he was talking to Kent Taylor, I listened shamelessly. Still, I was only getting half the conversation. This call most certainly went against every scrap of legal advice he'd ever received. I got the part where Ron asked straight out whether he was seriously considered a suspect. Apparently the answer wasn't 'yes' because Ron didn't explode on the spot. But it must not have been a clear 'no' either. He stayed quiet on the line for a full two minutes.

His next question, did they have any solid leads from the hotline, brought more of the same—a lengthy answer from Kent Taylor's end. At that point either Ron ran out of questions or Taylor came to the end of the answers he was willing to give because Ron thanked him and hung up.

"So? What did he say?"

He sighed. "Well, the good news is that I'm not really minutes away from being arrested as the damn *Killer Bridegroom*. And Taylor even promised to see if he can't get them to quash that description. At which point they'll probably scream about their freedom of the press and freedom of speech rights and the best I can hope for is a lengthy and expensive lawsuit later to gain back my good name. He did actually say that."

"At least he hasn't become your sworn enemy," I ventured as I took the spare chair in his office.

"What he actually said was that they are looking at all possibilities. Tips are coming in from the hotline, but so far none of them have checked out. Apparently people are so eager to get their name in the news that they'll call in almost anything. One lead came from Gallup and when the local cops checked it out, turned out the woman the guy spotted was really his neighbor. Seriously. Nothing but a publicity stunt. My life and Vic's life are on the line here, and people think it's cute to play jokes on the police?"

I could see his blood pressure rising again so I tried to distract him.

"The address book isn't yielding anything but what if we start going through things on her computer? There's got to be up-to-date information there."

He woke up the sleeping machine and I dragged my chair around the desk. Side by side we looked at the unfamiliar layout, getting a feel for the programs Victoria must have used most.

"Let's check email first," I suggested.

Ron normally doesn't have a lot of problem invading people's privacy—it's what we do most of the time—but he balked a little.

"I can do it in my office if you'd like," I said. Maybe he worried she would have private stuff of a very girly nature on there, or perhaps he was afraid she would kill him when she got back and found out what he'd done.

I agreed that it felt invasive but I forged ahead. "I'm just thinking this will be the place where her most recent correspondence is. We don't have a way to check her phone, so this is the closest we can come."

He sighed and entered the password, then pushed the keyboard closer to me.

Her inbox was fairly full but most of it looked impersonal. Your order from Amazon was shipped; Don't miss the big sale at Pier One; Have better sex!!

"She could use a better spam filter," I commented as I scrolled past that one.

Several messages seemed personal. I opened the first and skimmed the message. "Hi Vic, Congrats on your big day! In case you're checking email while you're on your honeymoon (you better not be!!), I had to tell you that Rick's surgery turned out fine. He's home and recuperating. Talk soon when you get home." It was signed with the name Ginny.

"You know who Ginny is?" I asked.

"Yeah, a lady she did a living room for and then they became friends. They have lunch once in awhile."

"Maybe we should try to contact her. If Vic is out there ..."

"If she can get to a phone, wouldn't she have called me?"

Good point.

"Even if all she could do was drag herself to Ginny's doorstep, someone would have contacted the police."

Very good point. Nevertheless, I wrote down Ginny's email address, thinking I might start a correspondence with her, just in case.

There were three other personal messages, which I skimmed. With each, I took down the sender's address as well. By the time I opened the third one, Ron was looking bored and had decided to refill his coffee. The note began much the same as the others and I'd almost breezed on, until I got to the last line. "Did you ever tell Ron about that call last week, you know, the weird one? Well, however it turned out, I hope all is well."

What call? I wondered. Victoria and I had spent quite a lot of time together in the days leading up to the wedding—picking up our dresses, checking with the florist, lunches, little bits of last-minute shopping. She'd taken quite a few phone calls but never referred to any of them as weird.

I thought back over the days, trying to remember her moods. She'd been on something of a roller coaster, I supposed. Wedding stuff, the way most brides must feel right before the big day. It was, after all, her first marriage and would be one of the high points of her entire life. There were quiet times; I remembered even asking if she was all right once or twice. And of course she'd answered with a bright smile and assurances. If she'd been having doubts about Ron, his sister was probably the last person she would admit that to. But she *hadn't*—I swore she had not experienced any doubts about going through with the marriage.

Besides, what would that have to do with some weird phone call that a friend named Emily would mention in an email? I glanced at the date on the message. It had been sent Friday evening, the night before the wedding would have taken place. I wondered if Emily had been invited. Surely, someone close enough to share these confidences would have been among the guests.

When he came back with his coffee refill, I asked Ron if he had a copy of the guest list. He gave me that blank male shrug, meaning: 'List? You mean there's a written list?' How do guys think this stuff comes together anyway? I swear, my brother can be one of the most observant people on the planet when he's being paid as a private investigator, and one of the most hopeless when it comes to life's really important things, such as his own wedding plans.

I found a folder on the computer labeled Wedding. That should do it. Sure enough, the highly organized Victoria had created complete lists for guests, ceremony, reception, and honeymoon. This last consisted mostly of a list of things to pack—it had been up to Ron to make the travel arrangements.

The guest list included an Emily Brackman, who lived in Los Lunas on the outskirts of Albuquerque, and a Ginny Fields with an address in the Tanoan Country Club area. I finally felt I was getting somewhere—at least I knew these were up-to-date addresses and the people on this list would have been in contact with Victoria in recent weeks. I picked up the laptop and carried it to my own desk.

I debated phoning. Oftentimes, you get better information when you can take someone by surprise, showing up in person. On the other hand, I could waste a huge amount of time driving from one end of the city to the other, only to discover my interviewees were not home. People had jobs, social plans ... this stuff gets so dang complicated at times. I picked up the phone and dialed Emily Brackman's number.

Starting the conversation was the toughest part. How much did she know, had she watched the news since the really vile accusations began, would she immediately hang up on anyone from Ron's family? I had to take the chance.

"Emily? This is Charlie Parker ... I was Victoria's matron of honor ... well, would have been ..."

From the amount of noise in the background I guessed she was at a mall and had at least one young child. Either that or she worked in a daycare center. She asked me to repeat what I'd said. Which I did.

"Oh, Charlie. Yes, of course, Victoria talked about you a lot."

Good things, I hoped, something that would overshadow the current media blitz.

"I feel so bad," Emily was saying. "Is there any news? I just hate what I'm hearing on TV."

"You and me both," I said. "Right now we're just trying to track down any information we can—"

A kid-shriek, the kind that tends to pierce eardrums, made me yank the phone away to a safe distance.

"Look, would it be possible for us to talk in person?" I asked. "I think it would be easier."

Emily chuckled. "It would. I'll be home in about an hour and will have the kids down for naps, if you want to drop by." The Los Lunas address matched the one from Vic's list, and Emily provided brief directions for how to find it. I gave it an hour and fifteen minutes—wanting those kids soundly asleep—then I pulled up in front of her house.

The small towns south of Albuquerque have grown tremendously in recent years and what I remembered as a sleepy little riverside burg in my high school days now featured such amenities as a Walmart Supercenter and a medium security prison. I mention these with no particular opinion on which is the better neighbor. Emily's home turned out to be in one of several new subdivisions which have boosted the local population, those who want out of the big-city bustle of Albuquerque.

The Brackman's home distinguished itself from the other cookie-cutter tan and brown houses in the neighborhood by having fairly mature trees out front and a neatly manicured, although winter-brown, lawn. Over the gate leading to the backyard I could see a brightly colored tangle of gymnastic/swing set equipment for the kids but at least the front yard was nicely uncluttered. I tapped lightly at the door, not wanting to risk a doorbell.

"Charlie? Hi, come on in." Emily looked like the kind of woman who would be Victoria's friend. Similar hairstyle, long and dark, dressed in jeans and a sweater. She was pretty but not gorgeous, the girl in high school who would shine at English and math and probably help on every committee, but wouldn't even bother going out for cheerleader. She had Fleetwood Mac playing in the background, subdued enough not to keep the kids awake but with enough volume we could talk without causing a disturbance either.

"I'm just making myself a cup of tea. Would you like one?"

I accepted and followed her into the kitchen.

"I think I only met Ron once," she said, her back to me as she worked at the counter. "Ran into Victoria once at Macy's and he was with her."

"Where do you know her from?"

"We met at UNM, interior design classes. Hit it off right away. We kept in close touch for awhile but our lives went separate ways. I married right out of school, worked awhile, followed my husband's jobs out of country. He works for an oil company. We were stationed in Saudi for fourteen months, Canada for awhile. When we finally decided it was time to get with the program if we wanted kids it seemed best to come back to New Mexico. Both our families are here, you know, keep the kids near the grandparents. Good thing we did—we ended up with triplets."

She set delicate china cups and saucers on the table, along with a beautiful sugar and creamer set. When I admired them she told me it was her daily indulgence, having a quiet cup of tea during nap time.

"Next year they'll be in kindergarten. I'm debating between going back to work, at least part time, or treating myself to mornings in my robe with dishy romance novels and plenty of cups of tea. I know what I'm *tempted* to do."

I smiled along with her and she sighed after her first sip.

"I don't want to take away from your quiet time," I said. "The reason I called is because I came across an email you sent Victoria on Friday."

"Oh gosh, I wasn't even thinking. She must have been so busy that day."

"It was a little crazy, but she's so well organized. Everything was coming together just as she wanted it."

"I don't know how you guys are coping. Between her

disappearing like that and then what they're saying on the news …"

"We're doing our best to ignore that. So much of it is speculation—we just really don't know anything. Ron and I've decided to piece together any information we can get. Which is how we got started on the emails. In your message you mentioned a call Victoria had received, something weird. Can you tell me about that?"

"She didn't mention it to you? In that case, it's probably nothing."

"Still, anything you remember could be helpful."

"Well, let's see. I met her for lunch last … last Thursday? I'm pretty sure. I'll look at the calendar. It was the day my mom agreed to take all three kids for an afternoon. Anyway, Vic and I met at Costell's. Have you been there? Cutest little place for salads and sandwiches—too girly for most guys, but we like it. I had this mango-avocado salad."

I guess my expression told her I really didn't need to hear the menu.

"So, she mostly talked about the wedding but at one point she brought up this phone call. I still don't know why, other than she seemed to be unsure whether to mention it to Ron or not."

"Who was it from? What was the call about?"

"She didn't know. She said it was a man, older-sounding, with some kind of an accent but she really couldn't describe it. He asked if she was related to … now this is the part I don't remember … what the name was. Victoria thought he was asking about her mother but he didn't quite have all the facts right. Vic's mother died a long time ago. I'm sure you know all this."

"Yes, she'd said it was when she was in high school."

It was one thing we immediately had in common when we met.

"That's right. Mrs. Morgan's life insurance was what allowed Vic to go to college with no student loans. I think she used part of it for the down payment on that cute little house of hers. I have to admit I was faintly envious of her financial position at that point. Of course, I wouldn't trade the time with my mom for anything."

She seemed to realize she was rambling again. "So, about the call, I'm afraid that's all I know."

"This man didn't give Vic his name?"

Emily stared toward the ceiling for a minute. "I'm sure he did. I'm just trying to think what she told me. It was kind of a weird name, I think, not one I'd ever heard before."

I drank the last of my tea, wishing I could prompt her or push her in some way to make the information come forth. But Emily seemed genuinely stumped. I ended up pulling one of my business cards from my purse and handing it to her.

"If you recall that name, please let me know. It's really important."

From another room came a child's voice and Emily's attention darted away from me. She saw me to the door but she'd already forgotten most of our conversation. I sat in my car for an extra minute, writing down exactly what Emily had said about the mysterious phone call and Victoria's reaction to it.

If Vic had been concerned about the man's intentions, why wouldn't she have immediately told Ron about it? We could have done some background checks, found information on the man. There must be more to this than I could see at the moment.

Chapter 14

Juliette yanked the tangled sheet from her legs. She hadn't slept well in the two nights since Friday's visit by Elmer Reddick at the office. She'd driven home in a blur, her mind churning with the lawman's comment. Al should have been at the condo and she would ask him, and he would no doubt have a simple answer to reassure her. But all she'd found at the condo was a note: *Sorry baby, got called out of town on business for the weekend.*

Business on Easter weekend? She phoned his house where Ernestina the maid told her she had not seen Señor Proletti since early that morning. If not for Reddick's remark, Juliette would have suspected another woman. But if Al really was being investigated by the sheriff's department ... everything took on a whole new meaning. What could he have done? It had to be something simple, such as not getting a required building permit. If only she could talk to him.

Of the possibilities—trouble with the law or seeing another woman—Juliette wasn't sure which disturbed her more. Her daddy, a preacher in Dalhart, would be horrified to see what she'd got herself into. Mama might once have echoed Daddy's words, although privately she usually offered a little sympathy. At least there would have been a shoulder to cry on. But his new wife, whom Juliette could not bear to think of as step-mom, was completely caught up in appearances and would see that she was disowned on the spot.

Juliette got out of bed and padded barefoot, wearing only a satin kimono, to the kitchen where she started the coffee maker. She reached for the wall phone and started to dial Carol Ann. Set the phone back. In their last conversation Carol Ann had been full of exciting plans for a weekend trip to St. Augustine with Tommy. She felt her eyes well up. There was no one she could talk to. She took her coffee to the living room, curled up in the corner of the sectional and stared out at the ocean. Easter morning.

The phrase brought back memories of sunrise church services under the trees in Texas, a bigger-than-usual Sunday dinner followed by an Easter egg hunt and baskets filled with cellophane grass and jelly beans, new shoes and dress—something frothy and precious. As for most children, the holiday had been a high point in her year. Now it was nothing but another day at a beach filled with tourists in bikinis, laughing too loudly under the influence of way too many drinks. A tear plopped into her coffee cup.

She set the beverage aside and walked to the sliding door,

eyeing her narrow balcony and looking down at the patch of concrete surrounding the pool, eighteen floors below. Laughter and shrieks from the crowd drifted upward on the warm spring air. She felt one moment's longing to simply dive off. A child's voice giggled and shrieked "Mommy!" and the feeling evaporated in an instant.

"I can't sit around like this and I can't just do *nothing*!" she yelled into the empty living room.

She took a shower and washed her hair. Under the steaming spray she made a plan. She dried off and slipped into a favorite pair of shorts and a T-shirt. Grabbing her purse and keys she headed to the office.

I can't very well ask Al what's going on if I don't have a clue where to begin, she thought as she cruised along Greenlee Boulevard. But down inside what she really wondered was whether she *should* talk to him or whether she'd better do as the deputy advised and stay clear. Either way, she needed to know.

The construction yard was dead silent. She'd never been here without the roar of big equipment engines out in the back lot and the bustle of men and vehicles moving in and out. The wide chain link gate leading to the back was closed and padlocked, a sight she'd never seen before. In fact, Friday afternoon was the first time she'd been left alone to lock up. If Al were to come in, she would have some explaining to do. She thought about this as she parked and unlocked the front door. She could say that she'd left a personal item behind and needed it. What item? She scrambled for ideas while she entered the alarm code at the keypad on the white box beside the door. That was another thing he'd only now begun to trust her with, a key and the code. A shiver passed through her as she considered his reaction if he felt she had betrayed him.

She left the reception room lights off and went directly to her own office. The two plants on her desk looked desperately dry. Good—that would be her excuse. She set her purse on the desk beside them and brought a cup of water from the kitchenette. The moment she heard a noise at the door she would be ready with her plausible justification for being there.

The building felt eerily quiet without the constant hum of the AC and fluorescent lights. Even her sandals on the tile made too much noise. She tiptoed to Al's office, chiding herself for being so jumpy. With the door to the lobby and the window blinds closed, there was no way anyone could know she was in there. She kept one ear tuned to the bell at the front door as she stepped behind Al's desk and reached for the center drawer. A tug. Locked.

She tried each of the file drawers to the left and right of the knee space. All securely locked as well. His credenza held two more file drawers and a center section with doors across it. Frustration mounted as she discovered all were locked. Come to think of it, she'd never actually had access to any of those drawers; each time she finished a letter or handled a file she brought it to his Inbox and set it there. He'd always done his own filing. The fact had never struck her as odd until now. What executive filed his own letters unless he was hiding something in those drawers?

She chewed at her lower lip for a moment. She had no idea if the drawers were locked during business hours or not. It could be that he'd simply taken the precaution because of the long weekend. She spotted the sharp metal letter opener near his leather-rimmed desk pad. A few stabs at the lock on one of the drawers yielded no result except some tiny scratch marks on the lock.

Stupid, Juliette. Don't do it. If he spots those he'll know what you tried.

She replaced the letter opener exactly as she'd found it and went back to her own office. Across the hall, Marion Flightly's door was closed, as usual. Hmm … Who would have better access to the business's innermost secrets than the bookkeeper?

She scooted across the hall and tried the door. Not surprisingly, it too was locked. She debated the letter-opener trick—maybe a door lock was different than a desk lock—but the sharp old bird would surely notice even the slightest difference in the appearance of the door or her office. She'd bragged in the coffee room, more than once, how easily she noticed discrepancies in figures and how her bank register was never out of balance. And she'd commented each time Juliette wore a new pair of shoes or carried a new purse. It wasn't worth the risk of being called out in front of the others.

Sheila's desk proved to be a much better target. None of the drawers were locked and Juliette rifled them guilt-free. Unfortunately, all she found besides the standard pens, notepads and message books were a bottle of Glowing Flame nail polish, a hairbrush, a box of tampons, two dried up tubes of Superglue and a spare Bic lighter.

The file-sized drawer held a few thin manila folders which seemed unimportant. Toward the back were spiral bound message books with yellow duplicates of the phone messages she took all day. This could be good, Juliette thought. The forms were two-part, four to a sheet. The upper pink copy was perforated so four separate messages could be written and torn out. A sheet of carbon paper copied the messages onto yellow duplicates which stayed in the book. She had one like it at her own desk. Al often asked for someone's phone number and it was handy to go back to those yellow copies to find it.

She paged through one of the books, looking for … what, exactly? She wasn't even sure. She came across familiar client names and others who were unknown to her. But what did that mean? Nothing, really. She'd been in the office twenty minutes already and knew she dare not stay longer, especially if someone saw her car, casually mentioned it to Al, and she were to try using her plant-watering excuse. That was a five-minute task. She needed to get out now.

She put the message books back in the order she'd found them, watered her plants, retraced her steps to be sure all lights were off, all trace of her presence gone. Her hand shook a little as she entered the alarm code and locked the front door, but no one was outside. Cars on the street roared past at their usual pace, no one turning a head to look her direction as she started her car and pulled out.

Across the street from her condo she spotted a little street fair with food vendors and crafts booths fronting the beach. She parked the Camaro in her underground spot and walked over, deciding to clear her head. Her stomach rumbled at the scent of grilled meat and she ordered something billed as the Latin Macho Burger, eating it as she walked the beach. Stretching her legs and breathing the fresh sea air felt good. Tossing the wrapper from her sandwich into a bin, she browsed a booth selling handmade bead earrings and bought herself a pair in shades of blue and purple.

She'd probably blown everything out of proportion this

morning. That deputy was full of crap and Al really did have a business trip this weekend. He loved her. She worked by his side every day and slept with him almost every night. Surely he had no secrets from her. She walked home, put on her new earrings and settled on the sofa with a book she'd been wanting to read for a long time.

Monday morning, Al put her mind at rest when he walked into her office looking jaunty and somewhat amorous. He closed the door and took her hand, pulling her up from her chair and pressing his body close.

"Umm, I missed you," he whispered in her ear, raking his fingers through her hair.

"I missed you too. The weekend was too long."

"Feel like company tonight?" he asked. He'd reached for his coat pocket and pulled out a small square box.

Her breath caught as he put it in her hand. She took a step back and lifted the lid. An exquisite heart-shaped pendant, covered in tiny diamonds, glittered under the lights.

"It's beautiful," she said, her breath coming quickly.

"For the most beautiful girl in the world." He pulled the delicate chain from the box and draped it around her neck, stepping behind to hook the clasp.

Juliette cooled slightly at his words. She knew good and well she was not the most beautiful girl in the world and the words were meant to pacify her when he knew she'd been peeved with him. But when he stroked her cheek and looked deeply into her eyes, she forgot all that.

"Let me take you to dinner, that seafood place you love so much, then we'll go home and ..." His eyebrows wiggled. Her body warmed.

She smiled and shooed him back to his own office, then immediately went to the ladies room to look at the necklace in the mirror. It was now the third time he'd given her diamonds. One of these times would the gift be a ring?

"Al's going down one of these days, hon, and you don't want to be there." The voice of the deputy intruded into her thoughts.

"No." She said it out loud to erase his voice and shake off the memory of his visit.

Turning her back on the mirror she left the restroom and went back to her desk. But Reddick's words would not completely go away. Why was Al's desk locked? What secrets were hidden in there or in Marion's office? She didn't like it that the lawman who'd known Al since they were kids now seemed intent on getting him.

She had a hard time concentrating on her typing and found herself whiting out a lot of mistakes. A picture of the florid-faced deputy stayed in her head. He was probably just jealous. Al had become hugely successful, lived in a mansion, bought lavish gifts for his girlfriend. And Reddick—his life must seem completely dull and dreary in comparison. Life in a drab brown uniform and squad car, a public servant's salary that probably didn't go far enough. There was probably a chubby wife and three extremely average kids at home. No wonder he was jealous of his old schoolmate. That had to be it.

Even if it is just jealousy, she told herself, the man could be dangerous to Al. Might try to frame him for something, just to make him suffer. She vowed to keep an eye on the situation. If she heard anything more, she would warn Al before Reddick could cause trouble.

She rolled a fresh sheet of stationery into the typewriter and redid the botched letter.

* * *

She arrived a few minutes late for work the next day. After their beautiful dinner together, they went back to the condo where Al had been especially attentive, with a special bottle of wine and a new tape of romantic music. They'd danced on the balcony and made love with a tenderness and passion that took her breath away. Midnight came much too quickly and she asked him to stay the night. At first he'd demurred but finally said he would call Ernestina and let her know not to wait up.

"She worries about me like her own son," he said.

He went into the living room while Juliette took off her makeup and finished her nightly routine, and he came back with two snifters of brandy.

"One more romantic touch for the perfect evening," she said with a luxuriant smile.

"I'll leave first in the morning," he told her. "You sleep in, baby."

And so she had. When she walked into the office she thought there was a knowing look on Sheila's face, even though she'd told Al to make the girls think she'd had an early dental appointment. She went first to the kitchenette for coffee, then carried her mug and purse to her desk. The connecting door was closed but she'd not seen any strange cars in the parking lot, so he must be alone. Maybe he'd like a good morning kiss. She opened the door.

"… not on the record," he said, pulling a sheaf of pages toward himself.

The other person in the room was Marion, who stood at the boss's side. She practically flinched when Juliette walked in.

"Oh, sorry. I didn't realize anyone was here."

Marion gave her a look that said, *obviously not*.

Al slid the papers under his blotter in a move so smooth most people wouldn't have noticed.

Juliette fumbled for words, being that the kiss offer wasn't exactly the thing to say now. "Just letting you know I'm in."

"Dental appointment go okay?" he asked with an impartial smile.

"Just perfect." She backed out.

A minute later she heard the other door open and close. Marion had gone back to her office. Al appeared at Juliette's door right away.

"Sorry, that was a little awkward," he said.

"Honey, it's your office. You don't have to explain to me."

Something in his expression told her those were exactly his thoughts. He'd merely been polite.

"So, what are we working on today?" she asked.

He stepped back to his desk and brought out two cassette tapes of dictation. She was debating whether to ask about the other papers, the ones he'd taken from Marion, but her phone rang.

"Al Proletti's office," she answered.

She didn't know the male voice and when she asked who was calling, he said, "Tell him it's New York."

Okay … She turned to Al. "New York calling."

His smile dropped away and he stepped quickly into his own space, pushing the door shut on his way to his desk. The door didn't click firmly and Juliette noticed that it gaped open about a half inch. In case he looked her direction, she made a show of putting paper in the typewriter and placing one of the tapes into the machine.

His tone started out jovially enough, a greeting to

someone he knew fairly well, but changed completely once the other man spoke.

"I know, but there were circumstances," he said.

Silence as he listened to the other man. Juliette began typing furiously, eyes toward her page, even though she had not yet turned on the machine with the dictated tape.

Al's voice again: "… had to ditch … not sure how much they left behind."

Again, she typed while he listened.

"That part of it's fine. I got all the paperwork."

More silence on his part, punctuated by attempts to interject, being interrupted by the man at the other end.

Juliette typed, caught no more before he slammed the phone down. Through the tiny crack in the doorway she saw him, elbows on the desk, fingers gripping the sides of his head. A violent oath, a palm slapping the desktop. He stood, his eyes scanning the room.

She quickly looked away from the door, sending her attention toward her work. If he spotted the fact that the door hadn't been closed, he didn't acknowledge it. A minute later she heard him telling Sheila he was going out. The Porsche started and left the parking lot with a roar.

Juliette wasted no time strolling into his office, all business-as-usual, with the fake typed letter in her hand. His lobby door was closed so she edged the connecting door shut as well. The mysterious papers were still under his blotter and she pulled them out.

Handwritten entries on some kind of crude form, each a half-sized sheet of flimsy paper. The printed information was in Spanish, the handwritten parts in some kind of sketchy code. 540 Kilo said one of them, 200 Kilo on another.

She heard a sound in the hallway, jammed the flimsy sheets back under the blotter and hugged her other letter to her chest as she walked back into her office, hoping her composure hadn't slipped too badly. Marion stood in the doorway to the hall.

"Hi Marion, can I help you?" Rarely did the bookkeeper come in here, and Juliette was certain her pounding heart must be visible.

"Just wondered if you wanted a cup of tea. I'm heading for the kitchen to get myself one."

"Thanks, but I still have coffee here." Juliette flashed her a smile.

The older woman gave her a hard look. Had she only now figured out Juliette was sleeping with the boss? Or did she suspect her younger co-worker of spying? Marion didn't say another word, just headed toward the kitchen.

Juliette practically fell into her chair, her knees felt so weak. She fiddled with the tape machine but her mind was on those pages under Al's blotter. What had he been talking about and how did those papers relate? She wished there was a way to get copies of the pages and study them, but she dared not handle them again, especially with Marion's eagle eye now trained on her.

Chapter 15

I sat in my Jeep outside the Brackman home a few minutes, deciding what to do next. The other email, the one from Ginny Fields, might be worth a follow-up. Her address was way across the city, so I called the number I'd gotten from Victoria's guest list. The call went to voice mail so I left a brief message and clicked off, fairly certain I'd never hear back from her—my same old worry about the reception any of Ron's family would receive from friends of Vic's who'd had an earful of the news. Halfway back to the office, my phone buzzed.

Not a fan of cell phones and driving, a quick glance showed Ginny Fields's number and I hit the button to accept the call anyway. I tapped the speaker button and set the phone on the console beside me.

"Ginny Fields here. I received a call from you."

"Yes, Ginny. Thanks so much for getting right back to me." I gave the quick introduction, approximately the same thing I'd said to Emily earlier. "I'm on the road right now, maybe twenty minutes from your address. I wonder if we might meet for a few minutes? I'm trying to track down any type of useful information about Victoria."

A long pause.

"I don't know what I can tell you, Charlie. She decorated my house and worked for some of my neighbors."

"But you became friends. You were invited to her wedding. You wrote to let her know about your husband's surgery."

"Well, all that's true. How did you know about my email and the surgery?"

"My brother and I are Victoria's family. We're scared to death and we're trying to find answers. Can you spare me even a *little* time? I can meet you somewhere—just name it."

A sigh she didn't bother to conceal came across the airwaves. "Well, okay. I'm just finishing some shopping at ABQ Uptown. Meet me at the Starbucks there."

Good—a lot closer for me. "I'll see you there in ten minutes."

Although I would have preferred a more private setting and a friendlier invitation, I was at the point where I would take what I could get. I spent an extra couple of minutes finding the coffee place and a parking slot. I hoped Ginny wouldn't be a stickler and leave before I got there. Lunch hour had slid right past me and my energy for dramatics was severely lagging.

I recognized her by the pile of shopping bags surrounding her chair. Plus, she looked like the Tanoan type, with chic casual clothing and a pricey manicure. She'd chosen a table in the corner farthest from the two other patrons of the shop. I grabbed a high-octane something-or-other, although it was probably the last thing I needed. To convince myself I was making a healthy choice I added a thick slice of banana nut bread to my order since it was the only thing in the whole place resembling fruit.

"Ginny? Thanks so much for meeting me," I said while the barista whipped my coffee to pure frothiness. She sent a tight smile my way and went back to something on the screen of her phone.

I took my seat across from her and offered to split the banana bread. She gave one shake of the head. Silly me. She was obviously one of those women who's always on a diet, despite her size six figure.

"So, as I mentioned on the phone, Ron and I are partners in a private investigation firm and we're trying to work along with the police and hotline folks to get any leads on what may have happened to Victoria and where she is now."

"I have to say I was shocked to hear it. I'd RSVP'd with regrets on the wedding invitation. My husband is still recovering from surgery and we're having to curtail our social engagements for a few weeks."

"I hope he's mending well?"

"Oh, yes. He's feeling much better, thank you."

"So the first you heard of the wedding being cancelled was on TV. That must have been startling."

"And, of course, the things they're saying about the groom. I'd never met him, but of course Victoria was obviously very taken with him."

Taken with him? Okay, I guess that's one way to say head-over-heels in love. I sent Ginny a prim little smile of my own.

"My brother is devastated, of course. To have something happen to his bride just hours before the ceremony …"

"So, what can I do for you? I'm afraid my recent contacts with Victoria consisted of a lunch about three weeks ago and my one email, simply because she'd asked about my husband."

"I'd gotten the impression you and she became friends after she decorated your home. I was hoping maybe she'd said something in recent days, maybe told you if anything was worrying her."

"Well, I've referred several influential friends to Victoria as clients. They all seemed happy with her work, except Ida Van Horn, who is something of a pill anyway. She threw a bit of a fit over a delay with the fabric for her sofa. I supposed Victoria was concerned about that, since she would be going away on her honeymoon, which would delay the job even further."

"I was thinking more along the lines of threats, danger … something life-and-death." I was beginning to tire of this self-indulgent line, where a late fabric delivery was as important as a missing person.

"Afraid not. As I said, Victoria and I were more on an occasional-lunch level than real confidants." She took the last sip of her coffee and began to shuffle in her seat, clearly as impatient to be out of my company as I was hers.

I managed to stick one of my business cards into the top of her designer handbag as she stood up. "If you think of anything—anything at all she might have said that could help us find her—please give me a call."

At last Ginny seemed to take me seriously. She sent me a genuine smile and patted my shoulder as she scooted by. "I do hope you get the answers, and I really want it to turn out that Victoria comes home safely."

She walked out and I saw her slip into a Mercedes parked at the curb. I doubted she would give our conversation a second thought. What a difference between this 'friendship' of Vic's and the relationship with Emily Brackman. The woman with triplets had given me more time and information than this society lady. Ah well, that was simply the state of the situation. I sat there a while longer, savoring my snack and coffee—both of which were very good—and making a few notes.

The only thing I'd gotten from Ginny Fields was the name of Ida Van Horn, and since this was a current client of Victoria's it seemed well worth the effort to contact her. I called the office and asked Ron to look at the wedding list I'd left on my desk to see if the Van Horns were invited guests. They weren't.

"Hold on a minute," he said.

I didn't remember that our phone system played classical music while a person waited. We must have chosen it for its soothing qualities. At least it worked that way on me.

"Would the listing be a Ralph Van Horn on Tanoan Drive?"

"It's gotta be." I wrote down the address he gave me. I miss the old days of carrying a phone directory in my car, since I'm still not great at finding everything in the world on my cell phone.

Rather than risk a rebuff over the phone from the woman known to be a "pill" I decided to head that direction and take my chances at her front door. I negotiated my way out of the shopping center's parking maze and stuck to major streets, heading east on Academy to Tanoan's residential entrance. A man stepped out of the guard house, asking my name and my reason for being there. I was afraid he would phone the Van Horns to be sure I had an appointment, but he just wrote something on his clipboard and let me through.

I followed the winding road where dozens of manor houses sit snugly near their fellow McMansions. Seems any of them would be more comfortable with a little acreage on which to breathe rather than standard city lots. But that's just my take on it. The address numbers led me around two curves before I came to the Van Horn place, a Spanish colonial reminiscent of those I'd seen in old Hollywood movies where stars of the '30s lived. I wouldn't say it exactly fit with its modern, boxy neighbors but it had a lot more character.

The beveled-glass door was answered by a woman in her late seventies who stood a smidge over five feet, even with her elegant peach-hued French roll and modestly high heels. Even at home, here she was in her Chanel suit and double strand of pearls.

"Oh my, yes, we know Victoria," she said when I gave the quick reason for my visit. "Ralph and I adore her. Do come inside." And here I'd been worried about getting an earful about sofa fabric.

Ida didn't seem like much of a stinker to me. Another way in which Ms. Fields and my perceptions differed.

"We're just having a little happy hour," she said, picking up her highball glass from the console table near the front door and leading me through nicely proportioned rooms with Saltillo tile and thick area rugs.

"Ralph, we have a guest. Make her a drink." Maybe the prickly personality had drowned in that glass.

She turned to me as we entered a solarium with a bar across one end of the room. "What would you like, dear?"

With my recent consumption of both tea and coffee I already felt as if my teeth would float, but I agreed to a small glass of sherry. Ida's own glass contained a martini and Ralph topped it off for her with a heavy dose from a shaker.

I begged use of the powder room before I picked up my glass, returned five minutes later and took a seat in the chair they offered, a blocky thing that was far too deep and soft.

"As I mentioned, I'm Victoria Morgan's sister-in-law— well, I would have been as of Saturday."

"Oh, dear, I imagine your family is worried sick."

"Yes, we are. My brother and I are trying to find out if there's anything we don't already know about how Victoria spent the past few days, anything that might have been worrying her, something she might not have wanted to trouble us with. Really, almost anything could be a clue for us."

She gave me a slightly blank look. I'd better phrase this more directly.

"When was the last time you saw Victoria?"

"Oh, well, I guess that would have been last Wednesday or Thursday. She was supposed to have some fabric for me but it didn't come in. I guess she wanted to give me the news in person because she stopped by. It was right after my tennis lesson, so that would have been Wednesday morning."

"Did she talk about anything other than your decorating

job? Maybe mention a phone call or anything?"

Ida shook her head. "She talked a little about the wedding. I had already told her Ralph had other plans that day." She took a hefty slug of the new martini. "Now that I think about it, she did receive a phone call while she was here. Normally, she'll ignore the phone when she's with me. She's the most polite young woman."

From behind his whiskey glass, Ralph nodded.

"Did she do that—ignore the call?" I asked.

"Well, I had gone off to the kitchen. She was in the salon, measuring for the new drapes, so I guess she knew I didn't need her right that minute. I heard the phone, then I heard her speaking. It didn't last long. Less than a minute."

"Did you hear what was said?"

She gave me a long look. "I don't eavesdrop."

"Oh, I didn't mean that. I thought maybe you walked into the room or something and might remember."

"Well, I was passing by the door. I heard her ask 'Who did you say this is?' and then she got kind of short with him. Said 'I don't know what you're talking about' and hung up. When I went in there she was rummaging through her purse and came up with a pen. She jotted down a name."

I wondered if whatever she'd written the name on was still in the purse. Not that it would do me a lot of good since the police had it now.

"I asked her if everything was all right," Ida said. "She seemed very distracted after that."

"You said she got short with *him* on the phone. Are you sure it was a man?"

"Oh yes, she told me that. She said 'That was odd, some older man. I'm sure I've never heard of him before.'

Then she put the pen and paper away and went back to the measurements."

"And she was distracted?"

"Definitely. She had to measure three times and then she went off and left her tape measure here. I still have it, if you want to take it back."

If only the forgotten item had been the phone itself. It could have given us a world of information.

* * *

I got back to the office to find Ron dozing at his desk. Sally would have left at one o'clock. Freckles danced in my path as I made my way through the rooms. She was more than ready to have her dinner.

"We should go home," I told him. "Maybe stop at Pedro's on the way."

He admitted he'd spent most of the afternoon staring at Victoria's computer screen without gleaning any solid information. This is not like my brother.

"I don't want to face those microphones again," he said. His face and posture seemed ragged.

"Maybe they're gone by now."

But when we switched on the office TV it was still the top story in Albuquerque and had now made the national networks as well. I could only imagine the new influx of vans, satellite dishes and cameras. It made me want to avoid home, too, but we had to go there sometime. Sleeping at the office held no appeal.

"Come on. We'll get out of our cars and walk right past them."

Ron made the stop at Pedro's after I phoned our take-out order. I'd created a stir with the reporters but I'm pretty quick and dashed right past them and into the house. The curtains remained closed but I peeked around the edge and was ready with my hand on the knob when Ron made his own run for the front door.

We ate Pedro's fabulous green chile chicken enchiladas but had to settle for homemade margaritas, since Pedro can't do those up to go. While we ate, I filled Ron in on my afternoon—the visits with Victoria's friends and customers, the phone call from the mysterious man who'd obviously worried her.

"Are you sure she never said anything about that call to you?" I asked.

He thought about it but shook his head. "Nothing. Do you suppose there was something going on that I never picked up on?"

"Doesn't make any sense. This was an older guy, for one thing, and the call was very short, according to Ida Van Horn. Plus, it is absolutely not like Vic to sneak around. She would have been up front and told you."

"So, why didn't she? If she was upset about something, that's what she's supposed to talk to me about, to share with me."

He had a point. Spouses should share. I couldn't imagine keeping anything of true importance from Drake. I cleared the Styrofoam containers, washed the silverware and glasses, spoke briefly with my hubby who sounded tired but happy to have had a productive day. I wished I could say the same. I went to bed with repetitive thoughts rattling around in my head.

What could someone have said during such a short call to upset Victoria so much?

Chapter 16

Six weeks passed. Juliette found her ears tuned to every conversation in the office. It was a miracle she could keep up with her correspondence, the construction bids and Al's complicated appointment book. Three times, she'd been able to catch brief glimpses of paperwork that passed through Marion's office, but none of them revealed anything. She'd not seen another reference to kilos, although a few things Al had said on the telephone when he thought the door was tightly closed led her to believe he was talking about shipments. Those shipments almost certainly had to be drugs, she concluded.

Everything else passing through the yard or the job sites was well documented. So many pallets of block, a certain tonnage of steel, quantities of glass for the windows in a high-rise. The amounts and costs were staggering, but they all made sense. The hushed conversations held a different tone and quality. But each time she'd fished for more information Al treated her comments as nothing.

"Sure, we buy some of the materials in kilos," he would say. "A lot of this stuff comes from Europe. You know that." Or, "Don't worry your pretty head about anything that doesn't cross your desk, baby."

Perhaps her mistake was that she always tried to catch him relaxed and talkative when she brought up those things. His response was always to distract her with a gift, an extra drink, or sex. He wasn't taking her concerns seriously, but what did she expect?

The calls from New York worried her most. During those conversations, Al's tone turned deferential. Whoever the man was, Al treated him as a boss. And yet, in every other aspect of his life, he was the leader, with no question who was in charge. Specifics were never given, nothing she could directly question. She wanted to be trusted, to share his burden, to offer advice and suggestions, but that was not happening.

Juliette finally quit posing her guarded questions. She couldn't express doubt in her man. Surely he knew what he was doing. She took to watching Marion instead.

The bookkeeper, as usual, worked with her door closed and rarely exchanged more than basic pleasantries with the other women. When she did, Juliette found it suspicious, as on the day Marion had offered tea—a once-only thing. Marion was in and out of Al's office quite a lot, but her official path rarely crossed Juliette's so there were no excuses for dropping off something at the bookkeeper's desk or handling her files. It was the most bizarre working environment Juliette had ever encountered.

She had lunch with Sheila a couple of times and tried to

hint at her concerns. Sheila's only comment had been, "I've learned that it's best to do my own job, collect my paycheck and keep office life separate from personal."

It might have been a way of telling Juliette that she disapproved of her affair with the boss. Maybe she was saying not to question or dig too deeply. Maybe Sheila simply had a philosophy that a job was a job and her real life took place at home. She was probably telling her young co-worker to get a life outside the office.

During a weekend when Al wasn't around, Juliette resolved to do that. She called Carol Ann who, miraculously, was free.

"There's a new Steve Martin movie out," Carol Ann said. "Let's go."

The show was called *The Jerk* and Juliette couldn't remember having laughed so much in ages. Maybe her Texas cornball humor was returning.

"Oh my god, there are some classic scenes in that movie, aren't there?" Carol Ann said as they emerged from the theater.

"The one where he's walking down the street …" Juliette caught herself giggling at the memory.

"'All I need is this thermos'," quoted Carol Ann, mimicking Martin's doleful tone. She paused as they approached Juliette's car. "Hey, let's go grab some tacos. We haven't done this in way too long."

Juliette felt her heart lift.

They chose a little Mexican food stand where they'd frequently gone together and found a table under the palm-covered patio roof. With orders placed and margaritas in front of them, Carol Ann suddenly got a coy look.

"I've been meaning to call you for a week, Jules," she

said. "I have some big news."

Before Juliette could ask, Carol Ann whipped her hand out from under the table and dangled it before Juliette's face.

"I'm engaged! Tommy proposed last weekend and I accepted."

Juliette took her friend's hand and studied the plain gold band with its small diamond, feeling an unreasonable flash of envy. She quickly covered the emotion with a smile.

"Congratulations, you two—that's great news!" She raised her glass, waited for Carol Ann to do the same, and they clinked them together. "To a happy marriage."

Carol Ann blushed a little. "There's actually a bit more. Tommy has been putting in applications all over the place for a better job. So, this one company accepted him, but they don't have openings in their plant here. What they offered him is in Alabama. So … right after the wedding we're moving to Birmingham."

"What? I mean, my god, that's sudden." Juliette felt as if the floor had shifted beneath her.

"Yeah, kind of."

A waitress walked up to them and placed plastic baskets with tacos in front of each place. An inquiry as to whether they needed drink refills or anything else. Asking if everything was all right.

Nothing is all right, Juliette thought. My best friend is moving away, my boyfriend hasn't proposed, and I don't even know what's going on in our lives anymore.

But Carol Ann had smiled at the girl and said everything was just great.

"So, my big question for you is if you'll be my attendant. Will you?" Carol Ann picked up her first taco and crunched into it.

Juliette suddenly couldn't look at the food.

"It's going to be a simple ceremony. I don't know if my parents can even come on such short notice. Tommy has to start the new job June fifteenth, so we have less than a month to pull this off. We're thinking of a small chapel or maybe even outdoors at a park or on the beach, or if we're really pinched for time just a little ceremony with witnesses at a judge's office." Carol Ann took a breath, picked up her second taco, and noticed Juliette hadn't taken a bite yet. "Aren't you hungry?"

She picked up her first taco. "Oh, yeah, sure." She took a bite for show but the food tasted like a ball of paper.

"And then I have to think about a dress. I'm thinking it'd be dumb to go for a long gown, even though I've always dreamed of one. But we need the money for moving—" Carol Ann set down her taco. "Are you sure you're okay?"

Juliette took a deep breath. She could not dampen her friend's big news with her own selfishness. She put on a bright smile. "I'm absolutely fine. I'm just so happy for you."

"Then eat."

"I guess it's just a little PMS moodiness. Keep telling me about your plans." She forced herself to finish two tacos while her friend went on with wedding details.

"I'll let you know the minute we set the actual date and place. Meanwhile, do not stress over a dress."

"But I want your day to be special. Tell me what kind of dress you'd like me to get. I want to do that."

"You're sure?"

"Positive." *Positively jealous that Al didn't propose to me first.* She masked her attitude by stuffing the third taco into her mouth and chasing it with the rest of her margarita.

They pooled their spare change for the tip and went back to the Camaro. All at once, Juliette couldn't wait to drop off Carol Ann at her apartment so she could be alone. Wedding chatter filled the fifteen-minute drive and they said a quick goodbye at the curb.

Juliette barely contained herself until she got back to the condo. She rode the elevator alone, luckily, and entered her spacious quarters. Two dozen red roses from Al—apology for being away for the weekend—sat on the console near the front door. A wave of bitterness overtook her and she flung the vase across the room. She screamed as it shattered, flinging glass and water across the marble floor, and she sank to her knees in the foyer.

The room was in full darkness except for the lights beaming up from the street when her frustration finally played out. She hauled herself to her feet, reaching for the wall switch, telling herself how stupid to create such a mess, all for a ridiculous emotional rant. She edged to the kitchen and got out the broom and dustpan, sweeping broken glass, letting the motion of the broom act as a catharsis.

Maybe I've been focusing on the wrong things recently. Why would Al propose when I'm so off-and-on. At the office she'd been suspicious and spying; at home in the evenings she'd been no better than a whore, giving herself cheerfully in exchange for the gifts and pleasure of his lovemaking. *If I want a husband, I've got to act like a wife—loving, caring, loyal and putting his needs first.*

Okay, the feminists would have a field day with *that* one. She laughed at herself as she put the broom away. After a stern lecture on being true first to herself, she got ready for bed and fell into a sleep riddled with images of Carol Ann as a bride and herself as a dull, spinster bridesmaid.

For the next two days she performed her office duties by rote and ignored the fact that Al had not been around after hours. Something was up but she couldn't bring herself to enter the intrigue of checking his files and spying. On Wednesday she spotted a sheriff's department vehicle across the street from the office. She couldn't tell if it was Elmer Reddick at the wheel but her suspicions were confirmed when, Thursday afternoon, she was shopping for something to prepare for dinner and the deputy stopped her in the aisle next to the potato chips.

"How are things, Miss Mason?" he asked, peering at a bag of Fritos.

"Just fine." *What do you want?* There was no one else in sight. Had he followed her or was this a chance encounter?

As if he'd read her thoughts he turned and faced her squarely. "Just wondering if you've been following your boss's activities lately."

"No more than usual. I answer phones, I type letters, I schedule appointments."

He seemed especially interested in that last bit. "What appointments does he have this week?"

"I'm not telling you that!" She hated his penetrating stare. "Business, that's all. Nothing unusual."

"Miss Mason, I'm not playing a game here. Al Proletti is a dangerous man, especially when he's pushed. He started out small potatoes with drug shipments but he's doing more and more of them all the time, directing airplanes to ditch in the swamps and offload big bundles of the stuff. It's gone beyond bales of pot. Now there's cocaine and heroin. It's not only local law enforcement with an eye on him, and he's handed out plenty of cash to get certain people to look the other way. He's working for a guy out of New York, and that bunch plays rough."

He glanced up the aisle, letting an elderly woman push her cart past them. Once she was out of sight, he continued. "Al has no loyalties."

She started to protest. Al was very good to his workers and office staff. Look at the generous raises he'd given recently.

"You haven't pissed him off yet. If he feels he's been betrayed, he'll stop at nothing. Ask Ronnie Delvecchio and Sal Oberman. Or, I should say, ask their widows. Both of those guys ended up in the swamp, pretty well chewed up by the gators, after doing some odd jobs for Al."

She felt her mouth open and close.

"Look 'em up, hon. You don't have to take my word for it. Those stories made the news—August, two years ago. All I'm saying is be careful. We're building our case, little by little. You don't want to be caught up in this thing." He grabbed a bag of Fritos and strode away from her.

Juliette stared after the lawman. He was obviously trying to scare her, maybe hoping she'd quit her job or call him secretly with information on Al's activities. He could make up anything about some guys being killed.

She steered her cart toward the dairy section. She would get the last items on her list and go home. Al was coming over tonight and she planned to make omelets for their late-night dinner, after she'd greeted him at the door in the black negligee from the little paper bag he'd dropped on her desk this afternoon. If the mood was right, she'd tell Al exactly what the deputy was up to. He wouldn't like it when he learned the man had followed her into the supermarket.

* * *

The moment Al arrived he was clearly in a mood. He hardly noticed the skimpy black outfit. She made his favorite drink and pushed him to the couch, loosening his tie and crawling onto his lap. It wasn't until she'd pressed her breasts right into his face that a smile appeared.

"Sorry, baby. I've been a grump, haven't I?" He began toying with the ribbon tie at her cleavage. "I need to take better care of my girl."

She dropped all thought of telling him about Reddick that night. They went to the bedroom almost immediately and she did everything she could think of to keep his mind off anything but her.

Later, she offered the omelets but he said he'd had a long day and his head was pounding. He'd better get home and get a full night's sleep.

"Stay here. Call Ernestina and let her know you don't need anything."

His eyes flicked back to the bedroom but he shook his head. "Nah, I'd better get going."

He'd picked up his jacket, kissed her forehead and was out the door before she knew it. She sighed, pulled her robe around her and went into the kitchen to make an omelet for herself. Well, at least it gave her an evening when she could catch up on her bills and maybe watch Johnny Carson. She sat on a barstool at the counter and pulled out her checkbook and the calendar she used to track bills and birthdays and such. She had the nagging feeling she'd forgotten to mail a card to someone back home.

Running her finger across the dates for the past few

weeks she got a tingle in her belly. She'd missed her last period.

"Oh, no," she said out loud.

She rechecked the dates. She'd always made a small mark on the date it began, usually for the purpose of being able to warn Al when the week was coming up next time. He didn't want details, merely to be warned.

She ran to the bathroom, checked her supply of tampons. Yes, there were too many. She'd definitely not used any in more than a month. Her pills were off schedule too. How had she messed up her routine so badly? Well, the answer was obvious—she'd had her mind on too many other things.

She went to bed but stared at the ceiling most of the night. What to do? Of course she would tell Al the news right away. Well, maybe confirm it with her doctor before springing the surprise. She would plan a beautiful dinner and really make the moment right. He would be excited— wouldn't he?—and they could make plans to be married. A traditional Italian man like Al Proletti, of course he would want them to be a family and be involved in his child's life. She could hardly wait to tell Carol Ann. It was so romantic that the two longtime friends would both be getting married so close together.

Elmer Reddick's face appeared in her mind, his warning about Al's being involved in drugs. Ridiculous! She knew her Al and he wasn't like that. And even if he was, he would change now, give up anything that would put the family in jeopardy. If there was even a hint of truth to Reddick's story, Al would just tell that man from New York that he was no longer interested. She sighed and eventually fell asleep.

* * *

She chose Saturday night for the big announcement. The test at the doctor's office had confirmed it. She was pregnant, due next April. She could hardly contain her excitement but she had to be sure Al was the first to know. When he agreed to spend the whole weekend together she said she would plan something special. They went to the arcade Saturday morning, then did a little shopping (she found herself glancing wistfully toward the baby department while he exchanged a shirt in menswear). They picked out steaks at the market and went back to the condo to lie around the pool for the afternoon. Soon, her body wouldn't be in such great shape for a bikini but Juliette didn't mind. She could hardly contain her secret until the right moment.

When Al brought the steaks in from the hibachi on the balcony she poured glasses of red wine (she would only drink half of hers—she'd read that alcohol was bad for the baby). She lit candles and dished up the baked potatoes and fresh asparagus.

"So, what's up with you tonight, baby? You've got some kind of gleam in your eye," he teased with a smile. "Got a sexy new outfit for me?"

She'd rehearsed what she wanted to say about the baby, upcoming parenthood and how wonderful marriage would be. She managed to deliver the little speech perfectly. What she'd not planned was his reaction.

"Babe, didn't you know? I'm already married."

Chapter 17

Juliette pressed her hands against her front door, chest heaving, eyes burning, her mind awhirl. The elevator bell dinged in the distance and she knew he was gone. Married? Children?

Where had the wife been all this time? Juliette had demanded details about her. The answer stung more than anything else—None of your business.

She sank to the floor, gripping handfuls of her hair with both fists. Her thoughts flew back to the times she'd been at his house—the initial tour, the Christmas party, New Year's Eve. Their first lovemaking in his bedroom. And all this time he—no one—had thought to mention a wife! Where was the woman on all these occasions? Why had she seen no evidence of a female inhabitant or children? It wasn't possible he had a family.

Here's what happened, she decided. He'd been so surprised by the news of their baby and her impromptu proposal he just didn't know what to say. Maybe he'd used the 'wife' excuse to get out of previous, unsatisfactory relationships. But this time was different—he would see, when she approached him calmly and rationally. Give him tonight to think about it, to begin making plans the way she had. He would come around.

She got to her feet and stared at the dining table. All her beautiful preparations, gone to waste. Ugly, wax drips ran down the sides of the candles. Fat had congealed on the untouched steaks and the butter on the baked potatoes formed awful yellow puddles. She blew out the candles and scraped the plates into the trash. Once the dishes were in the dishwasher, the table and countertops wiped clean, only then did the tears come. She found an old knitted afghan and pulled it over herself, bundling into the corner of the sofa feeling weak and bedraggled, unable to face going to the bedroom where she'd strewn rose petals over the bed and burned musk-scented candles. The romantic setting mocked her even more than the discarded special dinner had done. She dozed, waking when the sky outside began to turn peachy with the rising sun.

Her stomach lurched when she stood.

Well there's proof, she thought. I really am going through this. Her insides rebelled at the scent of last night's dinner in the trash, and she made her way to a cupboard where she found some plain crackers. A few of those and a swig of carbonated soda, and she felt a little better. She dragged herself to the bedroom where she erased all traces of the evening's intentions, tossing everything including the red negligee into the waste basket. The shower, running long and hot, soothed her body and her mind.

At her closet door, she debated carefully. How she presented herself at work today could make or break everything. She would be very businesslike and offer to take Al to lunch. In a public place they could speak calmly and rationally. She would not succumb, as she did last night, to hysterics in order to keep him. And he would surely be calm enough to talk reasonably to her about the future. She chose her best suit and a plain white blouse, then pulled her hair back the way he'd often commented he liked it.

When she arrived at the office, his car was not in the lot. She parked and walked toward the front door, her spine straight, her head high.

Marion stood beside Sheila's desk, the two conversing casually. For all Juliette's intentions of first speaking with Al, she couldn't help herself.

"Is Al married?" she blurted out.

Sheila was the first to look at her but Marion answered.

"He is." The older woman's expression held a trace of humor. "I take it he's only recently mentioned it to you?"

Juliette looked toward Sheila. Why hadn't she said anything?

Sheila shrugged. "I didn't know. Honestly. You've seen him around here. He doesn't confide things to me. It's all business."

"But you aren't shocked."

"Not especially." Sheila stood and came around the side of the desk, placing an arm around Juliette's shoulders. "Honey, guys like him do this all the time. It's in their nature to play around."

"Has his wife ever come here?"

Marion spoke up. "Al keeps business and personal

things completely separate. I doubt she even knows exactly what he does."

Juliette thought of the snippets of overheard conversation, the warnings from Elmer Reddick. She would bet the wife hadn't a clue about *anything* Al did.

"But the Christmas party at his house … was she hiding somewhere upstairs while we were all there?"

Again, that smug little pinch around Marion's mouth. "That mansion isn't where his family lives. He's got another house and he keeps them isolated in a country club setting and the kids in private schools."

"Where?"

"I'm not telling you that, Juliette. He's a private man and that's one aspect of his life he lets no one touch, especially not the girlfriend."

Sheila's comment about men of Al's type. "So I'm not the first girlfriend on the side, am I?"

Both women looked at her as if that were the stupidest question in the world. She lifted her chin and started toward her office.

"Don't start anything with him," Sheila called out. "It wouldn't be smart to fight with him over this. Just accept him and take what you can get out of the deal."

Marion was right behind Juliette in the hall. "Al's business is complicated, sweetie. Don't make another stupid mistake by asking too many questions."

Juliette went into her office while Marion continued to the kitchen.

How dare the old bat! Calling her sweetie was salt in the wound. The woman cared nothing for Juliette; she was just rubbing her face in her situation. She closed her door and sat down, letting out a deep breath.

She would show Marion. Being involved with Al wasn't a stupid mistake—he was her future, her baby's father. She would continue with her plan.

When he walked into his office an hour later, Juliette kept her head high and finished the letter she was typing before acknowledging him. She carried the letter to his desk for a signature and gave a tentative smile.

"I'm sorry about last night," she said. "Can we have lunch today and talk things out?"

If he'd been prepared for a screaming match he was pleasantly surprised by her attitude. "Sure, babe. I probably shouldn't have walked out on you."

He signed the letter and she went back to her desk. *See, Marion? We're adults and we can rationally discuss anything at all.*

They drove to the restaurant in his Porsche, reminding Juliette of the lavish lifestyle she had so quickly adapted to during the past months. He'd chosen her favorite place, which she took as a sign of his love and sentimental feelings for her. He held her chair, ordered wine while she placed the linen napkin in her lap. This was a good start.

During the drive she'd planned her words. Once the waiter left, she began.

"I have to admit to being completely surprised when you told me about your wife. Honey, why didn't you say something earlier? We're all adults. I'm sure we could have … I don't know … worked out something."

"You didn't need to know. One thing you'll learn about me is that my life is compartmentalized on a need-to-know basis. This was something you didn't need to know."

She took a slow breath. "I understand that *they* live in a different house, not the one you've taken me to?"

He tilted his head in acknowledgement as he buttered

the tip of a breadstick.

"Which works out really well. Your current wife won't even have to move. You can divorce her quietly and when we're married I'll move into the mansion with you."

He pointed the breadstick at her. "Won't happen, sweetheart."

"You can move into the condo with me." Her voice faltered only a little.

Al carefully set the breadstick on his plate, sending a look toward the waiter who'd started to approach. The young man veered away.

"You aren't getting it, baby. There will be no divorce. I'm Catholic, married in the church, with six kids at home. My wife is a lovely woman and she's a wonderful mother. I'm happy with that life."

"But, I—"

"You're my girlfriend. I'm happy with this part of my life too." His nonchalant attitude brought her emotions near the surface.

She looked quickly at the surrounding tables but no one seemed to have overheard. "I'm pregnant. We are having a baby, you and I. I want that baby to have a home and a father who is there for him."

He shook his head. "Huh-uh. Not this one. You'll have to get rid of it."

Her eyes widened. An abortion was something she could never, ever consider.

"Adoption, you mean?"

"Well, only if you want to ruin your body and not have me sleeping with you for a good long time." The implication being that another girlfriend would come along to fill her spot.

She clamped her lips together as the waiter returned. Al ordered for both of them, her favorite salad and the sandwich he liked best. Forced to sit silently, her temper smoldered. The nerve! Saying her body would be ruined by having his child. What about the wife? She'd borne him six children and yet he stayed with her. She almost felt sorry for the woman, wishing she could hear what he'd said. Too bad Juliette didn't have a way to record the conversation. Teach him a big lesson!

Al spotted someone he knew across the room and got up from the table to say hello. Juliette's insides churned— partly from the fact that breakfast had been only four saltine crackers, partly from the emotional upheaval he'd just put her through. Using his religion as an excuse for no divorce but ignoring it when it came to suggesting an abortion. The man had no morals whatsoever! She stared toward the table where he was laughing and patting the business-suited man on the shoulder.

Maybe she would teach him a little something, call his wife and tell her the whole situation.

He returned when their food arrived and immediately picked up his sandwich, biting into it with gusto. She picked at her salad with her fork, shuffling the bits of chicken and oriental noodles.

"Come on, babe, you have to eat," he mumbled with a mouthful.

If she'd brought her own car she would have upended the big plate of salad right into his lap, but she was at the disadvantage here. It would not be wise to play her hand too soon. She needed the veneer of calm to cover her thoughts and plans. Plus, he was right about her needing food. No dinner last night, no breakfast today—skipping meals couldn't be good for her or for the baby. She speared a hunk of the chicken and forced it down her dry throat.

* * *

Back at the office she began a search for the phone number of his other home. It was something she had to do on the quiet. The other girls didn't know yet about her pregnancy but being fooled by his lies hung over her like a neon sign advertising her profound embarrassment. Sheila sent pitying glances her way, while Marion had a smug little smile now. Juliette ignored them both and closed her door.

She started with the phone book but there was no listing. She tried directory assistance to no avail. Of course it would be an unlisted number. Rich people did not make themselves available for just anyone to find. Then she remembered his calls to Ernestina, supposedly to let the maid know she didn't need to wait up for him. What a fool I've been, she thought. Those calls were to offer some excuse to the wife.

Al sat in his office all afternoon, doors closed, talking on the phone. At times his muffled tone was belligerent, other times quiet. Was it the rough man from New York? Juliette found she didn't care if the man intimidated Al now. Let the rat be pushed around a bit. Let him see how it felt to be powerless.

She tried calling Carol Ann at work and was told Miss Dunbar had resigned on Friday as she was getting married soon. Her phone at home rang until the way-too-cute answering message came on. Juliette didn't even know where to begin and couldn't say a fraction of it to a tape machine. She ended up simply asking Carol Ann to call her at home tonight.

A tap sounded at her door and Sheila poked her head in.

"Be careful," she whispered, one ear turned toward the connecting door to Al's office. "I don't know what you're up to but just remember, he knows everything that goes on around here."

Juliette flushed. Had she been so obvious?

Sheila backed out and returned to her own work. Juliette tapped her nails on her desk, her concentration shot and her stomach churning. She wondered how much longer she could go on working here. The photo of her mother smiled lovingly from the corner of her desk. If only she could go home to Mom now.

Juliette took a deep breath and picked up her purse. She slipped the picture of her mother into it and walked out the door, telling Sheila the salad at lunch must have disagreed with her and she was going home early.

Gravel spun under her tires as she pulled away from the office, a horn protesting her quick entry into traffic. She didn't care. Al's attitude and betrayal angered her. She wanted to push, to get back at him. He'd made one of those Ernestina calls only two nights ago.

She drove home and went straight to her condo. She was fairly certain she hadn't used the phone since that night. She hit the redial button and the line began to ring. Now she would see who she reached. A woman answered: "Proletti residence."

"Is this Ernestina?"

"No ... we have no one by that name here."

"I'm sorry, I'm looking for Mrs. Proletti."

"She and the children are out for the afternoon. May I take a message?"

"I'll just call back later." She dropped the receiver to its cradle.

It was true, all of it. And she knew how to reach them. She paced the room, fury rising in her. She had to think about this. She went back down to where she'd left her car in a visitor space out front. Rather than putting it away in the garage, maybe she would take a drive to clear her head. Five minutes later she was headed toward the freeway,

She steered to the on-ramp and zipped across three lanes of traffic, daring anyone to object to her twenty-miles-over-the-limit attack. She drove south on Highway 1, screaming aloud as the wind whipped her hair across her face, railing against the whole damn mess. After twenty minutes or so, her anger had gelled into a hard knot of determination. She took an exit at random, circled and got back into the northbound lanes.

Al's going down one of these days, hon, and you don't want to be there. Deputy Reddick's voice came back at her again. The other day at the market he'd mentioned two names, said to check them out. Two men who had crossed Al Proletti.

The names came to her, Ronnie Delvecchio and Sal Oberman. Reddick had advised her to check them out. Well, she would just do that.

She'd been to the newspaper office once, straightening out a billing snafu for Al. The upcoming exit to the airport reminded her, as the newspaper office was only a few blocks farther. She whipped her convertible off the freeway and found the brown block building easily enough.

A middle-aged woman worked the reception desk and Juliette explained that she was doing some research and wanted to find the circumstances of two men who had either disappeared or died.

"Well, if they died, obituaries will be the quickest place to find them. Disappearances … well, that's more of a news story. When did this happen?"

What had Reddick told her? Her mind went momentarily blank but then she pulled out a date. "August, two years ago," she said.

The woman took her to a small room with video equipment and rolls of microfiche. Juliette had no idea what to do, but the lady thumbed through some metal boxes and came up with what she needed, even threading it into the machine for her.

"Just turn this dial to scroll through the pages until you find what you want." She left Juliette alone to figure it out.

It took awhile but eventually she came upon the story where a Ronnie Delvecchio's body had been recovered by search and rescue five days after his wife reported him missing. They'd pulled the badly decomposed body from the swamp, most of its limbs missing due to alligators feeding on them. The details were too graphic for Juliette to handle. She skimmed enough to learn that the man was a minor drug runner with two prior convictions and short prison stints on his record. An abandoned Cessna had been found less than a mile from the body, crash-landed in the same swampy area, with traces of cocaine in the emptied fuselage.

So what, she thought. Everyone knew those things happened. It didn't mean Al had anything to do with it. Reddick was probably just trying to scare her. He could have tossed out any name he knew had been in the news.

Out of curiosity, she paged to the end and found the obituary for Delvecchio. His surviving widow and children would be cared for by a cash contribution from the man's employer, Pro-Builder Construction. Juliette felt the blood drain from her face.

Two days after that particular account, the newspaper posted a similar death notice for Sal Oberman, also an employee of Pro-Builder.

She knew she could never return if she did anything to antagonize Al. And then she knew—she'd already done it. By calling his home. He had once bragged that he had ways of tracing every call that came to the mansion. Surely, he would have the same at his other home and he would know the call came from her condo. He'd read her mind on so many occasions and she, stupid young girl, thought it meant they were soul mates. He would know exactly what she'd had in mind. How foolish could she be?

Gotta get out—now!

She stumbled over the chair legs in the newspaper archive room, staggered her way out the door and to her car, feeling as if there were eyes in the sky that could spot her. She stuck to the main streets, looking for answers. At the first used-car lot she spotted she pulled in, made a quick deal for the Camaro and took the cash. A two-block bus ride later, she bought a used Jeep Wagoneer and for the registration gave the first name that came to mind, her grandmother's maiden name.

Dusk was coming on as she drove the strange vehicle away from the lot. Now what?

More than anything she was afraid to go back to the condo. Even if he suspected nothing, he might simply decide to drop by her place tonight anyway, out of habit. One look at her face and he would know.

She would head for Texas. He knew she came from there, but as long as she didn't immediately go to her hometown maybe he would never track her down. The whole incident would eventually blow over.

But she couldn't get to Texas without money and she only had the clothes on her back and less than a hundred dollars in cash. She could use her credit card. But what if Al's reach included people within law enforcement? Reddick had hinted as much. They could probably trace her movements through credit card purchases. She had some cash at the condo, plus her checkbook. She could clean out the account first thing in the morning. And, she would take the bits of evidence she'd collected as insurance.

The few items were in what looked like a high school girl's love-letter box with its flower-power green paper. She'd stashed it at the bottom of her clothes hamper but a real search of the condo would reveal it quickly. Every instinct made her want to race home to pack, but she forced herself to slow down and think clearly. Her life depended on it.

Chapter 18

Cold. Everything felt *so* cold. And dark, a blackness deep as a well.

Bright lights flashed across the far wall of her enclosure rousing Victoria from her fog of pain. She squinted, moaned at the intrusion. Her breath came shallow and hot. The burning pain in her shoulder ebbed a little. She tried to sit up but the fiery sensation blasted back at her, flattening her to the floor once again, and with it the fuzziness in her mind.

She lay there for a time—no idea how long. When her eyes opened the quality of light had turned from pure black to deep gray, a charcoal world. The cement beneath her felt like a slab of ice. Her extremities were numb. Her body shook with the intensity of the cold, except for the burn in her core, the fire coming from her shoulder. Something told her she was in shock but she hadn't the clarity of thought to decide what that meant or figure out what she could do about it. She drifted away once again.

Somewhat more lucidity when she woke. The charcoal air had brightened to deep gray. A cloth of some sort covered her body. It smelled acrid, of something like turpentine. Its texture was coarse—not clothing, not a blanket or drape. Her fingers touched the edge of it, opening and closing, pinching it. The fingers touched a softer fabric. Her bathrobe. She recognized this item. She ran her hand up the sleeve, reveling in the soft plush until she touched the source of fire at her shoulder. The stabbing pain blinded her and she lost consciousness again.

Images and dreams plagued her. Ron, kissing her goodnight at her own door. A white dress, a pile of items neatly organized, something blue, something old ... she tried to take a deep breath but it hurt so much. More blackness.

A sound at the back door, she in her robe turning to check it. Two men pushing their way into her home. Shock and fear. Backing away from them.

"Hi baby, it's me, your dad," said the one with silver hair.

"No ... no!" She cried out in her sleep and moved, sending a fresh bolt of fire through her body. She had no father. He'd died in Vietnam.

Darkness faded back into the dream.

"I won't hurt you sweetheart," the man said. "I only want what your mother left for me."

The other man said nothing, merely walked around her living room poking at things on the shelves, lifting a cushion on the sofa.

"Get out of here!" she shouted at them. "Get out!" Her

voice would not cooperate. The firm words came out only as high moans.

"Just give me the papers," said the man with the gentle voice. "Then we'll go away."

The other man now held a gun. The barrel seemed huge, aimed at her. Her heart pounded and she felt a real tear run down her face.

"No ..." she cried.

She tried to run but her legs were useless, barely moving, tangling in her bathrobe. She startled into a half-wakeful state, realized it had been a memory, felt exhausted by the struggle. Once again, unconsciousness.

When she woke, the place lay in semi-darkness. Something told her it was daytime. Would the men come back? She pushed herself upright, sitting with her back against a concrete wall. The pain had receded somewhat, although she knew it could return any time with a vengeance. The space was an almost-bare square room, maybe twenty feet on a side. High, narrow windows covered in grime let in the little light by which she surveyed her surroundings. Across the space from her, a short flight of steps made a turn and climbed out of sight. In the corner near them she could make out a pile of items—two sawhorses, some cans, tarps. Her head pounded with the effort of trying to figure them out, and when she closed her eyes she had the coherent thought that it didn't matter. She didn't know this place. However she got here, either she or someone else had placed one of the tarps over her for the small bit of warmth it might offer.

She looked down. She was in her plush bathrobe, the one that used to be pale pink. Stains marked it now, especially on the left sleeve. Her shoulder throbbed so painfully it set her teeth on edge. She hugged the arm to her body and tried to get her feet under her. The movement, slight as it was, sent fresh pain ripping through her and she sank back to the floor. Sparkles floated before her eyes and she closed them again.

The faces reappeared. The silver-haired man wheedling, asking for something from her mother, his ice-blue eyes unrelenting. His request puzzled her, but the other man's intentions were clear. Images of Ron, the boys, Charlie and Drake—this ruthless one would harm them all. She backed into the dining room, hoping to reach her phone and call for help. A firm grip on her wrist, pulling, dragging her to the sofa. The older man looking through her possessions, coming to the photo of her mother on the shelf, picking it up, smiling in a way that frightened her.

She told him to put it down, to leave her things alone. The scene shifted and she saw a box, cardboard, covered in brightly patterned paper—a gift? Then the memories again. The heavy man twisted her wrist, pulled her arm behind her back and she kicked out at him, grazing his shin. At once, the gun waved directly in front of her face. The percussion threw her to the floor. Her left side went numb, her ears rang.

The men were shouting at each other but she could not pick out their words. She got to her feet, hugged herself to stop the pain that roared through her shoulder and arm. Then she ran, knowing at any second they would surely catch up with her and finish her off.

When Victoria next looked around, the concrete room was in total blackness. The scenes from her delirious dreams felt disjointed, out of sequence somehow. Her head felt a little clearer; she wanted to search the room, look for something to take for the pain, but the darkness was too intense, the effort to stand too daunting. She gathered her few covers and fell into a deep sleep, this time without dreams.

Chapter 19

The days without answers were taking a toll on Ron—I could see it on his unshaven face and in his eyes, where new wrinkles appeared each time I looked at him. I'd awakened early Tuesday morning (noticing my own baggy eyes in the mirror), tended to the dog's routine and my own, talked briefly on the phone with Drake before he headed out for his second full day of flights for the Fish and Game Department.

Ron showed up in the kitchen in his bathrobe, reaching blindly for a cup of coffee. I toasted him two slices of bread, even though he swore he wasn't hungry. He showed no inclination to get dressed and it felt as if the day stretched out ahead of us with little hope. The one item I might follow up from yesterday's interviews was Ida Van Horn's mention of Victoria writing down the name of the man who'd called her. If the scrap of paper was still in her purse, the police had it.

At the very least I could ask Kent Taylor if they'd had a chance to check it out and I could tell him why it was important. I mother-henned Ron into eating his toast and practically shoved him toward the shower. Nothing would be gained by moping around the house all day.

While my brother was out of the room I phoned the police department and got Taylor on the line. I laid out my findings as succinctly as possible but he'd obviously been on some other mind-track and it took him a minute to respond. I could hear crackling sounds in the background and finally figured out he was handling plastic or cellophane.

"I don't see any little scraps of paper here among the contents from her purse," he said after a couple minutes of this rummaging.

"Maybe the witness was mistaken and it wasn't a scrap." I mentally grabbed for ideas. "Maybe she jotted it in a checkbook or on a matchbook." Of course, who carried either of those items these days? "Maybe on something—"

"Charlie—whoa. I think all that's been covered, but I'll go through everything again."

"Oh, wait! Her cell phone. You have it, right? The call came in Wednesday morning, according to Mrs. Van Horn."

He gave a patient sigh. "Charlie, we know how to check this stuff."

"I know, Kent. I'm sorry. I didn't mean to sound—"

"Worried? I know that's what it is, hon. It's just that right at this moment there's nothing else I can tell you."

Hon. It was the first time the crusty old detective had used any sort of endearment. Usually, he treated me like the pain in the ass that I am. I felt a catch in my throat as he went on to say the call I was asking about had come from a disposable cell that no one was answering. They were not giving up but there wasn't much to go on.

"How's Ron doing?" he asked.

"Not great. He's holding his emotions in check but this is ripping him up, especially the media's tone."

"I'll talk to them again," Taylor promised. "One thing we're doing is having the DNA tested from the bloodstain on the rug."

"Oh god, I hadn't thought about that."

"We need to know if it's Victoria's or if it came from her assailant."

"How will that help?"

"We might identify the intruder, if it's his. Otherwise, you never know—any little clue can help."

I thanked him, even though it felt as if in some ways the investigation had stalled. On the other hand I was amazed he'd shared as much as he had, and he'd offered to try to get the press off our backs. In the living room, I spied through the crack between the drapes, only to find the reporters were still out in force. What we needed was a super-frigid, sub-zero night to run them back to their hidey holes. Unfortunately, the forecast was for clear skies with temperatures in the fifties. A person could practically sunbathe out there.

I heard Ron's electric razor buzzing away in the bathroom so I shouted through the door that I was walking over to check on Elsa. I'd begun to worry how she might be coping with the onslaught across the way.

Freckles followed me, knowing a treat is always at hand from Grandma. I tapped at her kitchen door.

"Pretty exciting, isn't it?" Elsa said, handing the dog

her requisite cookie. "I mean, not that I'm wanting them to pester you guys … but did you see the crew from CNN? I know that anchor lady. I watch her all the time."

Her fluffy white head bobbed as she talked, the blue eyes definitely sparkling.

"Gram! You haven't talked to them, have you?"

"Well, no."

"Well, don't! I'm serious. They'll take any little thing you say and twist it around. Next thing, it'll be 'sources near the family say …'. And you can bet it will be something harmful to Ron." I found that I'd paced the length of her kitchen twice.

"Sweetie, I'd never do that."

I stopped walking and took her veined hand. "I know you wouldn't. You'd never hurt any of us in a million years, but you might say some little thing, something none of us could guess."

I realized I would be smart to take my own advice.

"Just be careful. It's better not to say anything at all."

"I'll tell them 'No comment,' just like on TV."

The great hide-behind, the thing that always planted a seed of doubt. But I supposed it was better than giving out a real remark that could be misconstrued or something requiring further explanation.

"Try to avoid them completely if you can," I said. "Ron and I will be their targets anyway. Every time we leave the house or come home it's a new round of shouts."

"I know, sweetie, I know." She came over and put her arms around my waist, mimicking the hugs I used to give when I was a kid. Now she's the shorter of the two of us. We patted each other's backs until it began to seem a little ridiculous.

"Are you and Ron okay over there? Got plenty to eat and all?"

"We're fine. I can hardly get him to eat anything."

"I'm gonna solve that with a big pot of my beef stew," she said. "He always loved it and that way you don't have to cook for several days."

I started to say that it seemed like a lot of work, but then realized she thrives on doing things for others and right now our household made a good cause for her. She was suffering and feeling as helpless as we were.

"Thanks. That would be wonderful. We need to get to the office now, but tonight you should come over and we'll eat your stew together."

The plan had such a ring of normalcy, I returned home with a better attitude than I'd had in two days.

Ron perked up when I told him about Elsa's offer. Freshly shaved and dressed for the office, he almost looked like his old self. Maybe we both could pretend this investigation wasn't quite so life-and-death depressing.

At the office, I picked up the items I'd taken from Victoria's, planning on resuming my phone call inquiries. The phone rang as I picked up the old address book—Sally informing me it was Kent Taylor on the line; Ron wasn't in his office at the moment. Did I want to take the call? I grabbed the receiver immediately.

"Charlie, that DNA test I told you about earlier? I've got results."

"Wow—quick." I hid my disappointment that he wasn't calling to say Victoria was found safe and sound.

"I pushed the state lab really hard on this one. Since it's evidence where a victim is missing and endangered, I got it moved up the chain."

I heard my brother clomping up the stairs, a breath of cold air wafting from his clothing.

"Thanks. Mind if I get Ron on the line to hear this?"

Taylor had no objection and I called out to Ron. "Sorry, I had to get outside for a minute," he said, picked up his extension without even removing his coat.

"Charlie probably filled you in," Taylor said. "DNA results came back from the blood on Victoria's living room rug. It's hers."

So she'd been taken from her home, wounded and bleeding. I couldn't bring myself to go the next step and consider she might be dead. The silence from Ron's end told me he was having the same thoughts.

"I know what you two are thinking," Taylor said. "Let me stress that we do not know yet. We aren't the only ones looking at this case."

"So, we can believe she's alive somewhere." I said it purely for Ron's benefit, I knew. Taylor dealt with death all the time and must have learned ways to be less emotionally involved. He didn't have anything else to offer so I thanked him for the information

Ron and I spent a few minutes debating what we might be doing, aside from waiting in hopes of another call from Taylor. I suggested Ron get back to the laptop and passwords while I would take up with the old address book again, as little as I wanted to spend my time dialing numbers which had been disconnected. I opened the book to the page I'd marked where I left off, picked up the phone and started again.

The results were becoming predictable enough that I nearly caught a little nap while listening to recorded messages. One listing under the name Henderson, I noticed, had been written in ink but was repeatedly scratched out and changed. When a woman answered she caught me by surprise. I went through my rote explanation of who I was and why I was calling.

"Morgan? I don't think—"

The hesitation in her voice gave me hope. I listened while she debated with herself a little, discarding ideas aloud.

"The only Morgan I can think of was a lady from my hometown. She was the grandmother of a good friend. I imagine she's been dead at least thirty years. I realize that's probably no help at all."

Yeah, she was right about that. I thanked her anyway and left my number, clicking off the call and dialing the next number. This one netted me another answered call—this time a man who loudly belched and told me Morgan beer was his favorite. Must be a local brew wherever he lived— I'd never heard of it.

Ron appeared at my door. "I'm not getting anywhere with the computer passwords. I got a look at her bank accounts and everything makes sense with what I already know—wedding plans mostly. Credit card charges that fit what we were doing last week. Not a single thing since Saturday, other than the recurring automatic payments she set up for utility bills and such."

I ran my fingers through my hair, raking it back from my face. "The address book looks like a dead end too."

"I'm thinking home and stew with Elsa," he said.

I hated the dejection I heard in his voice, even though most likely my own sounded the same. We put Victoria's stuff away in the safe and locked the office.

There's something about a bowl of stew on a cold winter

night. The moment Elsa came over—Ron carrying the heavy kettle and she with a basket of jalapeño cornbread—I felt like a kid in someone's loving care.

I set places at the kitchen table and Freckles helped by carefully watching placement of all the food items, despite the fact that she'd been given her own dinner the moment we arrived home. Elsa ladled the steaming stew into big bowls and we sat down, no one digging right in. We were all thinking of Victoria.

"We should talk about her," Elsa said. "None of us can pretend we aren't scared silly. Tell me what's going on with the investigation."

As Victoria was the subject on all our minds, there was no sense filling the evening with inane talk of useless topics such as the weather or sports. We filled her in with as much information as we had.

"Her father died in the Vietnam war?" she asked, sneaking a bit of cornbread down to the dog, hoping I didn't notice.

"That's what she told me," Ron said. "He'd died before he ever saw her. Vic's mother raised her alone."

Elsa didn't say anything for a couple of minutes, chewing on the stew meat, her mind clearly turning.

"I'm afraid he couldn't have been killed there," she finally said. "The Vietnam war ended long before that. I remember it well. The president going on TV, declaring the end of hostilities. It was in 1973 because I remember the company where I worked and the way we were all talking about it the next morning at the office. Of course, ending a war is not quite that smooth. I seem to recall the evacuation of more people when Saigon fell, and that was a couple of years later."

Ron's spoon clattered in his bowl. "Victoria was born in 1979."

"Exactly." She may be old but her math skills are still excellent.

Chapter 20

A sound brought Victoria around to consciousness again. Beyond her range of sight came the grating sound of a key in a disused lock, an old doorknob turning. The concrete room seemed tinged in pink. Late afternoon. What day was this? She had no idea. Grunts and groans, male voices, sent adrenaline shooting through her body. A picture came to her of the two men in her house. They'd demanded something, some tape recording they thought she had. What if they'd tracked her here? Worse—what if they'd brought her here and were coming back to torture her for the information. Oh god.

She suppressed a whimper and squeezed herself tightly into her corner, pulling the musty tarp over her head. Dust and flakes of paint filtered over her face and she pinched her nose to avoid sneezing. If these were the men who'd broken into her house her life depended on remaining out of sight.

Heavy boots stomped down the concrete steps. Two men, from the sounds of it, shuffling along, carrying something heavy.

"Whew, what a day!" said a deep, gravelly voice.

The other one, higher pitched, younger, grunted agreement. "Damn generator's a pain in the ass. When are they getting power to the building, anyway?"

"Boss says not 'til after the holidays."

"Shit."

"Yeah. At least we'll have the place enclosed by next week. Windows installed, locks on the door, we can start leaving all this junk inside instead of hauling it around."

Metal grated against concrete as they shoved the generator across the floor. Victoria held her breath, unsure if they would be friend or foe. By their conversation, they seemed more interested in getting out and grabbing a beer.

She debated calling out to them for help. She opened her mouth but her voice came out as a croak, scratchy with disuse. A moment later the heavy boots clomped up the steps and there was the sound of a metal door closing, lock clicking in place. They were gone.

Victoria pushed the tarp aside. Her left arm still throbbed but the adrenaline surge left her feeling energized. She had to get out of here. Find a phone, call Ron. She gripped her left arm with her right hand, holding it tightly to her body as she got her legs beneath her and stood. Her vision dimmed perilously. She paused, allowed it to clear, tried a tentative step. As long as she held her breath against the pain she could manage two or three steps without stopping. She made it to the stairs, noting the light had gone from pink to gray. The short winter dusk was coming on fast.

Gripping a flimsy wooden handrail she took the stairs one at a time, with a long pause after each exertion. At the top of the flight she reached a small, square landing. The metal door looked solid with a hefty knob and deadbolt. She twisted the locking mechanism on the doorknob, fumbling it with her frozen fingers. The thumb turn on the deadbolt was easier to manage; although crusted with decades of dirt and grime it creaked the ninety degrees necessary to release it. She edged the door open, peering out carefully. A blast of icy wind fluttered her bathrobe and she realized she was barefoot. A whiff of car exhaust remained as the only trace of the men who'd been here a few minutes ago.

The door opened into an alley. She stood at the threshold, debating which was worse, leaving or staying. Indoors provided shelter from the weather, although no warmth other than her own body heat. Outside, even that was borne away on the breeze. But the men could come back. She had to get help, no matter what it took. She stepped to the alley, her numb feet hardly feeling the rough surface and layer of dried mud on the multiple tire tracks that ran its length. She pulled the metal door shut behind her, not locking the knob. Listened.

In the distance, traffic. Engines revving, the toot of a horn. She looked toward each end of the alley. To her left, it ended at some kind of loading dock behind a big building. The high doors were closed, not a vehicle in sight there. To the right was a street. No cars had driven by. She began walking, taking stumbling steps on frozen feet. At the street she held back, watching for activity. There was none.

The narrow thoroughfare was lined with two- and three-story buildings of the office and warehouse variety, many of them appearing to be empty. She didn't recognize the area. Yellow-brick fronts with large windows, some of the glass broken and missing, others soaped or papered over. Graffiti on all. To her left she could see the next intersection, some sort of convenience store or package liquor place with a neon sign fizzling out a weak signal. She couldn't imagine walking in there.

But nothing else on the street appeared open. A phone. All she wanted was to reach a phone. Ron would come get her. She could have a bath and tend to her injured arm. Thinking of warmth and family carried her to the corner. Outside the store's lighted windows she spotted a pay phone. A laugh bubbled up—*haven't seen one of these in years, and now it shows up when I need it.*

She picked up the receiver. It had an oily feel in her hand and the parts that would touch her face smelled of grease, liquor and unwashed hands. Her stomach lurched but she forced herself to hold it. Then she remembered she would need coins and she had none. Maybe in the store, she could borrow some. But a glance at the clerk with long, slimy hair selling a miniature bottle of booze to a guy in an oversized ripped parka told her it would not be smart to walk in there. She gathered her robe more tightly and stood with her back against the wall, pressing 0 on the keypad.

"Operator."

"I need to make a call," Victoria said, suddenly at a loss for the number. Ron's apartment phone had been taken out. He might be at her house. She gave her home number.

"Please deposit fifty cents or insert a credit card," came the voice.

"I don't have any money. Please—I need to reach my fiancé."

"Please deposit fifty cents or insert a credit card."

She began to wonder if she was speaking to a person or if this was an automated system. She had no clue. Her head pounded and she couldn't think.

The stringy guy in the parka came out of the store and glanced her direction. His eyes were glazed and his grin revealed missing and rotten teeth.

"Hey sweetie," he called in a drunken slur, "I'll help you. Come home with me."

"Please!" Victoria said to the operator. "Please …"

The man started toward her and she realized how it must look, a barefoot woman in a robe out on a cold night. She dropped the receiver and ran.

Chapter 21

I turned on the TV, as I did every morning these days, while I scrambled eggs for Ron and myself and listened to the sizzle of bacon in the microwave. Freckles had made her rounds of the back yard and now sat with her floppy ears perked in my direction. Starting my day with the depressing news of the world was normally the last thing I wanted to do but now that our family seemed to be right in the midst of it, I had to know what was being said.

Kent Taylor had been amazingly open with us but there were a lot of things about the investigation we weren't being told. Such as the stunning announcement I caught as Ron walked into the room.

"Police are now openly saying they are searching for the body of Victoria Morgan, the Albuquerque woman who went missing sometime between this past Friday night and noon on Saturday, what

would have been her wedding day."

Ron reached for the remote but I waylaid his hand. I knew the announcer's gloomy tone was irking him as much as it was me, but we really needed to know what was happening.

"Search and rescue teams are combing the usual sites—the west mesa, nearby arroyos, and the foothills of the Sandias." Aerial shots caught bright-yellow jacketed people fanning out from some sort of command center. By 'usual sites' we knew the woman meant the places where murder victims are often found.

A second anchor person came on—a man with orangey makeup and perfectly sprayed hair. They went through a lot of back-and-forth speculation about how the search for a body must mean the police had given up all hope of finding Victoria alive. I nearly shut the stupid thing off myself at that point.

"Search and rescue incident commander Bob Perkins asks that anyone spending time in the outdoors please report anything unusual they might find. Mountain bikers, motorcyclists, hikers ... we're showing the hotline number at the bottom of the screen or you can always call 911."

When I looked away, the eggs had scorched but nothing seemed appetizing at the moment anyway.

"All it means," I told Ron, "is that we need to work harder than ever to figure out what really happened."

He seemed shell-shocked. "What really happened is that someone got into her house and abducted her. If she was on her own she would have figured out a way to contact us."

He had a point—a very depressing point—but I couldn't let it get the best of him. I gave the eggs to the dog and she gobbled them down while I pushed Ron to get his coat and go with me to the office. Although a couple of the reporters had figured out the connection with our business and where we went all day, most of them were still concentrated here near the house. I supposed they figured they could catch us at more vulnerable times that way. Who knew?

Sally had already made coffee and turned the thermostats up when we arrived, bless her. She'd also made some breakfast burritos that merely needed to be heated in the microwave and smothered in chile sauce—a much better choice than my own meager breakfast attempt earlier. I sat Ron at the table and actually placed a fork in his hand.

"You'd better eat," I lectured. "You've already lost all the weight you need to."

The feeble joke landed flat.

"Oh, some lady called right after I got here," Sally said. "She said you called her yesterday. I'll go get the message slip from my desk."

I sat down beside Ron and tried to talk strategy as we ate. My own plan was to go back to the old address book, hoping like crazy that someone, somewhere would be able to give me useful information. What that might be, I had no idea and must admit to feeling like I was spinning my wheels at times.

Sally came back with a written note. The caller was Carol Ann Henderson, which only vaguely rang a bell—I'd made so many calls recently.

"I'm calling Kent Taylor," Ron said. "Can't stand getting news from the media and I'm not waiting around for Ben Ortiz to go through *legal channels* to learn things on our behalf."

I understood his frustration. I just prayed he wasn't doing or saying anything that would crucify him later.

As it turned out, Ron didn't need to call Taylor. The detective was standing in front of Sally's desk when I walked through the reception area on the way to my office.

"Is Ron here?" he asked. "We've got some news that looks positive."

I didn't bother with niceties, just shouted for my brother from where I stood. He came out of the kitchen at a pretty good clip.

"Where can we talk?" Taylor asked.

I'll say pretty much anything in the world in front of Sally, but there wasn't time to waste telling him. The three of us walked up the stairs and ended up in my office, since it's less cluttered with Ron's perpetual piles of junk. I took my desk chair, Ron sat on the cushioned bay-window seat, Taylor remained standing.

"We got a hit from Victoria's bank," he said. "Someone logged into her accounts. Checked the credit card balance page and looked at her checking and savings. No money was moved. This was someone simply scoping out the status. It could mean Victoria is alive and well somewhere, checking on her own money to be sure it's okay."

Ron and I exchanged a glance.

"When did this happen?" I asked. After all, there was a chance it happened after our little snoop session.

"Monday morning. There's been activity on her internet account since then."

I looked at Ron. He looked at me. We were *so* busted.

He'd had a rough week, so I took the rap for it, admitting I had used my key and gone into Victoria's house.

"Where was the computer? Our team didn't find one." Taylor asked. I almost detected a hint of admiration for my detecting skills.

I told him about the floor safe. "I didn't mean to do anything wrong," I swore in my best preschooler's voice. "We only wanted to help."

"And what else was in there?" He almost—not quite—looked amused.

I was on the brink of enough trouble already so I told him everything—about the passwords, the money and credit card, the old address book.

He held out his hand, wiggling his fingers. "Give. Now."

Ron scooted over to his office to retrieve the laptop and notebook with the passwords. I got a lecture on entering a crime scene and contaminating evidence, a talk that ended with, "You are this close to being arrested for obstruction of justice, concealing evidence … not to mention breaking and entering."

"I didn't break—I only entered, using a key given to me by the homeowner. Besides, your team had been there already. I didn't know they were coming back right away, that they weren't finished yet."

"Don't get into semantics with me. You entered a crime sce—wait a minute. Our techs were finished. They didn't go back later. What did you mean?"

"Just as I was leaving—a car pulled up to the house and stopped. I didn't wait around, but I assumed your guys came back."

His face became thoughtful, his forehead wrinkles more pronounced.

Ron came back with the computer and other items, while I reached into my desk drawer where I'd been stashing the address book whenever I wasn't using it. See? I really was being careful.

As I picked up the book something fell out, a small

envelope. It must have been stuck between the final pages—
I'd been through most of the book already. Kent Taylor
hadn't seen it and for one split second I debated sliding
the drawer closed without letting him know, but then I
remembered the lecture.

I handed him the book as I picked up the envelope with
my other hand. It was once white, a little yellowed now,
the size to contain a notecard. There was nothing written
on the outside but a fifteen-cent stamp had been glued to
the upper corner. Not waiting for permission I opened the
unglued flap and pulled out a single sheet of paper.

"What's that?" Taylor asked, noticing my movements
for the first time.

I held it out of his reach and scanned the delicate sheet
of feminine writing. It wasn't Victoria's, that much I knew.

"It says, 'Albert, I wanted to let you know that you have
a daughter, born last week. I'm sorry you wanted nothing to
do with us, that you'll never know her.' It's signed with only
the letter J," I said.

Taylor held out his hand and took the letter, scanning
it for himself, as if I might have made up the contents.
"Who's J?" he asked.

I drew a complete blank, but I was getting used to that
when it came to this address book.

"I think Victoria's mother's name was Jane," Ron said.
"She so rarely talks about her mom. She died when Vic was
near the end of high school. Breast cancer, I think. I know
it really hurt Vic that her mother was too sick to attend her
graduation."

"Do you suppose this was a letter to Victoria's father?"
I said it more to Ron than the detective. "Maybe she learned

he had died before she could mail it."

For Taylor's benefit we went into the quick explanation of how we'd figured out that Jane must have made up the story about the father dying in Vietnam.

"It doesn't mean he didn't die, though. Just not in the war."

Kent studied the letter a moment longer. "I don't see how this has anything to do with our case. You want to keep it with family memorabilia or something?"

I took the thin page, refolded it and put it back into the envelope, dropping it on my desk. I wasn't sure what family memorabilia we were collecting here, especially if it turned out there would be no marriage. The thought of Victoria permanently out of our lives—never to help raise Ron's kids, never to light up Ron's face the way she did, never to take me shopping for another fabulous outfit. My eyelids prickled. I blinked hard and turned away for a second.

When I turned back, Taylor had tucked the laptop under his arm, promising Ron that a complete forensic investigation would be performed on it and if he found that anything—anything at all—had been erased or compromised, the two of us would most assuredly be doing jail time.

Chapter 22

Victoria ran until her lungs refused to take in another scrap of air; her bare feet screamed in pain. The drunk had taken a few steps after her and called out but she didn't hear him now. She slowed enough to turn her head and look back. He'd not followed her around the corner.

She rested her back against the nearest building but the glass in the old storefront swayed dangerously. She had a vision of herself falling through it, unable to get up, so she moved onward. Nothing in this neighborhood seemed familiar although she must be within blocks of her home. After running away into the dark night, her memories felt hazy. She'd lost track of the alley from which she'd emerged a little while ago, where she'd left the door to the concrete cellar unlocked. It occurred to her that she'd not had food or water in at least two days.

A blast of cold air came down the deserted street and she stumbled ahead, finding an alley with a large dumpster near the mouth of it. Beside the dumpster sat a large cardboard box; someone had been too lazy to flatten and put it inside. She tipped it to its side and crawled in, the small space and shelter from the wind a blessed relief. She thought of food but only wanted to sleep. Her eyes closed, the world becoming a black void.

* * *

"Hey, lady. Lady, wake up!" The voice came from very far away.

The sense of being jostled. Fear—those men—had they come back? Flashing lights, more voices. Movement. Her stomach feeling queasy. Bright lights. Urgent voices.

"...temp is only eighty-six....blankets! Hot packs.... Get 'em on her chest."

"... feet don't look good."

Were they talking about her?

She was home, feeling warm now. The silver-haired man came in, demanded the evidence. She didn't know what he meant, what evidence he wanted. She began to cry, hearing her voice as a small whimper.

"Gently with those hands and feet ... Crank up the heat in here! Let's get some oxygen to her."

She fell asleep again, despite all those voices in her head, the sensation of being shoved around. She was at home with her mother—Mom in a hospital bed set up in their living room, pill bottles everywhere. She held a bowl of soup, tried to get Mom to eat some of it. "Victoria, I need you to take care of something." Mom's voice so weak, her body so frail.

"Change out those packs …" An authoritative voice. Was he telling her to do something for her mother? The regular doctor never said those things.

The living room was overly warm but Victoria had no choice. Mom was always cold, always shivering. "Baby, I have to tell you some things … about Florida. It's a dangerous place for us … I have evidence of a crime …"

Evidence. That word again. The strange man wanted the evidence.

"Baby, get the box from my closet. Hide it. Hide it real good … man with blue eyes … he'll try to find me but he wants the evidence."

"Mom, what are you saying? Evidence of what?"

"Crimes. Bad things. He went to prison but he could get out."

Victoria saw herself walking into her mother's bedroom. On the closet shelf, a stationery box, flat, about nine by twelve inches, made of brightly colored paperboard. She pulled it down and carried it to the sickbed. Her mother's face relaxed.

"Yes, honey, that's it." Jane flinched as another spasm racked her body. She caught her breath and spoke again. "Keep it with you. If a man named Al Proletti ever comes around, take the box to the police."

"… conscious yet?"

"No, doctor. She's restless, though. Not comatose."

"… her name?"

"Still a Jane Doe at this point … checking with police."

Jane? Mom? She looked down at the sickbed. Jane

Morgan took her last breath. Victoria closed her eyes, wanting nothing more than to sleep forever.

Chapter 23

Kent Taylor's warning dimmed a little after he left. Yes, I got it that he wasn't happy about our looking through Victoria's emails, but he would soon know that we hadn't deleted or messed with anything. To save his own skin he'd have a police forensic team all over that thing. I took a slow breath and resolved not to let it bother me. Sally's message slip was still in my pocket so I pulled it out. The police had now officially shown no interest in the flowered address book so I fully intended to resume my mission—to either find something worthwhile or discard this line of thinking.

I picked up the phone and dialed the number Carol Ann Henderson left.

"Yes, Charlie. Yesterday you asked me to call you back if I thought of any more information about the Morgan family you'd asked about. I'm so sorry to say this, but I had to be sure I could trust you."

Her voice definitely had a Southern accent—funny how I hadn't especially noticed that the first time we spoke.

"And now you do?"

"Well, yes. I checked out your private investigation firm to be sure you were for real. See, I think I made a terrible mistake a few months ago. Someone else called, asking about my friend Juliette ... and I'm afraid I let it slip that she'd changed her name to Morgan. And then the man hounded me into saying she'd moved to New Mexico. Well, when you said you were calling from Albuquerque ... I don't know ... I got so worried you might be helping him. The man frightened me something fierce."

"Why is that?"

"I mean, how was I to know? Juliette died years ago and I—well, it just didn't occur to me that there was any way he could harm her anymore. Anyway, I'm sorry I said anything to him and I wanted to apologize to you, and that's really all I had to say."

She hung up before I could process her rapid train of thought. I stared at the dead phone in my hand, debating whether to dial her right back. Maybe better to let some time go by and try to catch her by surprise. If I could even begin to formulate questions to go along with the babble she'd just offloaded. I hung up my phone and headed across the hall to Ron's office to run it all past him.

Ron wasn't at his desk and when his cell phone rang it startled me. I reached toward it. The display said it was Albuquerque Police Department.

Uh-oh. Despite my bravado earlier the guilts came creeping back, along with Kent Taylor's lecture about our having searched Victoria's computer for evidence. We really should have told him about it, not acted on our own. Now, if he'd discovered anything he didn't like—well, he had mentioned jail time and I had no doubt he was serious. So, answer it or not?

On the third ring I succumbed to the need to shut the thing up so I answered.

"Ron, Kent Taylor here," came the familiar voice. Some detective—he hadn't noticed it was my voice.

"Sorry," he said, when I corrected him. "I called with some news."

Dread. Hope. Elation. It took all of one-point-two seconds for my emotional range to hit all of them.

"Where?" I asked, a moment after I'd shrieked for Ron to get to his office—now!

"UNM Hospital. She was brought in early this morning. Charlie, I have to tell you that she's in critical condition."

"Alive, though."

"Yes, she's alive. She has a gunshot wound and severe hypothermia. She must have been out in the elements most of the past three days."

Ron came into the room in time to catch my query. I had to stop and pass along what Taylor had said. I couldn't imagine poor Victoria out there in the cold and what all she'd been through.

Ron took the phone from my hand and hit the speaker button. "We'll be right down there," he told the detective.

"You won't be able to see her," Taylor said.

"I have to. I have to see that she's okay. I'll hold her hands—she'll get better when she knows I'm there."

"Ron, until we can talk to her and get her version of the events, I'm afraid you're still a suspect."

"What! Seriously?"

"It's procedure. I'm sorry."

Ron was breathing hard. I expected a temper explosion any moment so I stepped between him and the desk.

"I can't stop you from going to the hospital," Taylor said in a low voice, tossing us a bone I supposed. "But there are guards outside her ICU room. I'm asking you not to make a scene."

I tried to assure him it wouldn't happen but it was kind of like promising to hold back a raging bull. I would have to get Ron settled down before I dared let him walk into that building.

"The doctors have said they will call me the moment she's conscious," Taylor said. "Once I can talk to her, I'm sure we'll get the answers we need and—most likely—you'll get to see her then."

He was saying he didn't truly believe Ron to be guilty, which was huge. My relief must have been evident as I clicked off the call because Ron's whole demeanor changed. He rubbed his eyes, scrubbing at his face to hide the intense emotions.

"She'll be all right," he said in a ragged voice.

"She's alive. That's the important thing."

"I'm going up there," he said. "I know, I know." He held up a hand to quash my response. "I'll behave myself. I need to be there, in the same building, in the same place if I can. She'll come around and I have to be there for her."

Truthfully, I've never seen my brother so emotional and it hit me how very much Victoria was his whole world now.

"I'm coming with you." Finding Victoria alive, if not exactly well, was only half the equation, I realized. We still had to find out who shot her. What possible motive could they have had?

* * *

There are few places less fun to be than a hospital waiting room. Bright upholstery on the chairs and cheery pictures on the walls do nothing to dispel the weighty sadness and worry of the people who would pretty much give anything not to be there. It was nearly noon so added to the generally depressing atmosphere were overtones of cafeteria-cooked food, that mélange of flavors and smells that do not go together, no matter how much they try to spice it up.

We approached the ICU nurses' station but didn't have to ask which room was Victoria's. Armed policemen stood on each side of the first door on the left. Beyond the glass windows we could see a bundle of white blankets with a bank of blinking machines beside the bed. Wires and tubes ran everywhere. At this distance, the only real sign it was our girl was her long brunette hair visible in tangles against the pillow.

The nurse took pity, no doubt because of the ravaged looks on both our faces, and led us to stand in front of the window for a moment. Both cops straightened their stances, letting us know that breaking through and getting inside was out of the question.

"The blankets and heat packs are there to warm her up. Her core temperature had dropped dangerously low," the nurse said. "She may lose a couple of toes."

Ron and I both blanched a little at the reality of it.

"Once we get her warmed to a safe temperature and she's stable, she'll go to surgery for the gunshot wound. The bullet's still in there. We have to get it out and address any infection."

"How long—?"

"With luck, we can get all that done today. A surgeon is on call, waiting for us to let him know to come. We'll address the frostbite issues, and then it's a matter of recovery. Her own strength and will to live have a lot to do with it."

She glanced sideways at Ron when she said this, and I got the feeling she'd heard the news stories which had so badly branded him already. Luckily, his attention was so fixed on Victoria he hadn't really noticed the nurse's hesitation.

"I'm afraid there really isn't anything you can do but wait. The detective told us to notify him when she's conscious and able to speak, but I have to be frank. It's not going to be until later tonight, maybe tomorrow. You might as well go home for awhile."

She ushered us out of the forbidden zone and went back to her desk and all those monitors. I steered Ron toward the row of stiff-looking chairs.

"Should we do as she suggested?" I asked. "Go home, figure out what's next?"

"I can't even wrap my head around what's next," he said. "I can't imagine being anywhere but here until I get the chance to talk to her."

"Okay, buddy." I patted his arm. "Okay."

* * *

I discovered going back to the office with the hope of catching up on my accounting duties was useless. Businesses have so many little things to do at the end of the year, tax-wise, December is always a busy month. With the wedding plans last week and the heartbreak this week I was already hopelessly behind. I spent two hours doing what should have been fifteen minutes' worth of work, and I didn't make even a small dent in the whole job.

Finally, I closed everything up, ran by the house to take Freckles home, called Drake to bring him up to date. He told me he'd finished the game count and was now returning the Fish and Game crew to their headquarters, then would be on the way home. He would hangar the helicopter and pick up his truck then come join us at the hospital.

I picked up Ron's favorite burger—he's addicted to Whoppers—and found him in the same chair where I'd left him.

"Any news?"

He brightened at the sight of the food, dipping into the bag for the fries. "So far, so good. She's stabilized enough for the surgery. As soon as the doctor arrives they'll take her in and get rid of that bullet."

I had a feeling Kent Taylor would show up around that time. I knew he wanted the bullet for testing, to compare with ballistics tests from Ron's gun. My theory proved to be true, although it was still awhile before the nurse called him over and handed him a little baggie, the contents of which I didn't even want to look at.

I wondered if he would wait with us until Victoria came out of the anesthetic—it could prove to be an awkward wait—but he didn't. No doubt the hospital would call him again when she could talk.

Again, Ron asked if he might sit by her side. Again, the answer was no.

It was going to be a long night.

Chapter 24

Drake arrived sometime around when I might normally be thinking of bedtime if I was home. He looked slightly bedraggled after flying half the length of the state, not to mention two nights in motel rooms that surely were not four-star. His flight suit definitely needed a wash and he smelled of jet fuel. He apologized for this, saying he hadn't wanted to take time to go home and shower until he saw us. We filled him in.

Victoria's status was the same—surgery went well and recovery room time seemed to take forever, to us anyway. Eventually, we sensed motion around the nurse's station and I jumped up in time to see them wheel Vic's bed back to her ICU cubicle. There didn't seem to be any fewer machines or wires now but the mood of the nurses had definitely picked up. I hung unabashedly nearby as the nurse we'd spoken to earlier picked up the phone. I could tell she was talking to Kent Taylor. She granted him five minutes if he could get here within the hour.

I kept staring wistfully toward Victoria's little room but the nurse firmly shook her head. The two police officers came back. I supposed I should be grateful for them. We knew Ron wasn't the assailant but they didn't. And none of us knew who really shot her. The added protection was a good thing.

I'd rejoined Ron and Drake in the waiting area when Kent Taylor arrived. He greeted us.

"They say she's been able to speak a little," he said. "I won't learn much, I'm afraid."

"Can you at least tell her we're here," Ron asked, "and tell her I love her?"

If Taylor was uncomfortable with that request he didn't show it. He pulled out a small notebook and headed toward the desk.

"If he gets five minutes with her, I'm betting the rest of us will be allowed even less time, if at all," Drake said. "So, if you don't mind, I'm heading home for a hot shower and something to eat."

"Go," I said with a little laugh. "That fuel smell is getting a little overwhelming. Throw your clothes in the washer while you're at it."

Ron shook his hand and they turned it into one of those man-hugs that involves hearty slaps to each others' shoulders. Drake's elevator arrived and there was a slight commotion as four people emerged, one carrying a camera and one a microphone. They headed our direction.

"Oh, no you don't," called the head nurse. She buzzed around the end of that desk faster than I would have thought possible with her stocky body. "No press in here. This waiting area is for families and there's no way in hell you're getting near any of our ICU rooms."

The blond reporter opened her mouth, looking as if she would argue, but the nurse was larger, older and carried herself with a lot more authority. She placed herself between us and the media gang.

"Get, now! Go on out. If the police want to talk to you it'll have to be in the conference room on the first floor or outside the building." She swished her hands, the way you might send a group of kindergarteners out to play, and they minded.

I heard a couple of mutters as the group headed toward the elevator but none of them tried to get past Nurse Barricade to speak to Ron or me.

"Thank you," I said to her as the elevator door swooshed shut with them inside. "Dealing with them hasn't been fun."

"This ain't about fun, sweetie. It's about protecting my patients."

I wanted to bristle at 'sweetie' but her attitude was cool. I had to be happy she was there, along with the police, to stand guard over Vic. I paced the length of the waiting area twice. At this hour we were the only ones there. Kent Taylor's five minutes began to feel awfully long but finally he emerged and walked over to us. I found myself holding my breath.

"You're in the clear, Ron," he said.

I thought my big brother was going to weep. He blinked several times and swallowed hard.

"How is she?" he asked. "Is she in a lot of pain?"

"She's pretty doped up. No pain. But she dozed a couple times." He stuffed the small notebook into his inner jacket pocket. "What she did say was very clear. Two men, strangers, broke into her house and shot her."

"What did they want?" I asked.

He shook his head. "She didn't know. Usually with a home invasion it's druggies wanting cash, the kind of guys who'll take your TV set and jewelry and sell it to support their habit."

Something seemed off. As far as I'd noticed, nothing of value had been taken. Certainly the TV and other electronics were still in place. Even Vic's purse had been there.

"My guess," said Taylor, "is they either didn't think she'd be home or thought they could intimidate her into handing her stuff over to them. One guy got flustered and the gun went off. She said she got out of the house and ran for her life. I'm thinking once they'd shot her they didn't dare hang around. Late at night like that, any neighbor could have become involved. The men probably took off without getting what they came for. Anyway, once she's back home and feeling up to it, she can let us know what, if anything, is missing."

His conclusion about the men leaving quickly seemed obvious, but there were still a lot of holes in the scenario.

I wanted to ask more questions but Taylor was in a hurry. Most likely the hospital call had interrupted his own plans for the evening. He walked away before I got the chance to bring up the other thing I wanted to ask.

Ron was already on his way to the nurse's station, and this time he didn't really ask.

"I'm going to sit beside her for the night. She needs to know I'm here."

"No long conversations," said the no-nonsense nurse.

Remembering what Taylor had said about Victoria's drowsiness, long talks seemed unlikely. Still, I completely understood my brother's need to be at his fiancée's side. I followed him past the desk, across the hall and up to the two uniformed officers at the door. They'd gotten the word from Taylor, obviously, because they parted to let us in.

It's unnerving to see someone you love lying in a hospital bed, bandaged and hooked to strange, noisy equipment. Last time I'd seen Victoria she'd been glowing with anticipation of her wedding, beautiful and perfect. Now she seemed smaller, shrunken somehow under wraps and blankets. Her face had been washed, but not thoroughly, leaving ragged scraps of days-old mascara, and her hair's luxuriant waves had morphed into stringy dark hanks. A stickler for looking good in public, she would be horrified. A thick bandage covered her injured shoulder and both feet had bulky wraps of gauze and tape. I thought of what the nurse had said about her losing toes to frostbite.

Ron moved past all that, looking only at her face, reaching for the hand lying outside the blanket. He picked it up, stroking her fingers and being careful not to touch the IV line taped to a vein. His lower lip quivered and I looked away to give him a moment's privacy.

"She won't be able to talk to you," I said. "You might as well at least sit down."

I spotted a chair in the corner and shoved it close until it touched the backs of his legs. Like a robotic man, he bent at the hips and knees and sank onto the seat.

"She's battling infection," said a voice at the door.

The nurse who'd been such a drill sergeant with those media folks now had a voice tender and caring. She moved into the room and checked a bag of clear fluid hanging from a hook near the head of the bed. "That GSW nearly got her even though the bullet itself only lodged in muscle. We're pumping in the antibiotics and she should be a whole lot better in a day or two."

She touched a button here, a dial there, moving around the room efficiently.

Ron hadn't taken his eyes from Victoria's face.

"I'm gonna go," I said, patting his shoulder and giving the nurse a smile. "Call if you need me—otherwise I'd better tend to my hubby at home."

Ron tilted his head until his cheek rested against my hand and we held that pose for a moment.

"I'll come back in the morning unless you want a break sooner." I realized it was already nearly ten o'clock.

I drove through fairly quiet streets, avoiding the university. With some exceptions Albuquerque isn't a big night-life city. I made it home in about fifteen minutes and that was mainly because I'd hit three red lights in a row along Lomas.

The first thing I noticed on my own street—the news vans were all gone. Now that there was no killer bridegroom, apparently there was not much of a story. Sad but true.

Elsa's place was dark. Poor dear had probably not slept much with all the commotion outside, and I knew for a fact several other neighbors had pestered her for information about us. Yet another thing to deal with sometime in the future, the family reputation within our own neighborhood. There'd been so many home sales in the past ten years or so, nobody knew us long-term, the way Elsa did.

From behind our drawn living room drapes, I could tell the television was on which told me Drake was waiting up.

I let myself in, got jumped by the exuberant puppy, and greeted Drake as he came through the kitchen door.

"Want some hot chocolate?" he asked. He had a steaming mug in his hand.

"That's yours," I protested.

"Won't take but a second to make another one." He took my jacket and handed me the cocoa, then ducked back into the kitchen.

The show he'd been watching ended and a newscast came on, telling me what I already knew—missing Victoria Morgan had been found and the police were now considering this to be a case of home invasion. A couple of experts were brought on to give statistics on the shocking number of these crimes. I was just happy not to hear Ron's name on the news, for once.

I filled in Drake on Victoria's condition and Ron's reaction to knowing she would be all right.

"I never really thought Ron would find the right person," I said, "the way I did."

In quick order, the cocoa was gone, the TV shut off, and we found ourselves in bed celebrating the fact that we have each other—as only we can do.

* * *

Three days later, the doctors cleared Victoria to go home. She was considered something of a miracle patient having only lost one pinkie toe to frostbite and with what would eventually become a dimpled crease across the top of her left shoulder. There would be some physical therapy to make sure use of that arm had not been compromised and she might have to adapt some of her sandals and most of her strapless dresses. All in all, we were one very lucky family.

I called Kent Taylor to be sure it was all right for us to take down the crime scene tape and deliver Victoria to her own home. While I wouldn't have minded taking her in at our place, I know too well the feeling a person has when she simply wants to go *home*, to be in her own bed. With the detective's clearance, I headed over there. I had roughly four hours to clean the house and make it comfortable for our patient's recuperation.

Armed with a few bags of groceries and some basic cleaning supplies I parked in the driveway beside Victoria's now-dusty blue PT Cruiser. Ripping the yellow strands of tape away from the door frame was one of the most pleasurable things I'd done in the past week, I'll tell you. It shouldn't take me long to straighten the furniture, run a dust cloth over everything and vacuum up any stray footprints the police had left behind. I would stash her vacation suitcase discreetly away in a closet and put a roast in the oven so she and Ron would have a hot dinner tonight. All those great plans sort of went *whoosh* the minute I opened the front door.

The place had been ransacked. The hairs on my arms prickled as I looked around.

The hall closet door stood ajar, drawers in the console hung open, sofa cushions lay on the floor spouting tufts of stuffing. Books were strewn from the shelves. As I moved toward the kitchen I saw cupboard doors open and items from a linen closet flung about.

Nothing appeared as it had the night I made my little foray for business files and the contents of her safe.

I set down the items I'd carried—two food sacks and

my purse—and dashed downstairs to see if the intruders had also located the safe. The same disarray was evident here but they'd not moved the heavy lamp which concealed the opening to the safe. Not that it mattered—they would have needed a master safe-cracker to get into it, of that I felt sure, and I'd already taken the contents.

My mind whirled with the implications. I should probably call the police immediately and report this, but they were stuck on the random-home-invasion theory and might not even listen to me. Worse, they would be all over the place for hours, completely disrupting Victoria's homecoming. None of the typical burglary items were taken—two flat screen TVs and some other electronic gear were all in place. She was so desperately looking forward to being home again … I couldn't ruin that for her.

I started with the furniture in the basement, straightening and organizing, stuffing the filling back into cushions and pillows as best I could, working my way through the house. The jolt of fear, which ran like an electrical tingle throughout my body, propelled me to maximum efficiency. My hands worked coolly while my brain buzzed along at a zillion miles a minute.

The men who'd broken in, that fateful night, must have been watching the place and come back for whatever they wanted in the first place. The good news about that was they were obviously after something other than Victoria herself. Knowing they hadn't intended to murder her was some consolation at least. On the other hand, if she knew what they wanted and where they could get it, they might have plans to come back and force her to reveal whatever it was.

I couldn't get all this out of my mind as I neatened the

kitchen and put the new food away in the fridge. Every room had received the same treatment, telling me the searchers had spent some time. I'd already found their point of entry, the back door I'd left unlocked after my own hasty departure.

Oh my god. The knowledge hit me at once. The car that had pulled into her driveway the early morning I was there—it had to be those men coming back. I'd escaped with moments to spare.

The theory made perfect sense. Knowing the police were finished with the house and the owner was gone, they knew they had plenty of time to search at their leisure. It had been daybreak when I was there. They might have stayed all day, with no neighbors the wiser, perhaps thinking their car belonged to one of the relatives ... or maybe they'd only used the driveway to turn around, not left a car in sight at all.

I'd finished what I could do in the bedroom and office, forcing myself to stop guessing at what the intruders might have done. We needed facts, and the only place we could likely get them was from Victoria herself. It wouldn't be easy, but we would need to discuss this soon.

I'd plumped the last of the living room cushions and pushed the sofa back in place when I heard Ron's car in the driveway. By the time I reached the front door, he'd helped her from the passenger seat into a wheelchair he must have borrowed somewhere. One foot was encased in some kind of fat medical-looking 'boot' and her left arm was in a sling. She wore the new flannel nightgown and plush robe I'd taken to the hospital as a gift yesterday.

Getting the wheelchair up the front steps proved too

much of a challenge so Ron simply picked her up and carried her into the house, while I wheeled the chair along and set it to the side.

"We'll have to rearrange things a little," I said, "but that's no problem. I'll do it."

Victoria, without makeup or styled hair, still looked beautiful to us. She gave an almost-exact replica of her old smile. "I don't plan to be in that chair very long. The doctor said I could walk on this boot as soon as I feel ready. They just didn't want me going into a swoon the moment I stood up on my own."

"And I'm not leaving her side," Ron said. He stood beside the couch where he'd deposited her.

She gave him a scolding look. "We talked about that. I'll be able to get around the house in a day or two. You have your office to run."

No one mentioned that they'd both cleared their calendars, planning to be away on their honeymoon for another ten days. They would have been in sunny Florida until right before Christmas, coming back all tanned and fit and rubbing it in our pasty winter-white faces.

"I was just about to put a roast in the oven for your dinner," I told them. "Ron? Want to give me a hand?"

He sent a quizzical look my way. Since when did Charlie cook? Much less, since when did Ron ever lend a hand in the kitchen?

"You sure you're okay?" he asked Vic, pulling a cashmere afghan over her lap, tending to the pillows behind her.

"I'm fine. I actually just want to snuggle down here and grab a quick nap," she said, making little nestling movements.

I rattled some pots and pans, getting into kitchen mode,

and kept my voice low as I told Ron about the condition of the house when I'd arrived.

"I didn't call the police. Was that the wrong way to handle it?" I worked at the counter, chopping onions, carrots and potatoes with my back toward the living room.

He thought about it for a very long minute.

"I don't know. They seem happy enough to believe the whole incident Friday night was random. So far, she hasn't said anything to contradict that idea."

"We have to talk to her about it. Whoever came back here—I have to believe it was the same guys—was after something. Maybe they found it and will never show up again. But what if they didn't?" I saw his protective mode kick in.

"I'm not leaving her side, day or night," he said.

"I think that's a wise idea." The roasting pan went into the oven and I cleaned up my scraps while Ron practically tiptoed back to the living room and gingerly lowered himself onto a chair where he could watch Victoria sleeping.

With similar silent intentions I walked quietly across the room and picked up my purse. I signaled goodbye to Ron and blew a little kiss across the room to both of them. I'd just reached the front door when the doorbell rang. Ack! My thoughts ran the gamut—from the police, to the intruders (silly, I know, why would they ring?), to Drake showing up to be of help.

What I didn't expect, until I opened the door, was the sight of Gladys Peabody standing there with a plastic-covered plate of cookies.

"Hello, dear," she said. "I saw your cars here. Noticed that Victoria is home."

"She's sleeping right now," I whispered.

I could see she would have loved to come in but at least she took the hint. She held out the plate. "Give her these and let her know I'm thinking of her."

I thanked her as profusely as you can do in a whisper, took the plate, and closed the door before the conversation could go any further. When I turned around Victoria was stretching.

"Something's wrong with this couch," she mumbled, coming awake. "The cushions feel all wrong."

I covered by holding out the cookie plate. Ron took it and lifted the plastic wrap.

"I heard you guys talking in the kitchen," Victoria said. "You're wanting to know whether you should tell me something, and I heard the word police. What is it?"

I gave the quick and vague description of what I'd found and our dilemma. She'd pulled herself to a sitting position by the time I finished.

"I don't think we need to call the police," she said. "There are some things I need to tell both of you first."

Chapter 25

Ron helped Victoria to sit up. She swore her injured shoulder felt better in that position than lying down. I brought her a cup of tea and she began her story.

"I'm afraid I lied to the police," she said. "When the detective asked if I knew the men who shot me, I said no."

"You *did* know them?" Ron's arm holding the cup froze halfway to his mouth.

"Well, strictly speaking, no, I don't. But one of the men introduced himself. He said he was my father."

Now it was my turn to be shocked.

"There were two of them," she continued. "An older man with silver hair and a younger one, a big thuggish type. He's the one who brandished the gun. The older man told me he was my father. I don't know what he expected me to say or do."

"You'd never seen this man before? Not even a photo?"
She shook her head. "I sure don't think so."

"Vic," Ron said, "your mother told you your father was killed in Vietnam and we know that's not true."

She sent him a puzzled glance and he explained our conclusion based on what Elsa had told us.

"I never even questioned it. Mom rarely talked about him and never spoke of the war at all. I gathered they'd been married a very short time before he went, and then he never came home. It was just us two girls all those years. We laughed a lot. She was playful and fun. I lost her way too soon."

"Any idea why this man would show up now, so many years later? And why on earth would he bring along someone to threaten you?"

She gave a ragged sigh and handed her mug over to me. "He wanted something, some kind of papers. I don't know—I was so stunned at what he said about being my father that the rest of it kind of zipped right past me."

"Papers. What sort of papers?" Ron asked.

"He used the word evidence. Said my mother stole some evidence from him."

"Evidence of what?"

"I should have asked. I was just so … shaken. I was already in my robe, getting ready for bed, and these guys show up in my house and make this unbelievable announcement, and all at once he wants evidence of something. I couldn't think. I just kept shouting at them to get out, go away." Her voice rose, the panic of that moment still fresh.

"I was standing right there," she said, pointing to the kitchen island, "and I could only think I should get to my phone. When I started toward my purse on the dining chair, the guy with the gun got really anxious—or over-eager, or something—and the gun went off. I just remember being shocked to find myself on the floor by the sofa. Then they were standing over me. The older one was furious—kept talking about this so-called evidence—and the other one wanted to shoot me again. Somehow I got to my feet and I just ran, right out the front door. I remember thinking I had to avoid the street and the lights, get out of sight. After that, it's a blur."

I could see she was rapidly tiring and I suggested she sleep some more. She nodded but said the sofa wasn't comfortable. I could imagine—the stuffing in the cushions had been pulled out and hastily replaced by me. We would need to send it out to be reupholstered.

Ron helped her to her feet, asking if she was okay to walk on the big clunky boot. When she admitted to being so filled with painkillers nothing bothered her, he helped her to the bedroom. I cleared the tea things and tidied the kitchen, thinking about what we'd just heard.

Suppose this man really was Victoria's father. He'd been out of her life, living somewhere else all these years and had somehow figured out where she was. The fact that he described the items he wanted as 'evidence' led me to believe he'd committed a crime of some sort.

The idea shocked me but the possibility was certainly there. There was a lot more to this whole story and for the life of me I couldn't quite put it together yet.

I went into the bedroom where Ron had helped Victoria out of her robe and under the covers. Her eyelids were droopy but she came around a little when she saw me.

"Did I do the right thing, not telling the police the man said he was my father? Surely whatever he wanted from me couldn't be important after all this time." Her voice faded to a murmur.

Ron assured her everything would be all right, kissed her forehead and tucked the blanket up to her neck. We left the room, closing the door behind us.

"What do you think?" I asked, once we were back in the living room. "Does Kent Taylor need to know that part of it?"

He paced the length of the room. "The thing I can't figure is, unless his own life was on the line, why would this stranger have showed up with some big muscle man to help enforce his demand?"

"Right. Why wouldn't he have taken the time to get to know Victoria gradually, work his way into her confidence and then ask about the papers? He might have had her cooperation and even access to her house if he'd played it differently."

"I think we have to ask, what crime was serious enough the evidence of it could still hold threat over him after more than thirty years?"

I thought about that. There weren't many. The statute of limitations would have freed him from nearly anything, except murder. Did Victoria's mother know the father of her child was a killer? It would certainly explain why she'd rarely mentioned him and made up a story about his death.

Chapter 26

Now that Victoria knew about the condition of the house when I'd arrived earlier and the hasty cleanup I'd done I asked Ron again about involving the police. We knew the men wanted some sort of evidence, and it was pretty obvious who had done the searching.

"Kent Taylor needs to know about this," he said.

"He's convinced it was a random burglary."

"But now we know better. We know the guy was specifically after Vic and something he thinks she has."

He was right. I should have called the police right away and probably shouldn't have cleaned up.

"Maybe they found what they were after, took it and will never darken her doorway again."

"Let's hope so." By his tone, I didn't feel too confident about that. "C'mon, let's get that call over with."

He pulled his phone from his pocket and punched Kent Taylor's number from memory. Quick rundown of what I'd told him about the condition of the house and what I'd done about it. I had the feeling I was another five notches down on Taylor's list of esteemed citizens in this town.

"There's something else and we're not sure how it's related," Ron said. He passed along what Victoria had told us about one of the men claiming to be her father.

By the look on his face, I could tell Taylor had delivered some kind of bombshell. I waved my hands at Ron, signaling him to put the phone on speaker.

The detective's voice came through. "... drug runner in Florida. I'll get the local authorities there to check further. According to the rap sheet I got after we made the DNA match, Proletti was convicted on drug trafficking charges in 1981 and did twenty-five years at the minimum security Federal Correctional Institution outside Miami. It's the same place they held Manuel Noriega, so I wouldn't be surprised if the two managed to connect and Proletti kept his enterprise going. I assume he got out when his time was up. Maybe sooner if there were any good behavior points or favors done. The record I received didn't go beyond what I just told you."

I was practically tugging Ron's sleeve by the time he clicked off the call.

"DNA match? Tell me what I missed."

"You got most of it," he said. "It goes back to the DNA test they did on Vic's blood from the rug. Kent says the DNA result was run through a national criminal database and they came up with a parental match to her."

I was having a hard time wrapping my head around

this new information. Criminal databases—why on earth would the police have thought there would be criminal ties to Victoria?

Ron was still talking. "Turns out it was her father, one Albert Proletti, mobster millionaire drug smuggler. As soon as I mentioned Victoria's father, Kent clicked to it right away and knew that was who we were talking about."

"So it makes sense why there was no sign of him for most of Victoria's life, and why her mother didn't want her to know about him. But still—why would anyone think there would be a connection between Victoria and some Florida mobster? I just don't get it."

"I don't know," he said with a sigh. "He was a little cagey about that. Sometimes a victim's past leads to the reason a crime was perpetrated against them. He thought that might be true in this case since we can't find any motive other than a random home invasion."

"I thought that's exactly what they believed it was, someone breaking in and abducting her. It was the point of the posters and hotline and all." Or—the thought leaped into my head—maybe they thought Victoria had a past and wanted to check it out in case she'd purposely gone on the run. Maybe the prospect of marrying someone with friends in law enforcement suddenly became frightening to her.

"Anyway, Kent said once they knew the parental connection was an old one and the man did his time for his crimes, when Victoria showed up safely, he couldn't imagine any connection to this case." He seemed to shrug it off.

Goes to show you never know what little fact will be crucial—it was something both Ron and Kent Taylor had said to me at different times. I'd picked up my purse, thinking I should get home to my husband and my dog—they hadn't seen much of me in recent days—but I noticed Ron's demeanor had changed.

"Okay, what's up?" I asked.

"I feel so rotten about the argument with Vic Friday night. Here we were, about to get married, and I kind of wigged out when she said she didn't want to go to Florida. Now it turns out there was a reason."

"Yeah … what would that have to do with your plans?"

He lowered his voice. "How did she know Proletti was from Florida if she didn't even know he was her father? I just feel—felt—there were a lot of secrets that I was only now finding out. She told me she grew up in New Mexico, that she'd never been to Florida. Did she lie about that? Are there other secrets I still don't know?"

"Ron, everyone has a past. Sometimes it comes out gradually. No—*most* times it comes out gradually. I'm still learning things about Drake, and he's learning about me. Why would you think she deliberately hid things?"

I heard a slight sound behind me.

"Because maybe I did. Hide things." Victoria stood at the edge of the living room.

Chapter 27

She looked a little shaky on her bandaged foot and I rushed to her side to get her to a chair. Ron didn't sit but couldn't seem to stand still either.

"Honey, I'm sorry," Victoria said. "It wasn't like I was intentionally keeping things from you. Things came to mind, as Charlie said, gradually. And it really wasn't until this week I had much reason to think about that part of my past."

"Please sit down, Ron," I said, patting the spot next to me on the lumpy sofa cushion.

"For some reason your mentioning Florida brought back memories of my mother's final days," Victoria said, leaning back in the chair. "I was only eighteen when she died and it was so traumatic for me ... I got myself through it, watching the life fade out of her as the cancer took over, but after the funeral I never wanted to relive those days again. I blocked out a lot of the details."

"If this is too much for you now …" I reached out to take her hand.

"No, it's okay. I'd be better off if I'd talked about it much earlier. Something about having a parent die in your arms … it's horrible, but it's also special. Mom and I shared everything and there weren't many others in our world. It's why I have a hard time sharing it. I've always felt that no one else could possibly know what I went through. I know that's silly—many others go through losses every day. But at the time you feel all alone with it."

She reached for the afghan and pulled it over her lap, winding the soft fabric around her chilly hands.

Her gaze grew distant. "One day—it was near the end of Mom's time, although I didn't realize how close to the end she truly was. Anyway, this one day she asked me to sit beside her on the hospital bed we'd had set up in the living room. Said she had something to tell me. I remember how I approached, thinking she was about to give some kind of birds-and-bees talk or something. I'd graduated from high school that spring and my only halfway serious boyfriend was leaving for college out of state in the fall. We hadn't seen much of each other over the summer, what with my time being devoted to my mother. I knew the relationship was waning and I couldn't even imagine getting involved with anyone else for a very long time, which is why I approached this little talk with a very offhand attitude.

"Mom began with things about her early life, some of it stories I'd heard—her childhood in Texas, for instance. But she had so little strength, I could tell there was something important on her mind and she was determined to get it out. I encouraged her to skip ahead, and she told me that she and her best friend had left Texas right after their high school graduation and moved to Florida. With no college degree and only secretarial skills to her credit, she did all right for herself by working her way up to better and better jobs."

Victoria closed her eyes for a moment and I began to wonder if this was all a bit too much for her first day home from the hospital. I started to ask whether she'd rather get back to bed, but she readjusted the sling's pressure against her neck and continued speaking.

"Again, I could see Mom tiring but she wanted to tell me. After a few years in Florida she got a job offer that went beyond her wildest dreams, working for a construction company at more than double the salary she'd earned before. The man was rich, lived in a mansion, and it seemed he was more than a little bit attracted to her. She said he had the most dazzling blue eyes."

I glanced toward Ron. He's such a bottom-line kind of guy when it comes to long, drawn-out stories I expected to see impatience in his expression. There might be a hint of a yawn coming on, but he was definitely not distracted.

"Apparently, Mom became involved with this man although it was cute to watch how she avoided admitting to an affair. She only hinted around at the relationship. What she really wanted to talk about was how she eventually discovered how dangerous he was. Working in his office she'd apparently come across things—he was up to something illegal.

"She was very tired by then and I suggested the rest of the story could wait, but she said there wasn't much more. She told me to go to her bedroom and find a box she'd hidden away on her closet shelf. 'Bring me the box,' she said. I had to get a chair and then move a bunch of things out of the way. Mom tended to let junk accumulate. By the time I located the box and took it back to her bed, she was asleep. I set the box aside and as I went on with the day the whole thing slipped my mind.

"Mom didn't forget about it though. The moment she woke up she wanted me to show it to her. I remember cranking the head of the bed up and placing the box on her lap. She raised the lid and pawed through the contents. Once she was satisfied about what was in there she closed the lid and handed it back to me. 'Hide this very well,' she told me. 'If a man ever comes around, you use this tape and these papers to get rid of him.' She told me his name— something that sounded Italian—I'd forgotten it for years. The man is dangerous, Mom said. Another thing she told me several times during the conversation was that I should never go to Florida. This man's reach was apparently so vast that he was to be feared."

"What did you think about that?" I asked. I noticed Ron had finally snapped to the fact that this might be the reason Victoria had reacted so strongly to his plans for a Florida honeymoon.

Victoria gave a small one-shoulder shrug. "Truthfully, at that moment I kind of blew it off. I couldn't imagine how any of this related to me or why on earth someone from twenty years or more in the past would come looking for some box of papers."

"Did you go through the box's contents yourself?"

"Barely. I remember taking the box, briefly glancing in and then stashing it back on her closet shelf."

"What was in it?"

Her eyes aimed skyward for a moment. "Papers, as she had said. Some of them might have had writing on them in Spanish? I hardly remember it now. I think there was a cassette tape. My most vivid memory of the afternoon was that Mom suffered a relapse and I had to call an ambulance. I suppose I had put the box on the shelf before it happened, but it's not important now. They took her to the hospital and I sat beside her until the end. I hated all the tubes and machines—I suppose it's the main reason I wanted to come home today, those memories are still painful. Mom died the next day."

Ron appeared lost in his own set of thoughts.

"The rest of that year comes back to me in little snatches of memory—the funeral, sorting through her things, having to move from the rented house where we lived. I received some money from a life insurance policy and decided the best thing I could do with it would be college. I felt the urge to get away from Albuquerque, but that would mean leaving everything about my early life and all my memories of Mom behind. I ended up staying."

I didn't especially want to play This Is Your Life and cover the ensuing years. I brought her back to the thing that seemed most relevant.

"So, about this box ... do you still have it?" It seemed if the mysterious intruder came here demanding and searching for evidence, it might have to do with the papers and cassette in the box.

"I'm sure I do. When I moved into this house I came across it. I'm sure I stashed it somewhere."

"Okay, this isn't the best time for me to put pressure on you but if those men didn't find what they wanted, they're likely to come back."

"Charlie—" Ron laid a hand on my arm. "Not now."

"They've broken in, threatened Vic, come back and searched again. How much more immediate can the problem be?" I ignored his fingers tightening around my wrist. "Vic, can you remember where you put that box? If I can find it for you, we could stick it in a safe deposit box or in the safe at our office. It just needs to be out of reach of this guy."

I guess my premise made sense; Ron's grip loosened.

Victoria yawned and I could tell the conversation had taken a lot out of her.

"Let's get you to bed," I said. "Ron will be right here."

Tucked in once more, she immediately fell asleep and I closed the bedroom door before cornering Ron again in the kitchen. The pot roast in the oven was beginning to smell pretty tasty and I peeked at it to be sure it looked all right.

"Are you thinking what I'm thinking?" I asked Ron.

"That the guy who showed up here is the same rich guy convicted of old crimes back in Florida?"

Well, obviously. "And the rich guy from Florida is Victoria's father."

"So, this Florida guy was arrested for his crime. It could explain why he didn't marry Jane Morgan, or at least why she didn't stay in Florida to raise her daughter."

"They didn't routinely take DNA samples on prisoners in the '70s. I don't know if the testing had really been well-developed back then, much less widely used."

"So, he got arrested much later than that, sometime within the last ten years or so. Or maybe they took the sample when they released him. Just to have it on file."

I had no idea how all that stuff worked—having never been close to many hard-timers—but there was a simple way to find out.

"Call Kent Taylor," I suggested.

The detective said he was out on a new case and would be tied up well into the evening. "That's okay," Ron told him, "just whenever you can, come by with a picture of the guy whose DNA matched Victoria's. We think it ties in."

We, kemo-sabe? Wasn't I the one who posed the brilliant deduction? At any rate, Victoria would sleep awhile, the two of them had a ready-made dinner, and Taylor couldn't get here until tomorrow ... seemed like a good time for me to go home and tend to my own family, not to mention getting some rest. This had become quite an eventful day.

As it turned out, Drake had steaks thawed and a beautiful salad in the works when I walked in. Being pampered by an excellent cook is always high on my list and I totally relaxed into the experience. We were both ready to crash early and I fell into a deep sleep punctuated by snippets of today's conversations and scenes. I woke before daybreak, thinking of the box of papers entrusted to Victoria and wondering where it might be now.

As soon as it seemed a decent hour to call Ron and Victoria, I did so. She'd done fine through the night, he reported.

"Kent Taylor called five minutes ago. He's planning to stop by here with the photo of Albert Proletti for Victoria to look at."

She had remembered the name being Italian. I asked what time Taylor was coming and said I would be there. Control freak—I know. The police and Ron could certainly handle whatever would come up, but I hate getting news secondhand. Especially from Ron. He tends to leave out important things.

I arrived about two minutes after the detective and walked into the house to find him chatting with Ron. Victoria looked a lot perkier this morning, with freshly washed hair and a snuggly pair of sweats. She still wasn't spending much time on her feet; both were up on the couch and the afghan was over her lap again. I gave her a peck on the cheek and sat in the nearest chair.

Kent walked over and asked how she was feeling. At her positive response, he got right down to business and pulled a photo from his jacket's inside pocket. I caught a glimpse of a mug shot—never anyone's best pose—with faded colors. Proletti had dark hair, bright blue eyes, and Victoria's nose. I wondered if she would see the resemblance.

"It's an old picture," Taylor said. "From nineteen eighty-one. Sorry, it's all I was given. Even so, can you tell if this is the man who broke in the other night?"

She stared intently at it. "Well, this one's a lot younger so it's hard to tell. Thinner, too."

Ron peered over her shoulder. Taylor just watched her face.

She turned the photo over, but there was nothing written on the back. Turned it back again and stared some more. Ran her fingertip across the jawline, then pointed at the man's eyes.

"Yes, I'm fairly certain it's the same man. I mean, if I saw him in person in a lineup or something … I could be more certain."

"It may come to that," Kent said, "but this is helpful. At least we know who we're looking for. Helps narrow it down from the hundreds we have in our police files here."

"His name is Albert Proletti," Victoria said, taking in

the facts from the mug shot. "This says he was arrested in Florida. Is he still in prison?"

"No. He did his time—twenty-five years on drug smuggling charges."

Her face became still as she handed the picture back to Taylor. I wondered what her thoughts were. Something told me she was holding back.

Taylor turned toward the front door.

"Kent?" I said, catching up with him. "If this man served his full prison term why would he come here demanding some kind of evidence? Victoria used that word when she described what he'd said. He wanted some evidence. But how could old evidence hurt him now?"

He considered my question, obviously not having put it together until now. I gave him a minute on that one and came up with another question, keeping my voice low.

"You didn't tell her Proletti definitely is her father. Is there a reason not to?"

"No particular reason. I thought maybe it would be easier for her, coming from you or Ron."

It probably would. "Thanks."

"On your other question, Charlie, I'll get back to you. All I can say is that my request for this photo generated some interest. Florida authorities told me ours was the second department in recent weeks looking at Al Proletti."

Chapter 28

Ron took to the kitchen—a rare sight—as soon as Kent Taylor left, whipping up a batch of blueberry muffins from a mix. Even though he called me in there several times (how do I turn on the oven? what are these things they describe as muffin papers?), the gesture was very sweet and Victoria clearly adored his way of spoiling her.

Even so, between smiles in Ron's direction, I could tell she had something on her mind. I decided there was no time like the present.

"Are you thinking of Al Proletti's claim that he's your father?" I asked.

She'd only mentioned it that one time, when she first told us of the break-in. Now she nodded. "There was a phone call, a few days before. I'd nearly forgotten it. The man who called introduced himself as my father and I thought it was a crank call—I didn't want to believe him. If only I'd taken him seriously." A look of regret crossed her face.

"I have some of his features, don't I?" Her fingers played with the edge of the afghan, nervous little tweaks.

"It's true. The police identified him because of a parental DNA match with your blood."

"They tested my blood?" She seemed equally upset with that bit of information.

"When you went missing ... there was blood here in the room. They just wanted to see if it was yours or the assailant's. I supposed it could have made a difference to the outcome of the investigation or the case, in court."

She nodded slightly. "I suppose."

"Anyway, some brilliant computer came up with the match to Proletti."

"So my mother lied, all those years."

"To protect you, I'm sure. She figured out his crimes, maybe. I guess she thought coming to New Mexico put the two of you a lot of miles away from him."

"It wasn't enough," she said. "He found me."

I still wanted to know how that happened. Jane Morgan had been dead a long time, Al Proletti in prison. What bit of information had started him on the quest and led him to successfully locate Victoria?

"I dreamed about it last night," she said. "The box. I remember what it looks like—flat, like stationery used to come in, covered in some kind of bright paper. Lime green comes to mind. While I was out on the streets time passed in strange ways. I can't remember how I got where I was ... days and nights went by ... I'm still fuzzy on that part of it. I had a fever, was half out of it, and these weird scenes would happen as if I were right there. The box—it kept coming back to me but I didn't know why."

"This is good," I said, sounding far too bright and cheery after what she'd just said. "I mean, knowing what we're looking for is a big help. Did any of these visions show you where you put the box?"

She shook her head sadly.

"Okay. Well, after breakfast Ron and I can start searching for it." Even as I said so I realized how difficult it would be. Proletti and his man had pretty well ripped through the whole house. More than likely they'd already found it. If that was the case the evidence was long gone now.

A clatter of metal came from the kitchen and I looked up to see Ron working to get the muffins from the pan, managing to bang it against the stove burners as he nearly lost the whole batch over the edge. Good thing I hadn't brought Freckles with me this morning. She would have known exactly what to do with anything fallen to the floor. I joined him, suggesting he look for plates and find the butter while I managed to successfully transfer the rest of the muffins to a basket and cover them with a cloth.

Over breakfast, I brought up the subject of the evidence and the box again.

"I really have no idea where it could be," Victoria said, shaking her head woefully. "I'm usually so organized but I'm drawing a blank on this."

Considering her recent ordeal and the fact she was critical in the hospital only a few days ago, I could certainly understand.

"Okay, looking at it logically," Ron said, "if it was in any normal hiding place in the house, the men would have found it, so let's start with the places they didn't search at all—the garden shed out back, maybe? The garage?"

The outdoor thermometer had barely topped forty when we finished breakfast but Ron and I decided to buck up and get busy on the task. He had the heavier winter coat so he drew the garden shed. I'd never been out there but I imagined it to be the same model of organization as the garage, which had precisely labeled boxes and small tools hanging from pegboard on the walls.

Vic offered to come out with me but I immediately quashed that idea. She had no business climbing around or lifting anything. She picked up a magazine, looking guilty for doing so, and I parked her on the sofa with the afghan over her legs before I put on my coat and headed to the connecting kitchen door.

All those neatly labeled boxes filled shelves which ran floor to ceiling in the garage. I spent a good five minutes staring at her precise handwriting, hoping, you know, that one of them would say Stuff My Mother Kept Secret. No luck on that.

With no better system in place, I began at the east wall, lowest shelf, and worked my way up and over. One entire section was filled with white banker boxes of business records—the requisite seven years' worth, and then some. The labels said so, right there. To be on the safe side, though, I pulled each one down, lifted the lid, thumbed through folders well enough to know no lime green box was among the goodies.

Same thing with a box marked College Records. Tell me, fifteen years or so after graduating, what does a person need with transcripts and such? We've all gotten on with our lives once school is out of the way. I supposed Vic is just one of those thorough people who likes to be able to put her hands on any random piece of paper when needed. I restacked the boxes I'd moved, wondering if one hour into the job I could legitimately call a coffee break. Decided not—if I lost momentum I wouldn't want to come back to the chore.

The next section held a more miscellaneous collection. Two boxes of old clothing—perhaps for charity? I didn't recognize any of the items I pawed through as being things I'd ever seen Victoria wear. Could it be possible she had a fat-clothes box? Hard to imagine her as ever being other than her current petite size.

On to some canning jars and the huge kettle used for sterilizing them, along with instructions and recipes for home canning. Who knew this was an interest? Then there was a shelf full of camping gear—down sleeping bag and pad, bright yellow backpack in a frame, a drawstring bag that seemed impossibly small to contain a two-person tent (according to the label). Again, a surprise to me that these were among Victoria's interests.

I came down from the ladder and stared toward the middle of the garage. I recognized a bunch of Ron's things stacked in the center of the floor where Victoria's car normally stayed. I knew he'd been steadily moving in but hadn't thought about what all that entails—golf clubs, motorcycle helmet from the days when he rode, power tools, boxes of music CDs and stereo equipment. I wondered if he would keep it all and cram it into the existing space or if he'd decide he could live without a lot of the outdated stuff. At any rate, nothing Victoria hid away years ago would be among his junk so I turned back to the shelves against the wall.

Christmas tree—miraculously well fitted into the box it came in. I always wondered how people did that. I could take it inside and help set it up. Christmas was less than two weeks away, I realized with a bit of a jolt. I carried it into the living room, noting that my brother had no qualms about taking a coffee break.

"I'm done with the shed," he said. "Doesn't take long to look through garden tools and a lawn mower."

I made a face at him, vestiges of the big-brother/little-sister relationship always lurking just beneath the surface.

"Since you're lounging around, you could set up the tree," I told him. "There are a few boxes of ornaments out there—I'll bring them in."

Victoria brightened at the sight of the tree and offered to help, but Ron told her to stay put, at least until he got the lights and garlands on and was ready for the simple ornaments.

Back in the garage, I pulled two boxes labeled Christmas from the highest shelf and carried them one by one indoors. The third had managed to get shoved against the far wall and it was a tippy-toe operation for me to get my hands on it, but at last we should have everything Victoria and Ron would need for a perfect tree.

Ron had made good progress. The branches were in place and Vic was sitting up, directing him where to place it—near enough to the electrical socket, far enough that it wouldn't block the TV set. I set my box down, ready to postpone any more dusty garage duty in favor of helping with decorations.

"Let's see what we have here," I said, shedding my coat.

Going through someone else's collection of ornaments

and trims is so much fun. It's practically like having Christmas morning come early because each little bundle of tissue or bubble wrap reveals some new delight. Of course you don't get to keep them, darn it. Victoria had some beautiful Waterford and the kind of gorgeous pieces I love to look at but would never spend the money to own. I set them aside and found strings of lights for Ron to work with first.

Victoria had left the confines of the sofa and joined me. "Oh, that last carton … I don't normally use those. I think all that's in there are school-project decorations I made as a kid. You know, construction paper covered in glitter, popsicle-stick frames with my own picture in them."

I could envision it. My own second-grade photo with snaggletoothed smile and a horrid boyish haircut still haunts me.

"I haven't had it open in yea—" Her eyes went wide as she had the same thought I did.

We both pounced, pulling off the strip of barely-viable cellophane tape and folding back the cardboard flaps. She was right about the ornaments—the artistic hand of a child clearly at work—and we lifted them out carefully. Beneath it all, flat on the bottom of the carton was exactly the box she had described—length and width about the size of a sheet of typing paper, depth of about two inches, made of lightweight cardboard with a papered lime-green pattern worthy of the seventies.

"You open it," she said. Given the shaky timbre of her voice I suggested we carry it to the couch and sit down.

Ron had abandoned the Christmas lights and stood behind the sofa, watching over our shoulders as I opened the little treasure.

"This is definitely it," Victoria said in a hushed tone. "I remember that cassette tape."

She lifted a couple of the topmost sheets of paper. "Look—there's writing in Spanish on these flimsy ones."

Below those were two folded sheets of ledger paper about two feet wide and twelve inches tall, the old-fashioned kind with super narrow columns bookkeepers and accountants used to use. No matter how much my computer frustrates me at times, I'm thankful not to hand write and manually balance these old pages. I unfolded and smoothed the paper but couldn't make much sense of what the written entries meant.

The next item in the box was a photograph. The colors had faded, but Victoria gasped when she saw it. "Mom," she whispered. "Look how young you are."

The informal snapshot had been taken at an arcade or carnival somewhere. A booth with a sign "Shoot The Ducks" was visible in the background. Beside Vic's mother stood a handsome man with dark hair. Albert Proletti.

This seemed the final bit of proof.

Vic stared at the picture for a long time, barely breathing. At last she placed a very gentle kiss on her mother's face and set the picture aside.

"What's next?" she asked, her voice a little too chipper.

I reached into the box again.

Below the various pages was a steno pad—another dinosaur from an era before word processors. I pulled it out and opened the sturdy cover on its horizontally hinged spiral. It reminded me of an old Doris Day movie in which she was a secretary—again, just a bit before my time—I'd never actually seen one of these in use. Inside the cover was a neatly penned name, Juliette Mason. It appeared some of the sheets had been ripped out. The printed cover on the notebook claimed it contained a hundred pages, but now there couldn't have been even half that many. The same neat handwriting filled the remaining lined sheets.

"That's my mother's handwriting," Victoria said. "I always admired the slightly backhand way she made her loops."

This book contains my observations of the actions and crimes of a man named Albert Proletti from Miami, Florida … the written text began.

"I want to know what's on the tape," Ron declared.

"We need to call Kent Taylor and turn this ov—"

He wasn't listening to me—he'd already knelt in front of the television stand and was poking through the electronic components there.

"Don't you have a cassette player?" he asked.

Victoria and I both gave him a what-do-you-think stare. Everything is digital these days.

"Never mind. I do." He headed for the garage where I imagined him diving into that pile of old junk in the middle of the room.

Vic and I remained side by side, reading the neatly penned pages. In true good-secretarial practice, the first page was dated: *August, 29, 1979.*

I began work for Mr. Al Proletti at Pro-Builder Construction in the fall of 1978. My duties involved transcribing taped dictation, filing most of the business correspondence, taking calls and scheduling appointments for Mr. Proletti. By the end of the year, we had become lovers …

Pieces began to snap into place.

"Her name was Jane Morgan," Victoria protested. "Why is this written as Juliette Mason?"

I shrugged and kept reading, but before I'd come to the end of the page Ron was back with a small cassette tape player in hand. He brushed off a good ten years' worth of dust and found a wall outlet. He picked up the tape we'd found and inserted it, pressed Play, adjusted the volume.

The voice was male with a slight New York accent. I supposed a lot of northeastern snowbirds fled south in those days too. Right away, it became apparent the recording was a phone call. We were hearing only one side of it.

"Come to the city? You crazy? I'm not making the trip."

A long pause.

"Oh. Scarpone's order ..."

"It's his voice," Victoria said. "Al Proletti."

Another pause. The tone changed.

"Mr. Scarpone, sir. Yeah, yeah. It's all taken care of. Did it myself. Nah, we did a big concrete pour Friday." Pause. *"I swear, man, I was there. Saw the stiff, watched the truck dump the load."* Pause. *"Whataya think? Only my most trusted guys."*

A much longer pause while the other man talked.

"Don't worry about her. Yeah, she's young ... nah, she won't talk." Pause. *"Hell, I'm sure she knows nothing."* Definite uncertainty in that last statement. *"No, really, man. We're done with the guy. Problem solved."*

The voice at the other end of the line grew louder, a rant of harsh words that only came through on the tape as static. A sigh from Proletti.

"You say so ... sure I can do it. You think she means shit to me?"

A little more blustering, the sound of a phone handset being slammed to its cradle, a groan. A chair creaked. Another heavy sigh. Footsteps crossing a floor of tile or hardwood. A door opening and closing. The tape went dead.

"Must have been a sound-activated machine," Ron said,

pressing the rewind button on the player.

I stole a glance toward Victoria. Her face had gone marshmallow white.

"Okay, now we can call Kent Taylor," Ron said. He rewound the tape and plucked it from the machine, then set it on top of the green box.

I wanted to read the rest of the handwritten account in the steno pad but he was already dialing.

"You have a copy machine in your office?" I asked Victoria.

She nodded. "The printer. It does everything."

I squeezed her hand and took the steno pad with me. Once all the pages were copied I asked if there was anything else in the box she wanted to keep. Aside from the photo, the contents were all business—a nasty business, true.

"The only thing I still don't get," I said while we waited for Taylor, who'd said he would come right over, "is Juliette. This was your mother, but you said her name was Jane."

Victoria had seemed puzzled ever since we heard the tape. "I've thought of something I can check."

She got up and made her way to the bookcase at the left side of the TV set. Asking Ron to scoot the naked Christmas tree aside for a minute, she bent to one of the lower shelves and came up with a Bible.

"Mom once said to me, 'The answers are in the Bible.' At the time I thought it was a little strange because she wasn't especially religious, but I thought maybe she was trying to give me a little boost of faith or something."

She carried the book to the back of the couch where she used the cushion behind me as a platform while she opened the leather cover.

"Just now I got to thinking, what else is in a Bible besides a million scriptures that I can barely understand anyway?"

She found the page she was looking for, I could tell by the triumphant look on her face. Pointing to a spot, she showed me a family tree illustration. The name beside her fingertip was Jane Morgan.

"Two generations down … Jane's granddaughter was Juliette Mason."

Ron stared at the page, two deep wrinkles furrowing his brow.

"Your mother's real name was Juliette. When she ran from Proletti she took her grandmother's name and became Jane Morgan."

"Juliette's best friend was Carol Ann Dunbar, married name Henderson. I spoke with her a few days ago. She recognized the name Morgan but didn't quite make the connection to Mason." Something else about that phone call still nagged at me.

"I don't know how Mom managed the legal side of changing her name without letting anyone know," Victoria said.

"Probably stayed in a very small community somewhere and posted the legal notices for a name change in the local papers. I'm sure things weren't as strict in those days before terrorism concerns and computerized everything took over our way of life." Ron's point made sense, and I'm sure if we truly needed to know exactly what happened he could spend some time backtracking through old records and get the answers for Victoria.

The doorbell rang and I quickly stashed the copied steno pages in my purse while Ron went to admit Kent Taylor. We spent a few minutes explaining how we'd found the box and basically what the contents were. Ron went ahead and admitted we'd listened to the tape, mainly to be sure it would be useful to the police.

"Would you be willing to make a formal statement that the voice on the tape is Proletti's?" Kent asked Victoria.

She nodded, although I saw a lot of hesitation.

"Very good," he said. "The FBI will be very grateful for your help."

Chapter 29

FBI? I couldn't quite wrap my head around the shift in focus, imagining only that it must have something to do with Proletti crossing state lines to come after Victoria.

I watched her carefully as Taylor bagged the evidence and left. She seemed completely drained. What a gamut of emotions she must be experiencing right now. Learning of her mother's secret life, finding out her father was a murdering mobster, knowing he was still out there and still looking for the evidence from Juliette. In that regard it was a relief to hand it over to the police.

Compounding the air of exhaustion in the room was, I felt certain, the fact that it had been hours since we'd eaten. I warmed some soup while Ron finished stringing the Christmas tree lights and we all sat down silently to the meal.

Victoria didn't perk up a whole lot so I suggested she have a good, long nap in her bedroom. She made little protest noises, thought she should help with the tree.

"It can wait. You sleep. Now." I felt like a little nanny but sometimes you just have to be that way.

While she rested, I retrieved the copied pages and began reading.

I'm alone and afraid and can't think what to do. I have made such a mess of my life—my parents would have a fit. This last part was scratched through as she must have realized she didn't have the luxury of writing a personal diary; this was to be an account of Proletti's crimes.

I've begun to gather some evidence, the little bit I can get my hands on. Al guards everything so closely, I'm beginning to realize my job is all superficial. What goes on here behind the scenes is huge and it's frightening. Twice I've heard him refer to 'getting rid of' someone. I'm going to try to set up the dictation machine so it will come on sometime without his knowledge. Maybe I can catch a conversation that would provide evidence to the police.

What I have so far are a couple of pages that refer to drug shipments. He brings airplanes in from South America and the Caribbean—I don't yet know where they originate, will try to find out. He guards these papers printed in Spanish very closely so I couldn't take more than two, and I pray to God he doesn't miss them.

This poor girl!

Another entry, in September: *Around the office things are more tense than ever. Sheila, not so much. She answers the phones and smokes her cigarettes and shows up for the mandatory holiday parties and picnics. But I think Marion is very aware of what's going on. Maybe not the bodies, but for sure the drug shipments. I removed a page from her ledger one day when she inadvertently left her door open during her lunch hour. My heart was pounding—I knew someone would catch me. Marion might still figure it out. She would have had to redo a bunch of entries and not much gets past that old bird. I feel sure she keeps two sets of books, so maybe the missing page will slip by, at least long enough.*

September 10: *I had to get out of Miami last night. Al was on the phone with someone. He thinks someone has reported his activities to the law and I got a sick, sick feeling he thinks it's me. I didn't do it! But that doesn't matter. If he thinks I did, I'm dead.*

September 12: *I drove all night, heading for Texas. Starting to think that's not a good idea. Al knows I grew up there. He'll come after my family.*

September 13: *Talked to Carol Ann from a little motel in Louisiana but I didn't tell her where I was. She said an FBI man found her, asked all kinds of questions about me. I couldn't sleep after that—so afraid for myself and my baby.*

September 17: *Called Carol Ann again but she wouldn't say what the man wanted to know about me. She said she couldn't talk, that Tommy wanted his dinner. At nine o'clock at night? Just as I was about to hang up she lowered her voice and said, "Jules, you can't call again. That man has a lot of power, they may have bugged my phone. I don't want you hurt, but I don't want me and Tommy hurt either. That's all I'm saying."*

September 20: *Drove all the way through Texas without stopping to see anyone. I don't dare. If Al Proletti has found Carol Ann and sent someone to scare her this bad—I have to stick to my disguise and my new identity and not contact anyone I know.*

The entries stopped. I could only fill in the blanks by assuming that was about the time she got to Albuquerque and decided to take her chances and stay. For all I knew she could have roamed the highways all over the country until winter set in and then decided to stay. There was no way to know. I imagined Juliette—Jane—pregnant and scared, carrying around these pages of documents and feeling as if she couldn't trust anyone. As she'd said, if Proletti's reach went that far, he might track her anyplace. And if the man who'd visited Juliette's friend really was from the FBI … even if they offered to put her in a witness protection program, could she trust that the mob wouldn't eventually find her?

I hoped Kent Taylor would read the steno book before turning it over to the feds, just to get a feel for what Victoria was facing. They could breeze in from Washington and investigate all they wanted, but unless they hauled Proletti's butt back with them, he was still here in Albuquerque and Vic was still in danger. At the very least, we needed to be sure she had protection from authorities at the local level—police, local FBI office … somebody.

I had just picked up my phone to call Taylor and discuss it when the ringer went off in my hand. Drake. He'd been out at the airport nearly all day, performing some inspections on the helicopter and getting her cleaned up in readiness for whatever the next job might be. He reminded me that Freckles had been home alone all day, which of course made me feel all the guilt of a bad doggie-mom.

I left the steno pages with Ron, suggesting he read them and remain on alert. If he felt calling Kent Taylor was a good idea, by all means go ahead and do it. For now, I was off duty in the homecare and protection areas and on duty with my own little family.

Freckles was ecstatic to see me, wagging her entire body, her floppy ears practically flying behind her as she raced from one end of the house to the other. She could keep this up for quite awhile, I know from past experience, so I hooked on her long leash and we headed for the neighborhood park. The air was cold but blue sky and bright sunshine did a lot to dispel winter gloom. I zipped my parka and slipped on gloves, ready to get my blood circulating with a brisk walk.

Bare trees rimmed the park, punctuated with occasional evergreens. Kids aren't out of school yet so the swings were empty. With no one else around and the area fenced but for a couple of entrances, I unclipped Freckles's leash and let her run.

My mind was still filled with the morning's events at Victoria's house—the revelations on the cassette tape playing through my head and the written words of Juliette Mason floating around. I felt for her—the terrified young woman forced to change her name and run for her life. No wonder she hadn't wanted to discuss any of it with her daughter. And poor Vic, blasted with so much new information at once. She had to be wondering what other secrets could be lurking out there—how much of her entire childhood was based on lies.

I let myself worry the little details for a few more minutes, until Freckles brought me a decrepit tennis ball she'd found in the bushes. She dropped it at my feet, her intention clear. What can I say—I can't resist those soulful brown eyes, so I threw it as far as I could and laughed as she caught up to it, grabbed it up in her mouth and came tearing back to me. More! she said. By the time my arm began to ache and the dog's pace slowed a little, I had put the other situation in perspective.

As we headed home I rationalized: those notes were made more than thirty years ago. The criminal had served his time. It was ancient history. Except for his words on that cassette.

I unlocked the front door and Freckles raced me to the kitchen, blatantly reminding me it was time for her dinner. I set the bowl down but my thoughts wouldn't stop. Juliette's box of evidence referred to old news, true, and yet Albert Proletti gone to such great lengths to identify and find his daughter *and* to demand that she turn over the evidence. He must know something in Juliette's possession could still incriminate him.

Mulling it over didn't get me anywhere and it wasn't until I heard Drake at the front door I thought about hunger. As all smart women do when asked what they're making for dinner, I answered with, "Reservations!"

Even that part of it became super simple when we agreed what we wanted most were the green chile chicken enchiladas at Pedro's. The three of us were in the car before you could say margarita. As with her predecessor, Freckles knew exactly where she would be allowed—quietly sitting on the floor in the corner behind our favorite table. I pacified her with a couple of tortilla chips from the basket Pedro immediately brought.

While he blended our margaritas I filled Drake in on some of the news of the day. As usual, he listened, nodded, didn't offer much opinion. The door opened and I caught sight of Kent Taylor, along with two men I didn't know, both younger, both wearing suits and ties. Had to be from out of town—Pedro's clientele is generally way more casual.

Pedro brought our plates just then and I saw one of Taylor's companions eyeing the steaming concoction of tortillas, chicken, cheese and green chile. Kent noticed and steered the strangers to a table across the room. The men had *federal agent* written all over them—okay, not literally—and I mentioned it to Drake.

"FBI, ATF?" Drake asked after he'd taken his first few bites and decided he better slow down.

"I guess they're somehow becoming involved in Victoria's case. Taylor said something earlier and I couldn't figure out how it related."

"But I bet you'll figure out a way to drop by that table in awhile and see what you can learn."

He knows me so well. I ate the rest of my dinner, trying to work up an excuse to do just that. As it turned out, the men ordered and ate quickly and were making moves to leave before I'd drained the last of my margarita. Kent Taylor walked over to us while the others went to the bar and pulled out cash to cover their tab.

"Okay, I can see your little wheels turning in there, Charlie," he said, dropping his voice to barely above a whisper.

I perked up, certain he was going to fill me in.

"Huh-uh. These are the big boys, Charlie, and you're staying out of it."

Well, *that* stung like crazy. I watched them walk out, but I most certainly wasn't going to forget about this.

Chapter 30

Hon, are you familiar with the phrase 'drop it'?" Drake was driving while I sat in the passenger seat stewing over Taylor's comment. "The authorities have it. They're closing in on the guy and the danger to Victoria will soon be over. Relax and leave it alone."

He was right, of course. And in due time, after a restless night, I came to agree. Let the law deal with the criminals. If Al Proletti hadn't already headed back to Florida, the agents here would find and nab him. We all needed to simply put this behind us.

With first the hubbub over the wedding, followed by the horror of the past week, I'd done nothing toward being ready for Christmas. The idea of shopping held little appeal for me, but I knew it was one of Victoria's favorite activities. Now she was on her feet again, somewhat, maybe a short jaunt or lunch out would cheer her up. I stopped by their house at ten the following morning and proposed the idea.

"No long walks," Ron said. "No carrying packages, not much time out in the cold." The man was such a bright spot in anyone's day.

"Okay, then, a girl's day out at the spa. We can't possibly strain anything in a steam room or lying on massage tables, right? My Christmas gift to you," I told Victoria, feeling very righteous that I could cross one item off my shopping list.

I called the day spa at the country club—one of those privileges we get because of the neighborhood where we live. You'd think the holidays would be booked solidly but we had apparently picked the right day of the week. The lady said their real slam would happen right after Christmas when all the ladies called to use their gift certificates.

"It's settled then. Warm and cozy, not straining anything at all."

Despite her injuries, Victoria managed to look adorable when she emerged from her bedroom wearing skinny jeans and a fluffy sweater. A silk scarf—perfectly color coordinated with the sweater—made a fashionable arm sling, while her snow boots cushioned her tender toes in comfort. They managed to be just the right thing, even though there was not a flake in the forecast.

The drive went quickly and the country club staff was super-courteous. I had mentioned our guest was the lady whose picture had been on the news recently and in light of her ordeal she was looking for total seclusion for the day. Carmina, the day-spa manager, put on her most professional manner and led us to the changing room, provided us with towels about a foot thick and white fluffy robes that felt as if they'd been made from the down of baby ducks.

Victoria's wounds couldn't take immersion in water so we wrapped ourselves in our towels for our first stop—the steam room, where we stretched out on teak benches strategically placed below the level of the cloud which hovered near the ceiling.

"I can't tell you how good this feels," she said, laying her head down on a folded towel and closing her eyes. "Ron is such a love, but he's about to smother me."

I couldn't exactly picture my brother being a love or an attentive smotherer, but I learned awhile back I don't have the same viewpoint of him as she does.

"Enjoy it while you can. It won't be long before he's sitting in front of a football game on TV and wondering where his dinner is."

She chuckled. "I know. And I don't mind at all. It's taken me this long to be ready for those things in my life. Now I am. Plus, he's really sweet to me, not to mention being handy around the house. He'd surprise you."

Color me surprised already. I deftly turned the conversation toward the subject that continued to nag at me, no matter how much I intended to forget it.

"Drake and I ran into Kent Taylor over at Pedro's last night. There were a couple of very official-looking suit-and-tie types with him."

I sensed her looking at me now. "And you want to know if they've talked to me."

"No—no I want this day to be about relaxation for you."

She actually laughed out loud. "Charlie, I know you better than that. You're a dog with a bone and you want to know if they were able to wrap up the case."

"Well … yeah, I suppose so."

An indulgent smile. "Yes, the two men are with the FBI. Darren Montenegro is with the local office here. The younger one is Phillip Applin and he's from Washington." She shifted slightly on the bench. "Special Agent Applin says there's a new director of his division and this new boss wants to clear up a lot of old cases. One of those old cases involves Albert Proletti."

Her voice went a little quiet.

"How do you feel about that, knowing they are after him again?"

A long sigh. "Well, if I'd known him as a father and had ever been close to him I might be conflicted about talking to the police. But he's a stranger to me. Our one introduction wasn't pleasant so I can't really side with him. Not to mention the things we learned from Mom's notebook and what we heard on the tape."

"True."

"Mainly, they didn't yet know the connection between my mother and Juliette who wrote the notebook. I told them what we'd discovered in the family Bible."

"That was it?" Hardly seemed like enough to bring a federal agent out from the east coast. I supposed the real target was Proletti, though, bringing him in with or without the supporting evidence the green box provided.

"I'm not sure why Phillip Applin is so enthused about the case," Victoria said. "I mean, he's way too young to have been with the FBI back in the '70s or early '80s. It turns out his boss, Gilbert Ahern, was the one who originally investigated the drug charges that sent Al Proletti to prison. I got the impression Phil is out to do a stellar job to impress the boss."

"I wonder if the same team was looking into the murder we heard described on the tape?"

She didn't answer right away and a moment later the attendant tapped at the door, warning us we'd had plenty of steam. The next step was a cold-water plunge for me and a cold shower for Vic, her bandaged areas wrapped in plastic. I enjoyed the cold for about one-point-three seconds before I roared up out of there in shock. The attendant met me with my comfy robe and all was well again.

Stepping into a room with a small rock-lined pond and a waterfall cascading from twenty feet above, I stretched out on the curved chaise next to Vic's and we stared, in stupor, at the water and lush greenery all around us.

"I might be able to get used to this," I said, knowing full well that these little luxuries were always few and far between for me. I normally have one eye on work and the other on Drake and his helicopter business at all times. I'm not a good relaxer. On the other hand, maybe I should learn to be.

I noticed Vic had become quiet, but not in a relaxed way. Something was still bothering her.

"Okay, give," I said.

"Well, this morning … there was more." She adjusted the turban over her hair and shifted her gaze to me. "The three agents were talking to each other. I'd gone into the bathroom and Ron was in the kitchen getting coffee refills. As I came down the hall I heard them talking about really wanting to pin Proletti on some old murder charges. I immediately thought about the tape we listened to."

I glanced around to be sure the attendants were nowhere nearby. We were alone, and the splashing water worked effectively to muffle conversation.

"Where Proletti basically admitted he'd buried a body in concrete."

"Right," she said. "The agents sounded happy, I mean, practically gleeful to have that tape in their possession. The DC guy said his boss told him they'd never catch Proletti because he was always sneaky and very careful not to get caught."

"Well, it seems like he was." Going to prison on drug charges was far less serious than for a cold-blooded murder.

"I kept thinking of the way the notes tie together with the tape, how my mother had been visited by some local lawman, a deputy I think. I really got the feeling she was suspicious of this lawman, that she didn't fully trust him."

"I saw his name—something like Reddick? Maybe I skimmed over that part too quickly and didn't catch her underlying feelings."

"Or maybe I just imagined it. She didn't really spell it out, whatever she didn't like about him." She adjusted her robe and sat up straighter. "There was more. Agent Applin played the tape again. There were actually two phone calls on it. We had shut it off after we thought Proletti left the room … well, he came back and the tape started up again."

Proof that Ron's guess was right—the machine had been sound activated.

"What was the second call about?"

"He doesn't address the person he phoned by name, so it was obviously someone who would know his voice. I don't remember the conversation word for word but it was along the lines of, 'You better see that no one comes around causing trouble for me on this.' Money must have changed hands because he refers to 'making it well worth your while' and 'you owe me'—things like that."

I mulled that over. "Did the FBI men know who he was talking to?"

"If they knew, they didn't say so to me, but I gather they didn't. They asked me if I knew anything about it. Of course I didn't."

If she'd interpreted her mother's notes correctly, I suspected the other person on the line would have been this deputy, Reddick. If that was the case, the deputy could very well be back in Florida waiting for Al Proletti to be returned to the state, although it seemed hard to believe he would take the chance that Proletti wouldn't implicate him with the FBI and take them both down.

Then again, I didn't know any of the players in this game and had no idea what the situation on the east coast was. It could be that Reddick had died of old age in the thirty-plus years since these calls took place.

I chided myself for getting involved at all. When our spa attendant came back, informing us that our masseuses were ready, I gladly dumped the whole subject of criminals and evidence and gave myself over to the pleasure of warm scented oil rubbed into my skin, my muscles fully relaxing. Judging by the soft breathing from the other table in the room, I guessed Victoria felt the same.

All too soon we were back in the dressing room, sipping cool water from crystalline plastic cups.

"I think I'll ask Ron out on a date tonight," she said, finding her clothes and heading for one of the little cubicles to change. "Both of us could use a break from hanging around the house and feeling worried all the time."

"Sounds like a great idea." I dressed quickly and hoped her nonchalant attitude would carry her through the coming days.

With Al Proletti still on the loose, it worried me that he might confront her again. The thing to do would be to immediately tell him the FBI had all the evidence and law enforcement were keeping a close eye on her. Maybe that news would send him scurrying back to Florida if he hadn't already gone.

I rested easier that night, assuming the FBI men had gone back to their own territory and Al Proletti most likely was on his way back to Florida—I mean, who watches a mobster's business when he's not around? He can't turn important decisions over to just anyone, right? When you think of it, mobsters really must lead a restricted life, unable to travel freely if there are wanted posters out with their faces on them, stuck with a defined territory, afraid of both the law and the hierarchy of their mobster bosses. It was probably a fluke that he could break away long enough to confront Victoria and then search her house. The more I thought about it the more confident I felt that he'd left New Mexico days ago. By the next morning I learned I was wrong on nearly all counts.

Chapter 31

I baked cookies the following morning, two batches of our family's holiday favorites, then divided them and took one plate over to Elsa. She insisted on making me a cup of cocoa and, since she does hers the old-fashioned way rather than from those little powdered packets I buy, I couldn't refuse.

"What's the news on the wedding?" she asked once she had me hooked.

"I haven't asked. I assume they're waiting for Victoria's injuries to heal completely."

"Oh, why wait?" she said, helping herself to another biscochito from the plate.

I did the same—something about that cinnamon sugar coating goes perfectly with hot chocolate. About the wedding, I didn't know how to answer her question. But since I had another plate of cookies for the fiancés I would deliver them and make it my business to ask.

Victoria greeted me at the door and I saw she'd given up the sling and was now able to wear her normal soft, fuzzy slippers. I held out the cookies, which she took with her good hand.

"I'm glad you're here," she said. "Those men are back and Ron went to the office this morning."

For a split second I thought she meant Proletti and his thug, and I thought of my pistol which was very inconveniently locked in my glove compartment. Before I could react I heard male laughter from the living room and figured out she meant the FBI men. She pointed out agents Montenegro and Applin. Finally, it registered with me that two plain vanilla cars sat at the curb across the street.

"Have they been questioning you?" I asked, wondering where this was going—should we have an attorney present? It seemed they'd already asked Victoria plenty of questions.

"Not really," she said. "Well, they just got here."

I squared my shoulders and headed toward the men. Near the kitchen stood a third man, also obviously from the government. He stood a little under six feet tall, with a gray buzz-cut, brown eyes, and a straight line for a mouth. Montenegro introduced him as Special Agent in Charge Gilbert Ahern from DC. I remembered someone mentioning that he would be flying out west a day or so ago.

He shook my hand and gave me an appraising look, as if to determine whether I was important enough to give them any information. I supposed it was all part of his job. I also remembered Kent Taylor saying this older agent was due for retirement soon but since he was the original one to investigate Proletti's activities all those years ago had decided to follow through and see the case to the end.

Victoria had taken the cookies to the kitchen and kept sending quizzical glances toward the three men. I had to agree—what did they want with her now? Being the more brazen or maybe the less intelligent, I came right out and asked.

"We brought back a couple of items," said Applin.

For the first time I noticed the green box on Victoria's coffee table.

"We assumed you would need those papers for the case," I said.

"Well, yes, we've kept the papers. I thought maybe Ms. Morgan would have sentimental feelings for the box, and of course the photograph of her parents, so I suggested we return them."

Three FBI agents to return two items of memorabilia? Something didn't register right.

"We're on our way to the airport," said Ahern, stepping back into my field of view.

Montenegro shifted from one foot to the other. What was going on here?

Vic hung back, staying near the counter that divided kitchen from living room so I stepped up to take charge.

"Thanks for that. So, if there are no more questions, Victoria and I have plans this morning."

I thought the invitation for them to leave was pretty clear but it took a full minute for Montenegro to stop looking toward the senior man and make the decision.

"Yes, right. Well, we'll be getting along then." He moved toward the front door with Applin behind.

Ahern seemed to be studying the room but eventually he followed the others. I watched through the peephole until they'd gotten into the two cars and driven away.

"Now that was weird," I said to Victoria who had finally ventured away from the protection of the kitchen.

"It was. They just came in, kind of smiles and happy—well, except for that older one—and offered me the green box. I haven't actually looked inside it yet. I hope they really did give back the photo."

"Yesterday, when they asked their questions, did you get the feeling they wanted more information?"

"They asked me several times if I'd seen or heard from Al Proletti again, and they repeated the same question when they arrived today. Of course, I haven't."

"Maybe that's all there is to it. You know how, in the movies, the government agents are so all-knowing, all-seeing? I suppose in reality they do not have all criminals on cameras and under surveillance at all times. They probably wondered if he's still here in the city."

"Yesterday, one of them made several phone calls and I gathered he was checking airline flights for Proletti's name."

There are certainly ways to travel without buying an airline ticket or he could have a fake ID and buy his ticket under another name, I thought, but there was no need to hash it all over with Victoria. She was edgy enough already so I changed the subject.

"Elsa wants to know what your plans are for the wedding."

She chuckled. "Yeah, put it off on Elsa, huh. I *know* you are every bit as curious."

"Well, *yeah*. I need to know when I get to wear my gorgeous new dress."

Her face went sad and I remembered, too late, that her wedding gown had been taken as evidence by the police.

"We will get your dress back, Vic. They can't possibly need it." I spoke with all the assurance of someone who is all blarney. I really had no idea if I could accomplish this.

I distracted her with the cookies while I thought about how to approach the police. If I called Kent Taylor and asked permission to get the dress back he would most likely have some line of legal mumbo-jumbo that would be a denial. However, if I showed up at his office and begged … maybe threw in a wistful expression and a tear or two over how sad it was about the bride losing her gown … It was worth a shot.

I pulled my keys out of my purse and told Vic not to worry. I would accomplish the mission and be back before she knew it. A box of Christmas ornaments sat on the floor near the unfinished tree so I handed them to her and suggested the time would pass more quickly if she kept busy.

Twenty minutes later I was approaching the municipal parking building next to the police department. Being one of those places that charges you for an hour's parking even if you only rush right in and back out, I decided to make a call. Kent Taylor picked up as soon as the department operator transferred the call to his desk.

"Oh good, you're there," I said. "I need to pop up and see you. It won't take a minute."

"Charlie, what's this about?" I couldn't quite make out the joy in his voice, but surely it was there somewhere.

"I'm already at the parking garage and I'll be quick."

"Okay, you'd better be."

I hung up before he could change his mind, then pulled

away from the curb and whipped into the parking structure, taking my little ticket from the yellow machine that dispenses them. Another car waited impatiently behind me then tried to run the gate and sneak in without getting his own ticket. I remembered the elevator to Kent's department came out at the third level of the garage so that's where I headed, finding—miraculously—I had a shot at the one empty space. The dark car that had rushed in behind me at the gate apparently had the same idea.

Too bad. I got here first. I got out, locked my door and faced the building. The dark car stopped behind my Jeep, angling so I couldn't walk past him. Jerk! I turned to go around. The car's doors opened and two men got out.

That's when I knew I was in real trouble.

Chapter 32

The silver-haired man caught my attention first, although the other one held a gun and was definitely the more dangerous looking. About a dozen thoughts went through my mind in a nano-second: he looked just as Victoria had described him, complete with the vivid blue eyes; my gun was locked in the glovebox; my Jeep was blocked in; I'm on the third floor, way above the ground; it's the police department—surely someone will come along soon.

"All I want's that evidence from your girlfriend's house," Proletti said.

Vic was right—he did have a faint New York accent.

"I saw those agents go to her house. You leave there right after and come to the police? You must have it with you."

The statement made no sense. Why would one bunch of lawmen give evidence back to the victim, only to have her turn it back to another section of law enforcement? I only thought of this later. At the moment he said it, I was struggling to keep a clear head as the thuggish one came around the side of their car and held the gun on me. I knew with a sick certainty it was the same gun that had nearly taken Victoria's life.

A white car slowly approached, the driver probably looking for a parking space in the crowded structure. Proletti tensed and the thug moved in closer to me. I was just trying to think of a way—any way at all—to alert the driver and get him to go for help. When the car stopped and Agent Gilbert Ahern stepped out I could have shouted for joy.

"Al," he said.

"Gil. What are you doing here?" Puzzlement showed in Proletti's eyes.

"The other guy has a gun!" I yelled at Ahern.

When he didn't react the way I expected, all at once I knew.

"Put it away, Fausto," he said to the thug, who complied. Turning to Proletti: "What did you tell your daughter?"

"Nothing, man. I asked for the evidence, searched the whole damn place. She had nothin'."

"Don't worry about that."

I had no time to ponder the remark, not with Fausto giving me the evil eye, so I tried to deflect his attention.

"I thought you were on your way to the airport," I said to Ahern.

"Later. I'm on a different flight from Applin."

"So … Here are your suspects. Aren't you going to arrest them?"

My bluff didn't work. His stern mouth turned upward at the corners, his version of a smile. Ahern wasn't here to catch Proletti and his cohort. He'd followed them as they tracked me. They were on the same side.

I remembered what Victoria said about the cassette tape, where Al Proletti talked to someone they assumed was in law enforcement. It wasn't the Florida deputy, Elmer Reddick. It was the FBI man from Washington. Kickbacks, bribes, who knew what all—the agent had been in Proletti's pocket for decades. I didn't want to guess at the devil's pact the two had made. I only wanted out of there.

Ahern might be a crooked lawman but he wasn't stupid. He read my thoughts as surely as if they'd been written on my face in ink. He stepped behind me, effectively caging me among the three of them. Unless I could knock one of them down or kick 'em in the privates, I was stuck. I didn't like the three-against-one odds. Injure one of them and I still had the other two to deal with.

"You know the nice thing about working with a rube in a dink police department like this one?" Ahern said to Proletti. "The nice thing is I'm the one who ended up with the evidence."

I took offense on behalf of Kent Taylor. We didn't always see things the same way but he was certainly not a rube.

Ahern reached into his jacket and pulled out a zipper bag full of neatly folded papers. I recognized them as the ones that had come from the green box, including Juliette's steno pad and the cassette tape. In his other hand he had a plastic lighter. He held up the bag and flicked the lighter.

Proletti's eyes grew wide, his jaw slack. Fausto looked toward his boss for guidance but none was forthcoming.

Ahern was staring at Proletti now. "You know how much I've covered up for you over the years, Al? You have any idea?" He'd let the lighter go out, thank goodness.

Al held perfectly still. I wanted to turn into a tiny field mouse and scurry away. Something here was taking a nasty turn.

"If all that shit I covered up was to come out now—you know how bad that would be for me? My pension—pfft!"

"So, burn it! We're both in the clear then. Proletti tried to bluster his way through. "You got enough to retire five times over, without a government retirement fund."

"Only if I wanted to live on some godforsaken island where you sweat all day and the mosquitos eat you alive, looking over my shoulder all the time. No contact with my family. Never see my kids, my grandkids? Nah. I want to live where it's civilized, send away for a little of the money now and then, not enough to make anyone take a second look. I have to doctor this tape so the evidence sends you away but doesn't reveal anything about me."

So, why don't we all walk away and you can do that? I really hoped he could read my face as easily now as he had earlier.

"Give me the evidence, then," said Proletti. "I can go so far away you'll never see my face again."

"Huh-uh. No way. I'm not taking the chance. Ex-federal agents don't do so well in prison."

I saw where this was really going. Ahern wasn't here to capture Proletti and take him in. There was too great a chance, once arrested, the mobster would tell it all. This meeting should have taken place between the two of them, all alone. My very, very bad luck to be caught in the middle.

"So, what're you sayin'? You're not turning the evidence over?" The mobster's expression became hopeful.

My hopes sank. Without that documentation, all we had in court against Proletti were the pages I'd photocopied and Victoria's testimony. It might be enough to convict him for breaking into her house and harassing her, but the real proof of the long ago murder the new FBI director was investigating—that was inside the bag. I scrambled for ideas. How could I get hold of the bag and get out of here? The three of them would hold a contest to see who could grab me and throw me off the side of the building first. Or they would simply shoot me down as I ran.

Ahern flicked the lighter again and a flame rose to life. He started to wave it toward the bottom corner of the bag of evidence.

I don't know what happened next, what silent communication passed between Proletti and his thug, Fausto. I only heard a deafening blast that reverberated off the concrete walls. Gilbert Ahern went down and a red blotch spoiled the center of his pristine white shirt. I fell to the floor and rolled under my Jeep, holding my breath, squinching my eyes shut, waiting for the bullet that would either come at me directly or ricochet off a concrete surface somewhere. Shouts and pounding footsteps echoed from a hundred unknown places.

"Shots fired! Shots fired!" was what I thought I heard, but my ears rang so badly I couldn't be sure of anything.

Pure pandemonium reigned for what felt like a long time. Blue-clad legs and black police uniform shoes appeared when I first opened my eyes. The Jeep rocked with thuds. Proletti's face hit the floor, startlingly close to mine, his blue eyes pinning me. His arms were yanked backward, cuffs went around his wrists. Someone jerked him to his knees then to his feet.

Near the tire of the dark car I saw the same thing happening to Fausto. If I'd rolled over, behind me lay the body of Gilbert Ahern. I didn't roll over—I didn't want to see him. I massaged my ears, wishing they would stop ringing. Gradually, the scurrying feet went away and the ringing got better.

"Charlie? Charlie, where are you?" It sounded kind of like Kent Taylor's voice, a little more high-pitched than usual.

I bumped my shoulder on an extremely hard metal object under the car as I struggled to get out. Rolled away from the protection of my Jeep and stayed there on hands and knees for a second, until I no longer felt like I would pass out. When I finally stood, pulling myself upright by gripping the door handle, Kent Taylor was standing beside the dark car scanning the surrounding area.

"I'm here," I said, although I could barely hear my own voice.

"Charlie, my god!" He came over to me. "I got worried when you didn't show up and came down here looking for you. By then the situation had already blown up. Are you all right?"

I nodded. "Yeah, I'm great. Just great."

I started shaking so hard I could barely stand up. He caught me before my knees gave way. Then I really embarrassed myself by bursting into tears.

Chapter 33

The next week passed in a blur—police questions, family calls … I remember a lot of chicken soup delivered by Elsa. My brother credited Kent Taylor with saving my life.

Ron and Victoria walked around emanating a sort of glow. They'd decided the wedding would go forth and, miraculously, managed to snag a one-hour window of time at the same little chapel where we all would have walked down the aisle two weeks ago. The place was already beautifully decorated because of the holiday. No thanks to me, Vic had her gown back, cleaned and fluffed, courtesy of APD.

Most of the guests were able to get there long enough for the ceremony but since we'd not been able to book a reception venue, that part of it would be limited to family and closest friends at our house, where the wedding cake had come out of the freezer in plenty of time to be nearly as tasty as on the original date.

In the spacious ladies' lounge at the church, Victoria and I were alone. I pulled up the zipper on her gown and worked at the row of tiny satin-covered buttons concealing it. My matron-of-honor dress was a tiny bit loose on me, but hopefully no one would notice. I'd not been able to eat much since the shootout, plagued by persistent faint nausea caused by shock to my inner ear or something like that. According to the doctor it would go away with time.

"How are you doing?" I asked Victoria, noticing in the mirror that she seemed a bit wistful.

Her reflection smiled at mine. "Good. I'm happy we're going ahead with our plans."

"No regrets about Al Proletti and the big secret?"

"Oh no. My father, the dream man Mom came up with for me … she was right, he died before I was born."

I suspected her pensive expression had more to do with the fact that her mother never lived to see her only daughter marry. That was my guess, based on my own feelings at my wedding. We both felt a longing for the parents who had died far too young.

We picked up our bouquets and walked into the vestibule. Behind the chapel doors we could hear soft music from the string quartet. I knew Ron and Drake would be standing at the front, outwardly poised, inwardly wondering what they were supposed to do with their hands, standing around in those awkward minutes before the bride made her appearance.

Ron would be thinking it was kind of sad our brother Paul hadn't been able to fly back to attend and to walk the bride down the aisle, but he'd been chosen a long time ago as the lead singer in his home church's musical program and there was no way he could change plans on such short notice. We all said we understood.

I reached down to shift Victoria's train into position, then tucked her veil the way she wanted it over her shoulder.

"You ladies ready?" Kent Taylor stepped toward Victoria, extending his arm.

My eyes met hers and we both took deep breaths. "Ready."

I gripped my bouquet and nodded to the ushers, who pulled the double doors open, and then I took my first steps forward, in time with the music.

Get two of the recipes from this story
—Pedro's Chicken Enchiladas and Charlie's
Christmas Biscochitos—at connieshelton.com
and click the New Mexico Foods link.

* * *

Thank you for taking the time to read *Weddings Can Be Murder*. If you enjoyed it, please consider telling your friends or posting a short review. Word of mouth is an author's best friend and much appreciated.

Thank you,
Connie Shelton

* * *

Sign up for Connie Shelton's free mystery newsletter
at connieshelton.com
and receive advance information on new books, along
with a chance at prizes, discounts and other mystery
news! Follow Connie Shelton on Twitter, Pinterest
and Facebook

Get another Connie Shelton book—FREE!
Go to http://mysterywriter_0.gr8.com/
to find out how.

Made in the USA
Coppell, TX
14 September 2020